The Colonel Investigates

The Colonel Investigates

Syed Mustafa Siraj

Translated by
Nivedita Sen

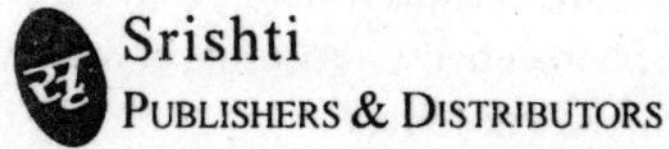

SRISHTI PUBLISHERS & DISTRIBUTORS
64-A, Adhchini
Sri Aurobindo Marg
New Delhi 110 017
srishtipublishers@yahoo.com

First published by SRISHTI PUBLISHERS & DISTRIBUTORS in 2004

ISBN 81-88575-31-3

Typeset in AGaramond 11pt. by Suresh Kumar Sharma at Srishti

Cover design: Vinayak Bhattacharya

Printed and bound in India

For Polu, Munnu and Milu –

C *hildren*

O *therwise*

L *amentably*

O *verstuffed with*

N *arratives of*

E *nglish*

L *ife-Language-Literature*

A window to the world, words and wit of West Bengal.

Contents

Acknowledgment

I am deeply grateful to my former teacher Rani Ray, not only for goading me on to translate these stories, but spending long hours, patiently reading, reworking and revising my rough renderings- literally teaching me as I tried to translate! To Syed Mustafa Siraj Saheb, I am indebted for the permission to translate his works, which I obtained over two delightful conversations and an exchange of letters with him. A special thank you to Jasjit Mansingh, Vinayak Bhattacharya and Shalini for addressing their varied range of talents to the specific job of putting together this book. And of course, I owe to my publisher and his team the freedom to do as I wanted, while we were all engaged in an unpretentious project that tries to broaden the base of popular stories in Bangla by making a few of them accessible beyond the ambit of the Bangla-literate reader.

Introduction

Most fiction writers in Bangla have not drawn the line at serious stuff for adults – they often not only take a break, but perhaps also want to reach out to the next generation of readers by writing for children. Some even dabble in the domain of detective stories which go back to Hemendra Kumar Ray's Bimal-Kumar and Jayanto-Maanik escapades of the pre-Independence generation, the Byomkesh series of Saradindu Bandyopadhyay, the Kiriti Ray cases of Nihar Ranjan Gupta, and the comparatively recent Feluda stories of Satyajit Ray, the Gogol episodes of Samaraesh Basu, Sunil Gangopadhay's Kaakababu's adventures, the Pandab Goenda mysteries of Shashthipada Chattopadhyay. These are only few examples, spanning more than half a century of serialized thrillers in Bangla; the more contemporary work has not been included in the above list. I have translated three such stories in this volume. Readers who do not have access to the Bangla script will now be able to enjoy the mystery stories of Syed Mustafa Siraj, who has written prolifically for adults as well as children and, continues to do so.

Siraj Saheb, one of the better known writers in the Bangla literary scene today, is a quiet, self-effacing person who was born in Murshidabad in 1930, and lives in Kolkata at present. He began his literary career with poetry and started writing fiction in the late fifties. He has written a lot for children; his most popular writings being ghost stories, mystery stories and adventures. His works have always been received enthusiastically by children. He is best known for his fictional work *Aleek Maanush*, which won, apart from other awards, the prestigious Sahitya Akademi award. His novel *Amartya Premkatha* won the Narsimha Das award of the University of Delhi. He has many other accolades like the Bibhutibhushan Smriti Puraskar, the Ananda Puraskar and the Sahitya Sampriti Puraskar to his credit.

Apart from the translations of some of Tagore's and Sukumar Roy's poems and Satyajit Ray's stories, the rich world of Bangla juvenile literature has yet to find its way to the library of the non-Bangla reading public. The collection of the three stories in this volume – the who – dun – its with the retired Colonel Niladri Sarkar as detective and his young reporter friend Jayanto as narrator and assistant, acquaints the reader with some of Siraj's popular fiction and could serve as a starting point. A unique feature of these stories is that although the detective in them is not young, except at heart, the adult and the adolescent reader alike can enjoy them . Although there are several stories with the coionel as detective in Siraj's repertoire, these were among the ones suggested by him for translation.

For a long time now, children's literature in Bangla has been sensitive to a simple need for a special sub-genre that the western literary world, with its intricate and sophisticated rubrication, has not distinguished in a way as to incorporate it within the everyday parlance of the common reader. It is a small detail that acknowledges the existence of a specific age-group, differentiating adolescent readers from child readers. In Bengali literary terminology, the generic name is *Kishore Sahitya*, literature for the young adult reader, of the age group of ten to eighteen or so. If at all I were to pigeonhole the stories in this volume, I would locate their place in *Kishore Sahitya.* The mystery stories here belong to this sub-genre, capable of arousing the adolescent reader's insatiable curiosity to find out who did it, as also why, when, where, and how, and simultaneously keeping their minds working as they read.

Although crime fiction in the modern sense of the term, written after the formal establishment of the police force, is a contribution of the early nineteenth century, mystery stories are believed to have existed in India from the Vedic times (about 800 B.C.), and have continued to enthrall generations of readers the world over, having neither lost their capacity to entertain, nor become redundant to mainstream literature. They are all-time favourites with readers both old and young. For the average reader, they offer a vicarious release from being hemmed in by the domestic space and a relentless regimen of work. The adventure or mystery becomes an agency that not only allows but celebrates the protagonist's transgressions from routine, and encourages the reader's imaginative participation in it. It lets the young and the not-so-young reader temporarily appropriate exciting and forbidden areas – replete with the perplexity of criminal goings-on – and experience the pleasures of unshackled time. Such stories challenge the domestic and the familiar, with it set rhythms of time, and its homogenous social spaces. In the serialized mystery story, space not only loses its confinement and is no longer restricted to the home and its neighbourhood; it also becomes attractive through the novelty in each new story. Although described in fastidious detail, this space is an outlet without any historical, geographical, economic, or sociopolitical concreteness. Time, too, is flexible and loses its regular regimen by allowing the protagonists to operate outside the routine parameters of their daily lives.

All this is true of the serialized mystery stories in this collection. The serialized mystery story also leaves no impact on the lives of its protagonist, and does not show him ageing in the physical sense of the term. The detective hero is as young (or young-old), fit, strong, agile and alert in the first story as in the last. With the complicity of his assistant/s, he not only physically vanquishes the enemy, whenever the occasion demands it, but also works out complex mental puzzles, culminating in exposing the criminal and his motive for the crime. Through all the spine-tingling drama, what keeps him going is his addiction to the exhilaration of the whole enterprise. In Hemendra Kumar Ray's *Sonaar Pahaarer Jatri*, the detective hero Bimal upholds his obsessive preoccupation with the thrilling life that the profession of a sleuth opens out to him, simultaneously repudiating the common insinuation that Bengalis are *gharkuno* or tied to their homes:

> Wherever there is a scent of adventure, we feel stimulated... we just want to plunge into the whirlpool of events, relish excitement after excitement... We desire a dynamic life, totally inundated by the fast pace of things around us, and crave to whole-heartedly celebrate the dangers that seem to overwhelm us [translation mine].

Despite being cast in the same mould as the thrillers that valorize a hectic, tumultuous and uncertain life full of potential dangers, the Colonel stories describe an ambience that might seem slow-moving to the contemporary reader. They belong to a period that has an old-world charm, reminiscent of the Sherlock Holmes stories. There is a conspicuous absence of women, as well a considerable representation of the landed aristocracy of yesteryears, who patronize the detective's ventures. The young reader might find the obviously bygone age they bring to life appealing despite or because of its leisurely pace – particularly when they concentrate on the mental and intellectual exercise of juggling with words in deciphering obscure riddles or rhymes that might help to solve the mystery. Unlike more contemporary detectives, the colonel lives a life that is unencumbered to a great extent by telecommunications – the audio-visual media or the electronic network – and has minimal access to any hi-tech infrastructure that can aid him in his work. Even when he needs a car to go around in the city, he has to depend on Jayanto, his young reporter friend, to drive him around. Notwithstanding the unhurried meanderings and the long-drawn-out cogitations, the benign humour of the stories keeps the reader's interest alive, provided s/he is willing to keep an open mind.

In my translation, I have hardly condensed or abridged anything; I have also retained archaic English words used by the last generation of Bengalis, like 'trunk call', 'kitbag,' and 'dak-bungalow' so as not to interfere with the flavour of the language used by the characters during the time that the episodes were supposed to have taken place.

The Colonel, retired from the army, is a self-fashioned sleuth who works on mind-boggling cases that cannot be solved by the police. He is tall, fair, of a strong build, and has a flowing beard. In his knapsack, he carries a pair of binoculars, some rope, a knife, a metal detector, and a few other simple implements. When the need arises, he can outwit or outdo any young and seasoned criminal without the use of any prop. He is idiosyncratic and, like some other fictional detectives, has a few strange passions. Apart from being totally addicted to coffee and also to cheroots – which may well dangle from his mouth unlit for all he cares – he is completely obsessed with tending exotic varieties of cacti and orchids in the garden on his terrace, and the pursuit of rare specimens of birds and butterflies. He is also taken up greatly with alliteration, anagrams, palindromes, puns, quibbling and other equivocation in words, particularly when they help him to solve a mystery in a way that he can not only trace the criminal but get to the bottom of the crime. His dedication to his work is quite evident in the scenes where he purses his eye-brows and frowns, self-absorbed and oblivious of anything except the riddle of the murder or crime. A combination of physical prowess and cerebral skills make him stand out like a heroic character among lesser mortals like Jayanto and Haldarmashai.

Jayanto, the narrator, is an ordinary, lazy and not-too-successful journalist in the Bengali newspaper *Dainik Satyasebak.* He cannot do without his afternoon siesta, and has such a phobia about the cold that he often shies away from baths during winter. He wants to play it safe most of the time, but when the Colonel decides to throw caution to the winds, he joins him in his reckless enterprises, despite his misgivings about the discomfort and dangers they might lead to. Self-professedly laid-back and of average intelligence, he is slow in comprehending solutions to problems that the colonel is able to work out within minutes in brilliant flashes of insight.

Sometirnes, the two also have Haldarmashai, a retired police officer – forever sniffing at his snuff – who runs a private detective agency, as an accomplice. Like the Colonel, his corporeal frame is colossal, but he is clumsy and constrained by his size, and his reflexes are not nimble. In fact, he is everything that the Colonel is not. I regret, that for obvious reasons, his hilarious ramblings in the east Bengali dialect could not be incorporated suggestively in the text in a manner that could, even remotely, capture their true colour and flavour. His long-winded linguistic articulation contrasts with the sophisticated Colonel's brisk, often brusque and businesslike queries and economy of expression – demonstrative of the latter's professional attitude to his clients and potential suspects. Although Haldarmashai tends to go on the wrong track at times, he is well-meaning and industrious. He is often made to do the major leg-work on behalf of the Colonel, thus contributing a great deal to the discovery of secret hide-outs of criminals and other such important information.

In the first story, 'The Wise Words of Ram Sharma', the Colonel and Jayanto follow a missing rare book to a palatial but dilapidated country house. The colonel intervenes to examine a series of thefts, impersonations and even a murder that take place in the light of the rare book, and the confounding magic square inside it.

In the second, 'The Inauspicious Goddess', after a brief encounter with an opium-addict who has a mysterious benefactor, the Colonel and his assistant are caught up in some eerie goings-on inside the palace of Lohagora, where an inexplicable clanging of utensils and tread of heavy footsteps are heard at night. To add mystery to the nocturnal horror, an anonymous letter dares Jayanto to be present at the deserted site of an ill-omened goddess at night. Despite Jayanto's apprehensions, the colonel pursues, probes and pierces the heart of the inscrutable tangle, which includes the decoding of an apparently meaningless rhyme and learning a magic trick with playing cards, to culminate in an exciting treasure-hunt.

The third story sends the Colonel, Jayanto and Haldarmashai on what seems like a wild goose chase to remote Raigarh, in search of the whereabouts of a kidnapped boy who is believed to have been murdered. More murders take place along the way, apart from the unfolding of a separate plot about the solving of a numerical riddle in an old manuscript belonging to the Raigarh palace, the salvaging of an inlaid box from an archaelogical excavation, and the constant and intimidating presence of a demon or deity in the forest of Harmatmatia, which looks like a bear…

Jayanto and the aged sleuth the Colonel
Penetrate these mysteries to their kernel
Focused, though quite foxed and fuddled,
They don't get completely muddled –
Solving them in ways that make you marvel…

Nivedita Sen

The Wise Words of Ram Sharma

I was quite taken aback when I entered Colonel Niladri Sarkar's museum-like drawing room the other day. The old nature-lover was sitting in one corner with a grim face. He seemed to be muttering something to somebody outside and frowning. A butterfly with black and white criss-cross markings sat still on his sage-like beard. It was, no doubt, one of the rare specimens in his collection. The Colonel, however, was oblivious of its presence.

Outside the window, there was a huge *Neem* tree. Swarms of pitch-black winter crows were screeching loudly there. Was that the reason for my aged friend's irritation? Was he cursing them? If so, they deserved it. Those ugly birds used to habitually attack the rare varieties of orchids and cacti in the carefully nurtured 'plant world' on his terrace.

Getting no response to my good morning wish, I hesitated somewhat, and then sat down on the sofa. A little later, Shashthicharan silently came and left a cup of coffee for me. His face too was quite sullen. I inferred that there must have been some altercation between the servant and the master, and the master was probably secretly cursing the servant.

But what could Shashthicharan have done to annoy him? Had he broken the leg of a butterfly? Or had he inadvertently opened the cage of the three-legged, ill-omened bat brought from the Tora islands? As far as I know, Shashthi cannot stand the grotesque, flying mammal.

Taking a sip of coffee, I looked sideways to find the colonel bending over the table and writing something. After about two minutes, he got up and sauntered towards me.

"Shashthicharan is really good-for- nothing..." I said

My friend seemed to be talking to himelf. He said, "But much worse than Shashthi is that creep – Jagamohan Bose."

"Who the dickens is Jagamohan Bose?"

The Colonel sighed heavily. He said, "Actually, the guy is terribly greedy for money. See Jayanto, keeping one's word is more important than money. There is no greater sinner than the guy who doesn't keep his word."

"Right, right. But what was the promise he failed to keep – this Jagamohan of yours?"

In a sad voice, the Colonel said, "He had done it earlier also. I had gone to him and we had agreed on the price of Emmanuel da Samsa's *The Flora and Fauna of Chrisso Islands*. When I went to get it the next day, I heard that he had sold it for a higher price. It was written in 1784, a very rare book. That is not the only reason for my indignation; he even had the audacity to bare his teeth and laugh. Can you imagine!"

Showing some sympathy, I said "It was really very wrong of him ..."

Seething with rage once again, the Colonel said, "Have you heard this proverb? The more the laughter the more the crying – Ram Sharma's ancient saying."

"I have. Really, it is not good to laugh so much. Jagamohan will know no end to his crying later on."

The Colonel said, "Ram Sharma alias Ram Shankar Sharma wrote his autobiography called *Atmacharit* in the year 1859. His life was very exciting. At a very early age, he ran away from home and took up the job of a sea-boy in a ship. He travelled all over the world. At a ripe old age, he returned to the village of Nadia and built a huge house on his ancestral land. The Sepoy mutiny took place in 1857. Ram Shankar used to secretly give financial assistance to the mutineers. As a result, he came to the notice of the British administrators, who sentenced him to death. While living in a solitary cell just before being hanged, he wrote the story of his life. After he died, his brother Shyamshankar took the permission of the government and got the book published. The book is very valuable and rare. I had been after Jagamohan for sometime now, to procure the book for me."

"Does Jagamohan have a bookshop?" I interrupted.

"Yes. If you go to College Street, you will see 'Lost Books' written on a signboard. A stuffy room stacked with books –

there isn't even a place to stand. You will have to talk to him from the kerb. But you won't be able to see Jagamohan fully. Only his nose will be visible through a gap among the heaps of books. You will have to take out money if you want to see some other part of his body. Then you can see the palm of his pale hand reaching out to you from a pile of books."

The Colonel smiled sadly. Then he said, "Yesterday evening he told me on the phone: 'Come quickly. The book has been found.' But in the meanwhile, this wretch of a Shashthi had committed such a mischief that I didn't even have the time to die. I was madly searching..."

"For what?"

"Its biological name is *Vanessa Artisi*. In English, you can call it Turtle-Butterfly. If you see it from afar, it appears like a lilliputian turtle. When it flies, it looks like a resplendent fairy. I firmly believe that damned Shashthi wanted to let it go. That's why it escaped. Oh Jayanto! I had got it after such a lot of effort. You know, the winter is when they hibernate. The poor creature was startled from its sleep by that rogue Shashthi!"

I stood up abruptly and said, "I don't know if you will be able to lay your hands on Sharma's book, but you will certainly get your butterfly back – if you can just stay still a bit."

I frightened him by suddenly grabbing at his beard and catching the butterfly. The Colonel squealed in delight and wonder, and ran into the other room, snatching the butterfly from my hands. A little while later, he came back, jubilant.

He put his arms around me and said, "My dear friend, I invite you for lunch today."

The old scholar of nature virtually became a child for a while. He forgave Shashthicharan, who smiled knowingly, and promptly brought in two cups of coffee and a plateful of snacks. While drinking the coffee, I reminded him that so much laughter was not good, because as Ram Sharma's ancient saying warns us – the more you laugh the more you cry.

The Colonel said: "Yes – I have really been hurt by Jagamohan's behaviour, Jayanto. Yesterday at nine in the evening, while shutting his shop, he called me to say that he has sold the book to another customer because I had failed to show up. See what he's done! At seven he tells me he's got the book. Two hours later, he announces he's sold it to somebody else, cackling with laughter!"

"What is so special about the book?"

The Colonel did not reply. Instead he suddenly got up and walked towards the table in the corner. Then he walked back with a piece of paper. He looked at the paper and muttered, "Okay Jayanto, name five birds whose names start with the letter 'ka'."

Thinking for a moment, I said, "*Kak* (crow), *kokil* (cuckoo), *kaththokra* (woodpecker), *Kakatua* (cockatoo), *kadakhoncha* (snipe)…"

"Great Jayanto, great! In our tradition, the letter 'ka' is very lucky. It is the first of the consonants. The Hindu god Krishna's name starts with this letter. There is a story about the devotee Prahlad, who would be moved to tears in school, just reading the letter 'ka'. So Jayanto, in the ancient Egyptian script, the five birds that you named were the symbols of five holy words – Sator, Arepo, Tenet, Opera, Rotas. In Egypt, during the reign of the Romans, an amazing puzzle was made out of these five words. Here it is."

So this was what had been occupying the mind of my clever friend! I was stunned to see the piece of paper. It said:

S	A	T	O	R
A	R	E	P	O
T	E	N	E	T
O	P	E	R	A
R	O	T	A	S

Observing my silence, the Colonel asked, "Do you notice anything special?"

"Yes. No matter which side I read from, I get the same five words. How the Egyptians must have activated their minds to get this extraordinary arrangement!"

"Not only that. The design is surrounded on all sides by the word 'Sator'. The Romans called this the 'Cirencester Word Square,' which is supposed to be a mysterious word square. During the fourth-fifth centuries A.D., this word square was possibly written in Egyptian word-pictures.It was deciphered in the nineteenth century. Then there was a rush to decode the puzzle. At first sight, if you arrange the words one after another in the Roman language, it reads: The sower Arepo holds the wheels carefully. In ordinary parlance, it would be: A man named Arepo, while sowing the seeds of the crop, holds the wheels of the machine which scatters the seeds, carefully. But what is meant by these words? Different people gave different interpretations. Then in 1847, an Englishman discovered a strange thing. Five leather pouches inside a trunk. A huge nail inside each pouch. And on the body of the pouches, they saw in the Roman script: SATOR, AREPO, TENET, OPERA, ROTAS. Each nail was bloodstained and had some words engraved in Roman. There was a great furore in Europe over this. Learned men unanimously gave the opinion that these were the five nails with which Christ was crucified. It was arranged to keep these five sacred nails in the Vatican. A special ship was sent for this. But while returning, the ship sank in the Atlantic Ocean due to some natural calamity. That's the end of the story."

"So we can infer that the five words are the names of the five nails. But who fixed those nails in your head after so many years?"

"Ramshankar Sharma alias Ram Sharma."

"What!"

The Colonel lit his pipe and said, "I saw the book in the

family library of the ancestral house of the royal family of Bhairabgarh. It is a book of 204 pages, and in a very tattered condition. I finished it in one night. It is about the wonderful doings of an extraordinary Bengali adventurer. But in one place, Ramshankar has written that while living in a village in Trinidad, on a stormy night, a frail Spanish priest took shelter in his house. Towards early morning, he breathed his last. In his robe, there was a leather pouch. Before depositing his belongings at the local church, Ramshankar opened his pouch out of curiosity. Inside it there was a nail about a foot long, on which some things were written in the Roman alphabet. The nail had no rust stains, but strangely enough it had blood stains on it. In the leather pouch also, it was written in Roman letters SATOR. He managed to unearth the mystery from a bishop. Which meant that during the shipwreck, at least somebody was able to save one nail – possibly that frail priest.

I asked, "What did Ram Sharma do with the nail?"

"That is the real question. It is not written anywhere in the autobiography. What is more, it is not even mentioned later." The Colonel blew some smoke from his cheroot and said: "The book was presented to the Raja Bahadur by a descendant of Ramshankar – Pranab Shankar Banerjee. A very rare book, that one. There was no provision there for microfilming it. I thought I would get back in time to make a copy on microfilm. But just my luck! A few days ago, the Raja Bahadur let me know by trunk call, that the book has been stolen. He suspects that Harisadhan, the gambler, drug addict son of a gentleman who was given shelter in the royal estate has done this. Earlier too, some rare books have been stolen from the library."

"Is that why you knocked at the door of Jagamohan of College Street?"

"Of course! The Raja Bahadur would be glad to get the book back, and I could have copied it on microfilm."

"And of course made some progress in retrieving the nail!"

Hearing my comment, the great detective smiled a little. "The case is not so simple, dear old chap! But reading the appendix of the autobiography, I had thought that the words seem to indicate something. So..."

Shashthicharan came and announced, "A gentleman has come. He is panting a lot. His eyes and face are bloodshot."

But the gentleman did not wait to take leave to enter. He walked in and sat down heavily next to me. Shashthicharan looked at him sternly and went off. The newly arrived visitor was rotund. He was wearing an expensive suit. In his hand was a briefcase. He was about fifty. He had a thick black-and-white moustache and was somewhat bald. He wiped his face with his handkerchief and said, "I am ruined! An order for the supply of goods worth two lakh rupees is about to be cancelled. Please save me!"

The Colonel was observing him with a sharp eye. He asked, "Who are you?"

"My name is Ramdulal Singhi. I have a business of supplying electronic goods to Arab countries. Sir, I often see you going to the chamber adjacent to my Sinha Trading Company in Park Street."

"Yes, Doctor Baidya is my friend."

"It was he who advised me to come to you."

"But what can I do to prevent the cancellation of your supply orders?"

"No sir, no! I did not come because of that. A book has been stolen."

The detective-supremo frowned a little. "Book? What book?"

"One minute, Sir! I'll tell you." Ramdulal Babu opened his briefcase and took out a piece of paper. He put it in the Colonel's hand and said, "See, it has the name etc. of the book. Jagamohan Bose of College Street is my daughter's father-in-law. I had asked for the book from him. Yesterday evening he phoned to say the book has been found, but he couldn't sell it for one paisa less than five hundred rupees. The party concerned was standing there with the book. For me, it meant a deal of two lakh rupees. I ran there with the money."

"Wait! Whose handwriting is this?"

"The person to whom I was supposed to present it. It was through him that I got the order."

"Why is it written in English?"

"Because he does not know any Bengali, Sir!"

"What is his name?"

"One Roderigue. A very stubborn man, Sir. He stays in Bombay."

"What will he do with a Bengali book?"

Ramdulal Babu shook his head and said, "That I don't know, Sir! A few days ago I had gone to Bombay. At that time he wrote in this paper and said that if I could procure the book, he would get me an order of two lakh rupees."

"Okay. Now tell me, how was the book stolen?"

Ramdulal Babu said, "I want some water, Sir."

Shashthicharan had lifted the curtain to enjoy the scene. He brought in the water even before the Colonel could ask for it. Ramdulal Babu gulped the water down, wiped his face with his handkerchief and said, "I had kept the book in the drawer of my table at the office and gone home. I had some work in the office because of which I was stuck in the office till ten at night. I was to go to Bombay with the book by the 12.15 flight. I also needed to take some papers from the office. Moreover, I stay in faraway Behala. I had thought that on the way, I would pick up everything from the office. When I stopped by at the office, I saw that the book was not there. I searched high and low, asked everybody at the office, but could not trace the book."

"Was the drawer locked?"

"I can't exactly remember, Sir! When I went there, I saw it was not locked. But the drawer lock had not been broken open."

"Does the key stay with you?"

"Yes Sir! But the office keys remain with the *chowkidar*. But why should he steal a book?"

"Who stays in the office at night apart from the *chowkidar*?"

Ramdulal Babu suddenly got frightened. "Nobody else stays there. But last night… Sir! Does it mean it was that guy?"

"What guy?"

"A representative of Roderigue Saheb. The gentleman came from Bombay yesterday. He showed me his card. He said he would stay the night and go to Gauhati by the morning flight. I asked him not to undertake the trouble of going to a hotel. There are two rooms in the office – there is a partition in between. I arranged for him to stay in the adjacent room. In the morning, I came and asked the *chowkidar*. He said, 'The gentleman's gone away in the morning'."

"What's his name?"

Ramdulal Babu thought a little and said, "What was it ... R. Maitra, or S. Maitra? But Sir, why would I disbelieve him? There are so many representatives of Roderigue *Saheb* who keep coming to Kolkata from time to time. They all spend the night in my office."

"What does he look like?"

"Slim and tall. Fair complexioned. Bearded."

The Colonel got up and said, "Okay. You can go now. I'll see."

Ramdulal Babu caught hold of the Colonel's hand and said, "I will run into a tremendous loss, Sir, if the book is not retrieved. Jagamohan Babu has said that even if we bang our heads, we won't get that book anywhere. There was only one copy. Moreover, I went to his shop again. In fact, I'm coming from there. Jagamohan Bose said the same thing again."

Ramdulal Babu tried his persuasive skills for a while longer and then took his leave.

The Colonel stood there with a serious face. I said, "Could it not be Jagamohan who's behind all this? May be he's got a wealthier customer."

The Colonel said, "In many instances, Jagamohan gets hold of books through people who steal those books. But this matter is very strange indeed! Why did a man called Roderigue need the book? Jayanto, do you have some time?"

"Today is my day off."

"Come, let us go to College Street at once."

There was a huge traffic jam at the junction of College Street and Mahatma Gandhi Road.

There were crowds of people. My car got caught in the chaos. Was it a procession or a streetside meeting? I asked a pedestrian, "What's the matter, *Dada*?"

The *Dada*-gentleman looked heavenwards and said, "What can I say, *Mashai!* What is happening here day by day? Murderous crimes in broad daylight in front of so many people! Oh! My head is behaving strangely, I hope I don't get a stroke."

Another pedestrian asked him, "Who got murdered? Where?"

"There! Go and see with your own two eyes. A masked man has shot the shopkeeper of the bookstore and fled."

Next to the shop was a hawker selling pens. He said, "I knew Jagaida would get killed. He used to steal one person's book to sell to another. No wonder I gave up being a salesman in his shop and took to the streets. Try and save your own skin first."

Peeping out of the car, the Colonel said, "I think Jagaida means Jagamohan, Jayanto! Most of the crowd is outside his shop. You keep the car nearby and wait. I'll just be back"

After a long time, my heart skipped a beat. I said, "Hell! Does it mean Jagamohan's got murdered?"

The Colonel walked away with an unperturbed face. The hawker of pens had heard my words. He said, "Yes Sir! A man, it seems, came in a jeep. Two shots were heard – *dhishum dhishum*."

The man was aiming to target me as a prospective buyer for his pens. But suddenly the traffic started moving. My ears got deafened with the sound of horns. Finding the left side relatively clear, I drove to the front of that line and waited for it to start moving. Then I started conjecturing all kinds of things.

A little while later, I saw the detective-supremo coming. He came and said smilingly, "Come. Let's go."

After he got into the car and sat quite comfortably chucking to himself. "How are you laughing? Did you see the body? Or have they taken it to the hospital?"

"Whose body are you talking about, dear? Jagamohan's?"

"Of course. Who else's?"

"He is a very shrewd man," the Colonel said. He lit a cheroot. The car had now turned onto Mahatma Gandhi Road. The Colonel said, "But it is true that a masked man attacked his shop. Also, two gunshots were heard. But Jagamohan is as fit as a fiddle."

My curiosity assuaged, I said, "So the poor man escaped narrowly."

"Jagamohan has got severely intimidated." The Colonel continued to laugh. "He started crying loudly on seeing me. He said it was his luck that he was sheltered behind the books, otherwise he would have been lying in a pool of blood."

"But this is a very serious case! Because the shot missed its aim the first time does not mean it will miss the next time also."

The Colonel did not say anything. He shut his eyes, leaned back, and started puffing mildly at his cheroot. Simultaneously, he started pulling at single strands of his beard. I have always observed, when the Colonel gets really involved in a mystery in a way that he can't find a way out of its maze, he plucks at his beard constantly....

I was invited to his flat for lunch that day. Shashthicharan had conjured up an elaborate meal. The veteran chose to remain silent throughout. He was not in a state to talk. After the meal, he went up to the roof, to his 'plant world'. I am heavily addicted to having a siesta after lunch. I managed a lovely nap, leaning on the sofa. The short winter afternoon passed me by. I opened my eyes to see the old man standing with his sage-like mien and a cup of coffee in his hand. Affectionately, he said, "Drink it, old boy! There is no drink like coffee to get rid of inertia. And listen, Jagamohan is sitting in the next room. I have made him wait for quite long. He can be called in now."

In accordance with the Colonel's instruction, Shashthi brought in Jagamohan. He also brought some coffee for him. Looking at his appearance, I could guess what mental state he was in. He looked like a sketch on wet blotting paper. He was a fat, roly-poly sort of fellow and had a pate of thick, unruly hair. His spectacles were just about sticking to his nose. On his forehead was a spot of fresh vermilion – he must have gone to Kalighat to offer his thanks to the gods. He was possibly coming from there. Looking at the coffee, for a few seconds, he could not seem to decide whether to have it or not. Finally, he concluded that he would, and draining half the cup in one sip, he said, "I am ruined! Really ruined!"

The Colonel screwed up his eyes and said, "If you would not be ruined, who else could be?"

Jagamohan gestured with his hands and screamed, "I will never do it again, Sir! If I do, please cut off my ears and hang them around the neck of a dog!"

The Colonel snapped, "Do you understand, then, who you had confronted?"

"Don't I, Sir! Of course I do," Jagamohan said quite pathetically. "There is no point lying to you. Yes, the book belongs to the royal house of Bhairabgarh. That damned Harisadhan brought me to this ruin. Just as you had ordered it, Singhi Babu had also done so. The question was..."

"The book has been stolen from Singhimoshai's office."

Jagamohan stared. Then he pleaded, "I will swear on anything, Sir! I would never stoop to swindling a relative, whoever else I might do it to."

"Listen Jagamohan Babu! What has happened has happened. Never go near Ram Shankar Sharma's autobiography again. Even if somebody promises one lakh rupees, do not try to procure that book again. Tell them straight, it will not be available."

"Again! the masked man said the same thing as he fired his bullet! The bullet hit a pile of books instead. That is how I got saved."

"Okay. You may leave now."

Jagamohan walked towards the door and suddenly turned. The Colonel said, "Is there anything you want to say?"

"I left out the very thing I came to ask." Jagamohan smiled a little. "I have grown old running a business of rare books, Sir! What is so unique about Ram Shankar Sharma's autobiography that it is causing so much trouble? Even you said that I fished in troubled waters. Why did you say this, Sir?"

"Jagamohan!," the Colonel admonished with a solemn face. "Actually, the book is really inauspicious. We shouldn't worry our heads too much over it. Do you know this 'the more the laughter, the more the crying' Ram Sharma's ancient saying? This is the same Ram Sharma. Therefore remember what I have said."

"Yes, I will." So saying, Jagamohan departed. Only he knew what he understood by that. May be he understood that he is forbidden to laugh.

The shadows were becoming darker at the end of the day inside the room. The Colonel clicked the switch to put on the light. Then he paced up and down as he said, "So the case seems to have got tied in a bigger knot, Jayanto! One Roderigue *Saheb* of Bombay keeps track of Ram Sharma's autobiography. He had asked for the book to be procured and given to Ramdulal Singhi. Jagamohan is related to Singhimashai by marriage. Harisadhan has stolen many rare books from the Bhairabgarh palace in the past. So Jagamohan appealed to him again. Harisadhan stole the book and sold it. Then there occurred two incidents. The stealing of the book from

Ramdulal's office, and the attack of the masked stranger in Jagamohan's shop. He didn't really shoot from a pistol. I could not discover any sign of a bullet among the heaps of books. That means, he had brought a toy pistol. Yes! He came to frighten Jagamohan. Jayanto, my guess is right. He actually wanted to warn Jagamohan and make him realise that he should not deal with the buying and selling of that book any more.... But why?"

"So that he would have no contender left."

"What do you mean? Contender for what?"

"The sacred, historic nails, whose price in foreign countries could be crores of dollars."

The Colonel laughed. "You have spoken intelligently, my boy! It is exactly that. Somebody or some people have understood that Ram Sharma's autobiography contains the clue to this priceless, antique nail Sator. Yes, one can see Roderigue's intention also. But somebody beat him to it and got the book."

"What about the man who stayed overnight in Singhimoshai's office – R. Maitra, or S. Maitra – could it be him?"

The detective-supremo agreed. "Right, right. Now this Maitra fellow, whoever he is, is known to Roderigue. Not only known, but intimate. He had got to know of the interaction between Roderigue and Singhimoshai. So he had come rushing to Calcutta."

The Colonel lit a cheroot and flopped into a chair. He shut

his eyes and smoked away quietly. Then he murmured to himself, "But where is that nail? Five birds in the Egyptian picture script. One meaning of it is: The sower Arepo holds the wheels carefully. At first, Jesus' body was taken from the slaughter-house in Golgotha to his grave. Somebody had taken the nails off the cross then. Does it mean that the nails were buried in the fields of a farmer called Arepo?... Then somebody discovered them and took them to a fort in Ethiopia... Ram Sharma got one of those...SATOR, AREPO, TENET, OPERA , ROTAS? A mysterious group of words. The words have repeatedly made use of the seven letters R,OA,T,S,E, P. 'N' is the only other letter, and it has been used only once. Lets us see how many meaningful words we can make out of these seven letters."

He suddenly got up and went and sat down at the table in the corner. Then he leaned over with his pen on the writing pad. I knew the old man was quite obessed by now. It might take the whole night to exorcise this demon. So I went to Shashthicharan and whispered, "Please tell your *Babamoshai* , I have gone."

Shashthi nodded. There was the trace of a smile on his face...

That very night, the phone rang at an unearthly hour. This is the eternal curse of being a reporter. It had to be some senior person of the *Dainik Satyasebak*. It must be some serious train accident, a bomb hurled at a minister, or some trouble in faraway Timbuctoo. May be I'll be ordered to go straight to the venue. Bother! Irritably, I picked up the phone and said, "What happened?" But, I could heard the voice of my wise friend.

"Jayanto! I'm extremely sorry to wake you up at two in the morning."

Hell! Old men often suffer from insomnia, and they make others suffer with them.

"Go on."

"Jayanto! I have just discovered a new word from those seven letters. It is an amazing coincidence! Do you know the older name of the village in which Ram Sharma's house was situated in Nadia district ? Satpur!"

"Great! But why call me in the middle of the night because of that?"

"Jayanto, Jayanto! I am talking about 'Satpore' pronounced with a British accent, and written in the Roman script!"

"Very good! But so what?"

"Sator, Arepo, Tenet, Opera, Rotas combined in a strange way to give me Satpore. The old world is full of mysteries, Jayanto. Listen! Be ready at nine in the morning tomorrow. We are going to Satpore , or the present Ramshankarpur. The train starts from Sealdah at half past nine."

"Tomorrow is not my day off. I just get one day off per week."

"Jayanto, a little while back a descendant of Ram Shankar

Sharma, Pranab Shankar Banerjee, phoned. The Raja Bahadur of Bhairabgarh is related to him by marriage. The Raja Bahadur had advised him to call me. At ten last night, the dead body of his missing brother Uma Shankar was found in the back garden of Pranab Shankar's house. Do you understand? Uma Shankar had been missing for three months. Suddenly his dead body..."

I snatched at his words and said, "Right. I'll be ready at nine." Then I hung up and lay quietly for some time. I could sense that I was getting inspired to surmise all kinds of things...

Ramshankarpur is another name for a concoction made up of a town and a village. On the banks of the Ganga, at one end of the place stands Ram Sharma's enormous, historic villa. It can be called a quiet place. In a fertile stretch of land next to the Ganga, it has a thick overgrowth of wild hedges and jungle plants. But if you step out of the Banerjee house and go a little northwards, a different scenery strikes your eyes. It is bursting with the life of a market-place, a hospital, a police station, and law courts. Like a town, it is full of people and the arrogance of vehicular traffic.

It is a huge, two-storeyed, old-fashioned house. It is surrounded on all sides by empty fields, vegetable farms, and decaying gardens of flowers and fruit. There is even a pond there. The square place is bound by a wall. But the wall is in a greater state of decrepitude than the house. It is broken in some places, at others weeds have made their way through holes in the wall. On the western side, the state of the embankment of the Ganga is also pathetic. With the passage of time, the Ganga has also moved away from the bank a little. The gate leading to the estate has been missing for a long time. If you enter from there, there is a jungle of Burmese bamboo. Adjacent to that is an ancient fountain, which has been long dry. Some parasitic plants peep through its stone body. An angel standing on a crumbling pillar seems to be bending to fill water in a vessel. But the head of the angel is missing.

Seeing me stare at the headless angel, the Colonel said, "After returning home, Ram Sharma wanted to live like a king. You can see one example of that. This statue is certainly not Indian. Sharma*moshai* undertook a lot of trouble to bring it all the way from his house in Trinidad. If he had been alive, he would have been sad to see the headless angel."

Pranab Shankar was standing next to us. He said, "In the 1942 storm, a huge gum tree fell over there. The head broke due to the impact of a single branch."

"I see that the fountain has five corners....Hmm, I have seen a fountain exactly like this one in Venice. But the brass statue within it is that of the Goddess Istar. Istar was the war goddess of ancient Sumeria. The five-cornered fountain at her feet is symbolic of the holy stars of Christianity. The wise men of the East knew of the birth of Christ by gazing on those stars. By following the stars, they reached the manger in Bethlehem." Saying this, the Colonel picked up something from the grass next to him. It was a shred of paper, yellowed by time. He examined it thoroughly and put it in his pocket. Then he started looking all around the grass – probably for grasshoppers. I know he studies grasshoppers. But Pranab Shankar seemed to be disturbed by the Colonel's behaviour. Soon after we had reached around twelve, he had brought us to see the place of the murder. His missing brother had been killed next to the fountain. His body had been taken to the morgue by the police. Uma Shankar had suddenly been hit on the head, possibly by an iron rod. He had died of one blow, because there were no other injury marks on his body.

The Colonel had not paid any heed to these descriptions. He was only talking about Ram Sharma. I was also beginning to get irritated by this. The Colonel then started looking at birds through the binoculars slung round his neck. To show some sympathy for Pranab Shankar, I asked about his brother, "How long ago was it when Uma Shankar was found missing, Mr. Banerjee?"

"About three months. There was no question of any quarrel. But Chotku was a little obstinate. Now and then, a trivial thing would infuriate him. But on the night before he disappeared, I had seen him very much at peace with himself. The two of us had dinner together. He chatted with me quite normally. Then he went to bed. In the morning, Gangadhar took his tea to his room but didn't see him there. He thought he must be in the bathroom and waited for him for a long time..."

Pranab Shankar sighed. After staying silent for a while, he said, "I do not have children. My wife died about two years back. I am getting to be 65. Only he made it worth my while to be alive. Yet I am so unfortunate, am I not, Jayantobabu? Suddenly, even that Chotku disappeared from my life! I left no stone unturned to find him. I even advertised in the papers. Then, after so many days, I have got his dead body back."

"Who saw the dead body first?"

"Gangadhar." Pranab Shankar wiped his eyes with a handkerchief. "Gangadhar has been with this household since boyhood. He used to love Chotku like a son. Last night – it must have been eight or eight-thirty – Gangadhar heard a faint cry from his room. He thought some thief has broken into the garden – they come in quite often in the dead of night. Gobindo the gardener must be shouting out to him, he thought. It was a moonlit night. Gangadhar came out into this verandah in the east. Immediately, he saw someone running away. Rushing out, he came and stumbled against Chotku's dead body, and fell. Then…"

The Colonel moved forward and said, "Mr. Banerjee, there is nothing else to note here for the time being. Come now, I want to inspect Uma Shankar Babu's bag."

Pranab Shankar stepped forward and said, "Come. I'll show you."

While going in, the Colonel said, "What does the police think, Mr. Banerjee? Have you learnt their opinion on the matter?"

"Yes. They think Uma Shankar had hidden himself because he was afraid of some one. That enemy had targeted him. Otherwise, why should he enter the house from the back gate?"

"What do you think?"

"I also think so. I am only surprised that if Chotku had enemies, why did he not tell me?"

"Mr. Banerjee, Uma Shankar Babu before disappearing, did you notice anything unusual about his attitude?"

"Not really. But he had been somewhat absent-minded of late. He used to silently brood over something. He used to stay awake at night, working on something. I have seen the light on in his room very late into the night. If I asked him, he would laugh and say it was nothing."

"But who could have any enmity with Uma Shankar Babu?"

"That is what I can't figure out. But he was a young man of this generation. I can't say anything for sure; perhaps he had secretly got involved in some party politics. However, I had never seen him openly involved in any political affair. He did not discuss any kind of politics with me."

It had been arranged for us to stay in a big room on the ground floor in the southern part of the house. Pranab Shankar showed us to the room and went to get his brother's bag.

Gravely, the Colonel sat in an armchair and lit his cheroot. I said, "You probably collected a clue near the fountain. I'd like to know what it is."

He smiled from the corner of his mouth. "Detectives find clues as soon as they look for them. This is the old-fashioned method, dear boy! Yes, I have also got something. But I don't know if it is a clue. A piece of a torn, dirty paper about a square inch in area. However, the paper is very old and it crumbles under a little pressure."

Pranab Shankar came into the room with an ordinary cloth bag. He said, "The bag was lying a little way from him, in the undergrowth. Gobindo picked it up a little while before you came in. The bag is indeed Chotku's. You can see his pants, shirt, towel and other odds and ends... Oh! What's this?"

Pranab Shankar was taking out the things and keeping them on the table. On seeing the thing, the Colonel said it was a battery-operated metal detector. If there is a metallic thing hidden anywhere, it can be located with the help of this.

I was startled to hear this. I said, "Does it mean Uma Shankar Babu..."

The detective-supremo gave me such a forbidding look that I shut up immediately. Pranab Shankar said with astonishment, "What did Chotku do with a metal detector?"

The Colonel did not condescend to reply; instead, he fumbled in the bag and said, "Yes, I have understood. Okay Mr. Banerjee, when did you present Ram Shankar Sharma's autobiography to the Raja Bahadur of Bhairabgarh?"

Pranab Shankar tried to remember and said, "Last August. He had come to these parts on some work. He stays at my house whenever he comes this side. We are related by marriage."

"Was Uma Shankar sore with you for giving the book to the Raja Bahadur?"

"Yes, yes. He was very indignant." I tried to reason with him that the book would just get ruined here. It would be much better cared for in the Raja Bahadur's library. Moreover, the Raja Bahadur had said that he would arrange for the book to be printed again."

"How were Uma Shankar's relations with the Raja Bahadur?"

Pranab Shankar said a little hesitantly, "I can only say that whenever the Raja Bahadur came to this house, Chotku would avoid him. Behind his back, he would make fun of his pompous manner. He used to say that he is like the king in a streetside performance. Actually, Chotku was always something of a rebel. He would always show contempt for a person who was revered by everybody."

"Did he visit the royal palace at Bhairabgarh?"

"Who? Chotku?" Pranab Shankar shook his head. "The last time he went was with my father in his childhood, not after growing up. He used to say, 'These Rajas have such an air about them; if I go there, they will ask me to press their feet, treating me like a servant. I have no reason to go'."

The Colonel expressed his opinion. "Yes, I can reconstruct the mental make-up of Uma Shankar Babu." Then he took out a piece of paper from inside the bag and started examining it.

Pranab Shankar was absent-mindedly folding his younger brother's shirt lying on the table. He said, "I haven't yet seen what is in the bag. Of course, the wallet has been found. It was in the hip pocket of the pants he wore. There wasn't much money in it."

"Could you take the trouble to get the wallet here?"

"I'll get it." Saying this, Pranab Shankar left.

The Colonel now left the bag aside and started on the pants and the shirt. He scrutinized a small notebook that he took out from the pocket of the shirt. I was sitting quietly, observing the actions of the old veteran. When his eyes met mine, he said, "I don't believe in after-life. But I have actually seen it happen in a few freak instances. For example, take the case of Ram Shankar Sharma! He was a man of exceptional courage, and fond of adventure. He was prepared to take on any hardship. It seems that he has been reincarnated in the person of his descendant Uma Shankar. It is amazing..."

As Pranab Shankar came in with the wallet, the Colonel stopped talking, took the wallet from him, and said, "Nothing's been taken out, I hope?"

"No, no! There is no question of taking out anything."

The Colonel took out a few coins from inside the wallet and said, "Hmm! Just as I thought. Two out of these coins are from Trinidad."

Pranab Shankar stared blankly. I said, "Where did Uma

Shankar get Trinidadian coins?"

The Colonel said, "In Trinidad. Where else?"

Pranab Shankar said with surprise, "Did Chotku go to Trinidad?"

"Yes, Mr. Banerjee. The reason for his disappearance is now clear to me."

Pranab Shankar said, "My brain is getting fuddled. I have heard that Ram Sharma lived in Trinidad. He had a house and property there too. However, I haven't read his autobiography carefully... Yes, I remember, Chotku used to sometimes say, he would go to see Ram Sharma's estate. But that is far away, at the head of South America. In West Indies."

"Then he ought to have had a passport with him. Where is the passport?" I asked.

The Colonel replied. "It is not clear to me what happened to the passport," Anyway, Mr. Banerjee, the murderer wanted to lay his hands on one thing. And he has been able to get that ... I have found two separate shreds of it, one inside the bag and another near the fountain."

"What is that?"

"The autobiography of Ram Shankar Sharma." Saying this, the Colonel started turning the pages of the pocket notebook. Hmm...the passport number is copied here. It means he did have a passport... Here I see a two-line note to the police in English. 'Reported to Police. Trabanka P.S. case No. P.F. 223

dated 15.10.80.' Which means the passport must have got stolen. The entry was made in a police station diary of a place called Trabanka. What date did he disappear on, Mr. Banerjee?"

"It was the 7th of October."

"Hmm... Oh! Look what I see here! 'Appointment with F. Roderigue at 6 p.m.' That Roderigue! The one who asked Ramdulal Singhi to procure the book for him!" The Colonel looked up and said, "Your brother probably ran into trouble in Trinidad by getting his passport and possibly his money stolen. There he was introduced to somebody called Roderigue. This much I have understood very well, that Roderigue is a wealthy businessman. His trade and business extends to many countries. Uma Shankar Babu got some help from him, and was able to stay on in Trinidad for three months, thanks to him. He only made one mistake. He should not have confided in Roderigue about the autobiograbhy. The thing costs crores of dollars-if it can be retrieved...Hmm...the knot seems to be getting disentangled. But Roderigue is now in Bombay. To send a man in good time so that he can snatch the book from Uma Shankar...No! it remains as knotty as ever."

Pranab Shankar was staring at him with his mouth open. Just then Gangadhar came and announced, "All arrangements for the meal have been made, *Barababu*. *Pishima* said that it is getting to be two, and I should go and tell you."

Pranab Shankar got up. "Oh yes! Sorry, sorry- it is very late for lunch. Please come, Colonel! We can talk later. We are not eating cooked food, of course, as we are in mourning. I just arranged some rice and lentils for you people."

The Colonel asked me, "Jayanto, do you want to have a bath? I, of course, got out after having a bath in the morning."

"A bath with the cold water of the mofussils in this bone-chilling winter? How cold it is here!"

"Shall I heat some water for you, sir?" Gangadhar asked.

"No. Let it be."

The Colonel laughingly said, "You must have been a cat in your previous life, Jayanto! No wonder you don't like water."

"You must have been a wild cat in your previous life," I retorted. "That is why you like giving yourself a water massage on a winter morning."

During the meal, we were being looked after by an old lady. Pranab Shankar introduced us. She was a distant relative. Apart from her, there was no woman in the house. Her name was Kumudini. A very affectionate lady, she was. She was really feeding us with a lot of care. She said sadly, "When Chotku was alive, he used to run around so much for his guests. I asked Paritosh to arrange everything, but Paritosh has so many things to attend to. Besides, nothing was to be cooked at home today, as we are all in mourning. We had to break the rule for you."

Pranab Shankar said, "Poor Paritosh is not to be blamed, it

took all night yesterday. Dealing with the police and police stations is no small hassle. In the morning, he went to the police station again, and from there to the morgue. He will not get any peace till they bring the body home. Didn't Paritosh come after that?"

"He came a little while back," Kumudini replied. "He went out again."

"Today he won't be able to go to the farm. Who knows what is happening there! Nobody dares touch the crops for fear of Paritosh!"

The Colonel asked, "Who is Paritosh?"

"You can call him the caretaker or the manager of this house," Pranab Shankar said, "He has been in the house since childhood and is a distant relative of ours. He also looks after the fields which I have sown with crops. He supervises everything in the house also. Had it not been for him, I would have been on the streets. Chotku was always incompetent – he couldn't care less about any financial matter. He used to say, 'Why ask me while Paritosh is around! Paritosh is like a hundred of us.' It is really that. But one can't bear to look at poor Paritosh now. This Chotku affair has almost torn him apart. The two grew up together. They played together and studied together. They were very close to each other. When Chotku disappeared, Paritosh went all over India looking for him. He almost stopped eating. What a state he was in!"

"When Paritosh Babu comes, will you please send him here?

I want to talk to him a little."

"Let him come. I'll tell him."

After the meal, the Colonel said, "In which room is your telephone, Mr. Banerjee?"

"It is downstairs. Paritosh has a kind of office there. He is responsible for everything. I am now quite old. I can't look after anything."

"I want to book a trunk call."

"Of course. Come, come."

I did not go with them. My addiction for an afternoon siesta had got the better of me. I went down and returned to our room straightaway. Before going to bed with a blanket, I sat in the sun in the verandah, and smoked a cigarette with great pleasure. That has always been my habit. After finishing the cigarette, I was looking at the blanket longingly when the Colonel came back. He frowned and said, "No! It is not a good thing to sleep in the middle of the afternoon. You lose your longevity. Come on! "We'll quickly go to Bhairabgarh and back instead."

"Bhairabgarh! Now where is that?"

"Not very far. You just have to cross the Ganga. By bus, it is about four or five miles."

I cursed the old man in my mind as we stepped out. While walking through the market-place, I said, "Could you please tell me what is going on in Bhairabgarh now?"

"Let us go and meet the Raja Bahadur- since we have come so close. Besides, we will find out about Harisadhan also."

"Harisadhan! Do you mean that addictive book thief? Has he ever been let into the house by the Raja Bahadur again?"

"Let us go and see for ourselves."

We worked our way through the crowds in the market-place and reached the bank of the Ganga. It took us an hour to cross the river by boat. But the journey was very beautiful. The Colonel kept his binoculars fixed on his eyes and managed to see many aquatic birds in the winter twilight.

I was shocked to see the crowds in the buses. The buses in Calcutta are also crowded, but they are nothing compared to this. The bus was full of people from one end to the other, and there were people on the roof too. Even so, the conductor was yelling, "Come on! Come on! It is leaving! Leaving for Bhairabgarh- Daihat-Katwa-a-a-a!"

It was perhaps because of the Colonel's appearance and western attire or his beard that two poor fellows were asked to get down to make place for us. God knows where he accommodated them! Seeing my face, the Colonel smiled wickedly at me and said, "It is sometimes necessary to experience the world as a downright comfortable place, darling!"

"But is it right to deprive others and grab their seats?"

The driver smiled broadly and said, "Don't worry about them, Sir. They are my own people. They are going free. After you get down at Bhairabgarh, I'll call them back again."

The tarred road with trees on either side curved as it went along. The bus stopped at least five times in going those five miles. Some passengers disembarked, but more than twice their number embarked. After we got down, the bus was looking like a mobile beehive – except that the bees were people.

From the corner of the bus station, we took a cycle-rickshaw and got down at the gate of the royal estate. A *chowkidar* promptly did a military salute as he saw the Colonel. I realized he had recognized the Colonel. In the verandah outside the row of rooms on the other side, a gentleman was standing with a cup of tea in his hand. He hurried forward to welcome us.

A little later, while we were waiting in the spacious drawing room, the Raja Bahadur appeared. He was slightly built, and was about as old as Pranab Shankar. He was wearing a simple pajama and kurta. He wore thick dark glasses. He said, "You have arrived very early. I had thought that you wouldn't be able to reach before six. But Colonel, it is no fault of mine. I wanted to send my jeep; you refused."

The Colonel smiled and said, "This young friend of mine is a reporter. I gave him an opportunity to experience the real state of our country. After going back to Calcutta, I hope he will write about the passengers of suburban buses in the *Dainik Satyasebak*."

I understood from this conversation that the Colonel had called from Pranab Shankar's house in Ramshankarpur to say we were arriving. After the preliminary introductions and a round of coffee, we brought up the topic of the Uma Shankar murder case. The Raja Bahadur said, "The incident is very strange. Uma Shankar was always a little headstrong by nature; but one can't imagine that anybody would murder him. Besides, it is a mystery to me why he stayed incognito for three months. As soon as Pranabda informed me about it, I thought we should seek your guidance. I don't trust that the police will do much in this case. So I myself tried many times to get you on the telephone. The telephone exchange here is worthless. I couldn't get through to Calcutta. So I called Pranabda again and said, 'You try and see. I'll give you the number'."

The Colonel asked, "What news of Harisadhanbabu?"

"Harisadhan? The Raja Bahadur's face contorted a liittle as he said, "After stealing the book, the rogue hasn't entered this house. He has understood that if I see him anywhere near the house, I'll take him to task."

"I want to know one thing Raja Bahadur! You got Ram Sharma's autobiography as a present from Pranab Shankar last August. After keeping it in your library, did you give it to anybody to read?"

The Raja Bahadur shook his head, "No. I had kept the book in the rare books shelf in the library. I didn't lend it to anybody except you. I don't think anybody knows about the book except you. Otherwise, those who are doing research on the nineteenth century would have tried to keep track of it. I read a lot of books. I have never seen any mention of this book anywhere. There can only be one reason for this. Although his brother Shyamshankar got the book printed, nobody dared buy even one copy of the book about the man who was hanged by the British government. Even this Jagamohan Bose, who keeps track of rare books like these, had never heard of the book. But why are you asking this question all of a sudden, Colonel?"

The Colonel smiled a little. "The book is connected with the murder of Uma Shankar."

"What!"

"Uma Shankar had been concerned about this book for a long time."

"Don't tell me! Why?"

"Do you remember I came and discussed with you about the sacred, historic nail 'Sator'?"

"Yes ... yes. You had wondered why Ram Shankar suddenly became silent over the subject of the nail."

"When Pranab Shankar suddenly presented the book to you, Uma Shankar was annoyed, because he was trying to find out the whereabouts of the nail from the book. But later, somehow he got it into his head that the nail is hidden somewhere in the house that Ram Shankar built in Trabanka, Trinidad. That is why he went off to Trinidad. He didn't tell his elder brother, because he would not have let him go."

"But he could have informed them after reaching Trinidad. Everybody here was sick with worry."

"You know Pranab Shankar. My opinion is, the man doesn't know how to keep a secret. His mind is an open book. May be Uma Shankar didn't tell him because he didn't trust him to keep the information to himself."

"You are right. Pranabda can't keep anything under his hat."

"Uma Shankar got into a tight spot after his passport and money got stolen in a foreign country. There, he had got to know a big businessman from Goa called Roderigue. We can guess that realizing the frustration and futility of his venture, he had openly told Roderigue the reason for his going to Trinidad. As of now, the nail costs millions of dollars. Which rich man would not want to keep it in his collection! The governments of many countries would want to keep it in their museums. Christian spiritual leaders would make a claim for it to be kept in the Vatican."

The Raja Bahadur agreed. "Yes, you had said these things even then."

"With the help of Roderigue, Uma Shankar tried to find Ram Sharma's house. I can't claim to know anything in detail but I can guess what must have happened. After he failed to find the nail, Uma Shankar came back to India with Roderigue. After that, we have seen certain things happen. Soon after his arrival in Bombay, Roderigue asked the Calcutta businessman Ramdulal Singhi to procure the book. In exchange, he tempted

Singhimashai with a contract worth two lakh rupees. Uma Shankar somehow got to know of this and became cautious. He rushed to Calcutta. But as chance would have it, that is the very day on which Singhimashai managed to get the book from Jagamohan."

"Right, right. Jagamohan got this done through Harisadhan ... Now I see!"

"Uma Shankar , under the alias of some Maitra, introduced himself as Roderigue's representative, spent the night in Singhimashai's office and got the book. Then he masked himself, intruded into Jagamohan's shop, and threatened him with a toy pistol never to buy and sell this book again. It was dark when he returned to Satpore. As he was quietly entering his house from the back gate, somebody was waiting for him. After hitting him on the head, he snatched the book for himself."

"Must be somebody connected with Roderigue?"

The Colonel shook his head. "It is not clear – the reason for Uma Shankar's entering the house quietly is that he probably did not want to face his brother in fear of being reprimanded by him. Although he was thirty-five or thirty-six years old, Uma Shankar was a bit whimsical. He would behave very childishly at times. I heard all this from Kumudini *Debi.*"

"Okay, that may be true. But who, apart from Roderigue, could be bothered about the nail? And how would that person know that Chotku would enter the house from the back gate at that time?"

The Colonel sat up straight and said, "Exactly! This is the real question. That is why I have come to ask you in confidence if there is anybody connected with Ramshankarpur who came to ask for the book from you?"

"Nobody at all." The Rajabahadur spoke with a worried face.

"Please try and remember!"

Thinking about it for a while, the Raja Bahadur said, "No! I can't remember any such thing."

"Did you want to print the book again?"

The Raja Bahadur said, "Yes. I thought I would do it around March. I had told you about it also. I would have gone to Calcutta this month and got in touch with a good printing press. Only a few days ago Pranabda phoned and wanted to know when I was getting the book printed again..."

The Colonel moved restlessly in his seat. His eyes became bright. "Did you say that Pranab Shankar wanted to know?"

"Yes."

"Why did Pranab Shankar suddenly want to know about this? He is not the kind of person who bothers his head about books. He stays quite aloof from most things."

The Raja Bahadur smiled. "Yes! I told him jokingly that the book has been getting destroyed bit by bit for such a long time, and that he should have got it published. A book written by ancestors! If it had not caught my eye, it would definitely have got destroyed... Pranabda said, 'You are right. I didn't understand the value of the book then'."

"Did Pranab Shankar say this?"

The Raja Bahadur was surprised by the Colonel's excitement. "Are you suspecting Pranabda..."

The Colonel stopped him and said, "No, no. It is not that." Then he stood up. "However, this is what I wanted to know. Whatever it is, I want to get back to Ramshankarpur right now. This time, I want your jeep."

"Certainly, certainly. One minute, I will tell Ramen. He will drop you to Pranabda's house. There is a ferry that can accommodate the jeep while crossing the Ganga. You won't get held up."

While going back, I did not ask the Colonel anything. It took less than twenty minutes to reach the bank of the Ganga by jeep. To cross over with jeep and all, it took ten minutes. In these motorized boats, there is a provision for carrying cars also.

The Raja Bahadur's jeep went off after dropping us to the gate of the Banerjees' house. It was past seven. The house was silent as night. In the combination of moonlight and fog, it seemed that the house was already asleep.

But Pranab Shankar was standing in the verandah outside the drawing room. He said, "You've come back from

Bhairabgarh! Were you able to meet the Raja Bahadur?"

The Colonel said, "Yes. Hasn't Uma Shankar Babu's body come back from the morgue?"

"It came at four. Everything was ready. The cremation was done immediately. It is about twenty minutes since we returned from the burning ghat."

While talking, we went to that room towards the south which had been given to us. A little later, Gangadhar came and gave us tea. After a few preliminaries, the Colonel asked, "Mr. Banerjee, did you ask the Raja Bahadur on the phone about the printing of the book some days back?"

Pranab Shankar was suddenly taken aback and said, "Yes, yes. I did. But why are you asking? Did I make a mistake?"

"No, no. Not a mistake." The Colonel said with a smile, "The reason for my asking is, why did you suddenly want to know about this from the Raja Bahadur?"

Pranab Shankar was shaken. "See, I don't understand anything about books and things. Neither am I interested in most things. One day Paritosh said that we should have got the book printed again. After all, Ram Shankar was the founder of this house and our ancestor. Who knows whether the Raja Bahadur will actually print it? Hearing that, I said, 'I'll find out'."

"Could you call Paritosh Babu once?"

Pranab Shankar said a little anxiously, "I have told him about meeting you. But so much strain has caused him a fever. After returning from the ghat, he has got into bed with a quilt. Come, let us go to his room."

We went round the southern and eastern end of the house and reached the outside of a room to the north-east of the house. A light was on in the room. Pranab Shankar called, "Paritosh! O Paritosh!" Then he knocked on the door. When there was no response, he pushed open the door. Since the door was only put together, it opened easily.

In the bed, somebody was lying with a quilt that covered him from his head to his toe. Pranab Shankar got very worried. "Goodness! Has he fainted from the convulsions of his fever? Paritosh, O Paritosh!" Saying this, he removed the quilt from the side of the head.

But on the pillow, instead of Paritosh Babu's head, there was a bolster. Pranab Shankar was totally taken aback. When the Colonel removed the quilt in one movement, we saw that the bolster had been placed on the bed longitudinally to give the impression of a man. Pranab Shankar gasped, "What is the meaning of this?"

"Quite clear," the Colonel snapped. "Seeing the difficult situation, Paritosh Babu has made himself scarce."

"Impossible! This can't be." Saying this, Pranab Shankar angrily went out. His yells could be heard outside. He was shouting for Gangadhar. "Gangu! See where Paritosh has gone."

I looked at the wise old man's face. He was observing

everything in the room in detail.

After upturning the pillow and the mattress, he went to the table. He pulled at the drawer and found it open. He handled some things inside. Then he went to the bookshelf on the other side of the table. Taking his torch out of his pocket he said, "My goodness! What is all this? Can you see Jayanto, what an affair this is!"

Not following anything, I said, "No indeed. Nothing makes sense to me any more."

"Can't you see these books? *The Mystery of the Egyptian Picture-script* by Morehead? *The History of the Process of Mummification* by Lord Carnarvon? And see, *The History of Egypt in the Roman Period*? This is a famous book – *Jesus Christ and the Five Lost Nails*. This is a strange collection Paritosh has!"

Saying this, the detective-supremo pulled out a waste paper basket from under the table. Then he started to collect crumpled bits of paper, cigarette butts thrown away from the ash-tray, and garbage like that.

After a while, I saw that he had straightened out a few crumpled papers and put them in his pocket. Then he picked up torn shreds of paper, spread them on the floor, and tried to join them together. Pranab Shankar came running in agitatedly and said, "I can't understand head or tail of why Paritosh behaved like this. Why did he do such a strange thing?"

Not replying to this, the Colonel stood up and said, "Mr.

Banerjee, did any trunk call come from Calcutta yesterday morning or the previous night?"

"It did. At that time, I had just about woken up. Gangu had said, 'A phone has come for Paritosh Babu from Calcutta.'"

"Didn't you hear what conversation was going on?"

Gangadhar was standing near the door. He said, "Paritosh Babu was saying to someone, 'The elder Babu is angry. Come stealthily under the cover of darkness.' He also said, 'Outdoing the thief in his own game?' He was laughing a lot. I remember these two statements of his."

The Colonel remarked, "This was Uma Shankar's second mistake…"

After we got back to our quarters, the Colonel spread the bits of paper on the table and said, "Now see, Jayanto!" I was quite astonished when I saw the word square that I had seen with the Colonel written on a piece of paper.

SATOR

AREPO

TENET

OPÈRA

ROTAS

In the other paper was written: Crow, cuckoo, woodpecker, cockatoo, snipe…

AEÓRPST SATPORE …

Ramakanta Kamar/ Subal Basu/ Raimani Maira/ Sada Das...

The Colonel smiled a little and said, "These Bangla names are probably pure games. When you read from right or left in Bangla, the words remain the same. Why I call them 'game' is because under them is written: Ka-na-k, Ja-la-j, Na-tu-n, Na-nd-an, Ka-nt-ak, Cha-m-cha, Ma-la-m ...After trying to solve a very complicated puzzle, it's a bit of a distraction, what else?"

Pranab Shankar was looking at his face pleadingly. He said, "Colonel! Have some mercy! Please tell us, was it Paritosh who murdered Chotku?"

The Colonel said, "Yes. Paritosh's primary intention was to get hold of the book. The second intention was to finish off his rival."

"Then we need to tell this to the police immediately. I reared a venomous snake- it is necessary to break his fangs."

Pranab Shankar was shaking in his rage. The Colonel tried to calm him a little. "Please, bear with us a little. We have not been able to establish the vital proof yet."

"What is that?"

"The murder weapon with which he was struck."

"Does anybody keep such a thing? The Ganga is one step away from the house. He must have thrown it away."

"In fact, he had a greater chance of getting caught if he had thrown it. Because Gobindo the gardener... One minute, I'll just be back. Saying this, the Colonel dashed out in a flurry.

Pranab Shankar said with surprise, "Where did he rush off to like that, can you tell me Jayanto Babu?"

"I think he has gone to Gobindo the gardener." Pranab Shankar stood silently for a while and then walked out slowly.

It was becoming colder. I had not guessed that it would be so much colder in the suburbs.

I was wearing a windcheater that barely kept out the cold. I picked up my blanket from my bed, wrapped it around myself and was just going to sit in an armchair when the lights went off. It must be some kind of load-shedding routine, I thought. I heard Pranab Shankar call out from the upper floor of the house. He was telling Gangadhar to light the hurricane.

Outside, the fog had thickened in the moonlight. Looking at the trees on the horizon, one had an eerie sensation. Five minutes passed, yet Gangadhar did not bring us a lamp. I thought I should call out to him and ask him to give us a candle at least. At the door, I had just yelled 'Gangadhar' when there was a faint sound in the room. The door leading to the inside was also open. I turned round and saw an outline of a form doing something, and heard a rustling sound. Whatever brightness the dusky moonlight outside was able to reflect was like darkness itself... "Who? Who is there?" I asked.

Immediately, someone seemed to whisper to himself, "Shut up. Or I'll finish you off."

Why had I not taken out my torch from my attaché-case!

But I am also not one to get intimidated. As soon as I screamed "Gangadhar! Gangadhar! Thief! Thief!" the wretched thief ran out after flinging me to the ground with a push. In my blanket-wrapped state on the floor, I resembled a fox in a trap. When I was able to stand up, I could hear Gangadhar. He was hurrying forward with a hurricane light.

Gangadhar panted. "What happenend, Sir? Was it an intruder?"

I said "Yes" seriously and pointed towards the table. The papers were not there. I understood that the thief had watched them from the wings. But what was the purpose of taking them? To do away with the proof? What else could it be?

Gangadhar was watching me sullenly. He said, "There's another mess on the other side. That's why it took me so much time to get a light. An intruder got into Paritoshbabu's room also."

"What are you saying?"

"He has emptied the bookshelves and taken away the books."

"Hmm, trying to do away with the proof."

Not comprehending, Gangadhar said, "I beg your pardon?"

I said. "Can you make some strong tea for me again, Gangadhar?"

"I'll get it, Sir." He disappeared.

My brain cells got activated only after the thief escaped. I took out my torch and my revolver of .22 caliber. Sometime later, Gangadhar came and gave me tea, saying, "The elder Babu is not feeling well. He is lying down. He asked me to request you not to mind..."

The Colonel returned after about two hours. He said laughingly, "I heard everything from Gangadhar. I hope you are safe and in the pink of health, darling!"

"I am. But the thief has run away with those papers. On the other hand, from Partitoshbabu's room also..."

The seasoned detective raised his hand and said, "I have heard. So what?" Saying this, he sat down and slowly lit a cheroot.

I asked, "Where did you go?"

The Colonel leaned as he sat down and said, "I suddenly realize that I am getting quite senile. The oldest inhabitant of this house is Gobindo Das. No, not the poet who wrote the *padavalis*, this one is a gardener. You can say he is my prototype, because he recognizes cacti. He also recognises orchids. On the trunks of the oldest trees in this house and on different branches, there is an orchid of a curiously beautiful variety. The bottom is red, the tip is blue. They flower during winter, and blossom into white clusters of flowers. Gobindo said that Ram Sharna had got them from some foreign country. They have been growing on this or that tree for five generations. They die out, and then flower again."

"Were you listening to stories about these orchids from Gobindo?"

"Yes. But the sad part of it is that in this house, Gobindo is like an old-fashioned, redundant piece of furniture. Out of pity, he has not been thrown onto the garbage heap yet. If his shovel gets rusted or it breaks, a new shovel is not bought for him. The elder Babu is as good as not being there. The manager Babu is more inclined to farming. What is more, he has even threatened to grow potatoes in what remains of the flower gardens and the fruit orchards."

"Who is the manager?"

"Paritosh." The Colonel shut his eyes and mildly puffed at his cheroot as he said, "Poor Gobindo's small crowbar was missing since this morning. He is reeling under the menace of cows and goats. He had thought he would put a fence all around. But somebody had stolen the crowbar with which he wanted dig a pit. He doesn't know when it was stolen. He remembers seeing it as late as yesterday evening."

"Colonel! Are you..."

The wise detective said, "The happy news is that before he could complain to the elder *Babu* about the crowbar, he was surprised to see it in its place. Yes dear, if it didn't come back, Gobindo would have complained to the elder Babu about it. There would have been some conjectures about the crow-bar suddenly disappearing like that – particularly against the backdrop of Uma Shankar's murder."

The Colonel blew away some smoke from his cheroot and said again, "But Gobindo was glad to see the crowbar in its usual place. So he has no reason to complain. Yes ... That is why Paritosh did not throw the crowbar into the Ganga. He knew Gobindo would not bother his head over that. In fact, he would have got more worked up if he did not get it back. He would have told the others."

"Did you see the crowbar?"

He nodded and said, "Gobindo told me about the crowbar while confiding his woes in me. Otherwise, it was not an important incident for him – at least not after getting the lost treasure back. Now the point is, if you hit somebody with a crowbar behind his head, the crowbar may or may not have bloodstains on it. It takes a little time, though very little, for blood to spurt out. It is an injury over the crop of one's hair with a blunt instrument. Say, it will take 3-4 seconds for the blood to ooze out. By that time, the thing has moved away a little. So it need not have had any bloodstains at all. Or if it does, you cannot often see it with the naked eye. The only thing to do in such cases is a forensic examination. I flashed the bright light from this torch on Gobindo's crowbar and saw through a magnifying glass, there were faint traces of blood on it."

Saying this, the Colonel took out something that was wrapped in paper and about a foot and a half long from his pocket and kept it on the table. Then he took out a book. Although it was leather-bound, its condition was tattered. Surprised, I said, "What is that? Where did you get it?"

From your second question, it is evident that you have

realized what book this is. Jayanto, this is that lost book. Ram Shankar Sharma's autobiography."

"First please tell me where you got it."

Ignoring my question, the Colonel proceeded, "Gobindo knows orchids. He keeps an eye on the family of the orchids brought by Ram Shankar. And you should see him when they blossom, he dances with joy. When I talked about orchids, he said happily that flowers came out this morning on the orchid plant that are creeping up the trunk of the *shirish* tree. 'Would you like to see it, *huzoor*?' Why me, anybody who dresses like a *sahib* is *huzoor* to him. My torch is very bright. Looking at the flowers, my eyes suddenly spotted something inside the curtain of orchids. Was it a bird's nest? I asked Gobindo if he had a ladder. Gobindo said , 'I'll just bring one, *huzoor*'."

I interrupted him and said, "Was the book hidden inside the orchids?"

The clever old man did not answer. I snatched the book from his hand. He shut his eyes, puffed at his cheroot and said, "First I want to hear you read the appendix."

I started reading. It was torn in some places. I could not read all of it.

> ...I advise my future generations that they should respect all religions. I specially say that Jesus Christ has also been accepted as another incarnation of God in our country. The sins of mankind were washed away by his blood.

> Moreover, the two communities that received the blood of his sacrifice have been blessed by his awakening them from their stupor… In the garden, all kinds of birds fly. They are symbolic of five kinds of beauty. Those five forms are the five nails. The five nails stained with the blood of Christ… About the protection of this angel in the garden that is an embodiment of beauty, I say that her beautiful mien is blessed in a way with the touch of that same self-sacrifice. I undertook a lot of trouble to establish her here…

The Colonel sat up straight. He took the book from my hands and started reading the appendix. Then he said, "Jayanto, possibly Ram Sharma has hinted at something here ... The angelic form – it must mean the statue on top of the fountain. The five-edged fountain…. He is giving instructions for its protection to his future generations… her beautiful mien is blessed with the touch of self-sacrifice. Jayanto! Does this not imply the self-sacrifice of Jesus Christ on the cross?… But notice the words 'mien' which means 'face'. Face means the inside of her head."

The Colonel stood up excitedly. My brain also made a connection. "But that angel on the fountain does not even have a head. It was broken long ago by a storm. Wasn't Pranab Shankar saying that?"

"But that means somebody must have got the nail. Despite seeing it, he didn't even realize what it was," the Colonel said restlessly. "A precious, historic relic!"

One could hear the sound of shoes outside. Then I saw the light from a torch.

A deep voice asked, "In which room?"

We heard the voice of Gangadhar. "There, Sir. Where there is a hurricane light."

The Colonel peeped out of the door and said, "Is it Mr. Sanyal? Come on in."

"Hello old dove!" A police officer entered the room and shook hands with the Colonel. Four other officers entered the room after him. Immediately, I understood that in the last two hours the detective-supremo had not only been chatting with Gobindo, but must have contacted these people also.

The Colonel said, "Mr. Sanyal, let me introduce you. My young journalist friend Jayanto Choudhuri. And Jayanto, this is police superintendent Mr. Ajitesh Sanyal."

After introductions with everybody else, the business started in right earnest. Station house officer Indrajit Bhadra said, "Paritosh has been apprehended in the fields inside Mr. Banerjee's farm. Colonel, you got the bull's eye! We have just arrested him and come here. The criminal is by now in the police station lock-up."

The Colonel said, "Take this murder weapon. We have to send it for a forensic test. There is blood and the criminal's finger prints on it. Gobindo the gardener is also a witness."

An officer took away the crowbar carefully wrapped in paper. At last, Pranab Shankar came down. Panting, he said, "Has the rascal murderer been nabbed? Has the deadly snake been caught?"

Mr. Sanyal laughed. "Yes. Sometime back. He was thinking of spending the night in your farmhouse. Our men had already laid a trap there. Don't worry, please go and sleep peacefully."

Pranab Shankar sat down. He said, "Tea is coming. Please sit down."

As though thinking aloud, the Colonel said, "I hadn't thought of this aspect even after coming here. I had thought that Roderigue's men are here but what I couldn't figure out is how he established a connection here so speedily from Bombay... Besides how did he find out about the stealing of the book? Everything seemed a bit confusing. In the evening, after going to Bhairabgarh, when I found out that Mr. Banerjee has been trying to find out about reprinting the book, I realized that somebody is goading Mr.Banerjee on to do it. After worrying a lot about it, he needs the book very badly now. However, Paritosh was desperately trying to do away with the incriminating evidence, taking advantage of the load-shedding. He would have grabbed the book from the *shirish* tree but he could not, because I was there. He thought he would return to take it later. Now let me ask Mr. Banerjee something."

Pranab Shankar said, "Please ask, Colonel."

"The head of the angel on the fountain was destroyed in the

storm of 1942. What was your age then?"

"About twenty-four or twenty-five."

"Then you should remember. After the head of the angel was broken, did you see anything like a nail inside it?"

"Yes. Yes. There was a spear-like object... to join the head."

The Colonel said with a heavy sigh, "No, Mr. Banerjee, that is the sacred, historic nail."

"What are you saying!" Pranab Shankar said with wonder. "That is why something was written on it in very small letters."

"Do you remember what happened to it after that?"

Gangadhar said from the doorway, "Why *Barobabu*, didn't Gobindo's wife take it out and bring it in? She made it a clasp to tie her goats with. It was a long nail. There were some engravings on its bottom."

The Colonel said, "Then it should be in Gobindo's room."

Gangadhar shook his head and said, "The nail was very unlucky, *huzoor.* Whichever goat his wife used to tie to that nail would get carried away by a fox or die of some disease. Finally, Gobindo's wife also died. Then Gobindo went and threw it into the Ganga. After that there were no losses, Sir."

The Colonel asked with disappointment, "Threw it in the Ganga?"

At last I saw a very old man sitting wrapped in a cotton blanket near the door. He first cleared his throat, and then said, "Sir, that nail engraved with a magic spell has been the bane of this house. *Barobabu* does not have children. He had one brother who also got murdered helplessly. On the other hand, see my situation. I am somehow surviving. I have no peace or happiness. That is why it is believed to be Ram Sharma's ancient saying that the more the laughter the more the crying. Somebody had carved a magic spell on the iron nail. That is why he also had to lose his life by getting hanged."

Everybody in the room was quiet for a while. Then the lights came on. Pranab Shankar said, "Gangu! Where is the tea?"

"I'll get it, *Barobabu*!" Saying this, Gangadhar went off.

I looked at the Colonel and saw him sitting quietly with his face resting on his hand. I felt sad. If he had recovered the sacred, historic relic, he could have shaken the entire world with the tremendous excitement of its discovery...

We had got ready for the morning train. The Colonel said, "Come Jayanto! Let us go and bid farewell to the exotic angel of the fountain."

After getting to the fountain, he said, "Jayanto, I am really getting to be senile. Otherwise, I should have realized yesterday afternoon after seeing the five-edged fountain, that the key of the mystery lies here. I thought of the five holy stars of Christianity immediately. Yet I did not realize that the nail should naturally be connected to all this. SATOR, AREPO, TENET, OPERA, ROTAS! One minute!"

Saying this, the Colonel stepped inside the fountain and

removed the grass and weeds from one side of the broken, concrete pillar. He took out a knife from his pocket. He kept rubbing it with his knife for a while.

Very soon, he came back with a bitter face. I saw that on the body of the pillar, the terracotta figure of a crow had emerged. That meant that on the other side, there must be similar figures of a cuckoo, a cockatoo, a woodpecker and a snipe.

But my aged friend was not prepared even to turn around and look. He said, "Its time for the train. Come on Jayanto."

I knew that it was that crow which had started it all. The Colonel can't stand crows…

The Inauspicious Goddess

Due to some mysterious reasons, Colonel Niladri Sarkar had recently spent some time at the Tora Islands in the Indian Ocean. Apparently, a strange creature moves around there in the night. Its face is that of a horse, the body that of a man – in one word, one might describe it as a horse-man. I was listening very intently to the thrilling story and wondering whether these horse-men could be the descendants of the *Hayagriva avataar,* described in our Puranic tales. Just then, Shashthicharan came and presented a card to the Colonel and said, "*Babamashai*, a gentleman wants to see you".

The little card was almost crumbling like dust. The Colonel turned it around and asked, "Is he tall and thin, with a middle parting?"

To my amazement, Shashthi said, "Yes".

"Black coat, loose trousers, a sling bag on his shoulder?"

"Yes *Babamashai.*" Shashthi's face expanded into a toothy smile.

"Bring him in." Saying this, the Colonel passed on the grimy, tattered card to me. "It is the only card he possibly has, darling. Handle it carefully – otherwise, you'll have to get some cards printed at your own cost for the poor man."

The visitor's name was printed on the card. Professor Tanacha, the great magician. "Is he a Chinese or a Japanese?" I asked.

"No. A genuine Bengali."

"Strange name! But have you lately acquired the skill of being able to see beyond the wall?"

"I went to scare a crow away a little while back, when I saw Professor Tanacha standing and looking pathetically at my flat. He must have been in a quandary as to whether he should come to me for a trivial matter… Here he is. Come in, come in, Professor Tanacha. Please sit down."

If the person who entered had been wearing a dhoti and a punjabi, I could have sworn that he was a percussionist in all-night musical soirees – he had a parting in the middle, a drowsy look, the air of a philosopher, and a smile as soft as butter. But the condition of his coat and pants was as pathetic as that of his card. He kept the dirty bag on the coffee table, smiled sheepishly and said, "May I speak frankly? "

The Colonel said, "Say what you have to without fear, Professor Tanacha. And er… will coffee be alright for you?"

"Of course. But two parts milk and one part coffee." Professor Tanacha gave a throaty laugh, making sounds like the wrenching of violin strings.

He should be drinking milk instead of coffee, I thought. I kept staring at Professor Tanacha. If one is not a habitual coffee drinker, he may as well not have it. I don't know why, but one could smell a mystery just by looking at the chap. Even if he was not a magician, there was some magic in his drowsy look.

After ordering Shashthicharan to make some coffee, the Colonel said, "Let me introduce you to my young friend Jayanto Choudhury, special correspondent of the *Dainik Satyasebak.*"

Professor Tanacha was full of joy. "What good luck! In all truth, I decided to come to the Colonel only after reading your article 'Ghostly Commuters in Nocturnal Taxi'. I managed to get the address from your office after a lot of effort. I had enquired after you. I heard that you had gone to Santhaldi, and would be late getting back. Have you found out if we'll have any respite from load-shedding?"

The Colonel smiled a little and said, "Even if we do, what makes you think that the menace of ghosts in your house will stop? That depends entirely on the intention of the ghosts concerned."

Professor Tanacha's face lit up with wonder. "I decided to come here only after reading in the papers about your supernatural powers. I admit, Colonel Saheb, at one time I have displayed many supernatural tricks here and abroad – but I'm not a patch on you. I have left the trade long ago. You can say I developed a kind of contempt for it. Not to talk of insomnia, things like mental tensions and poverty made me.... So..."

The Colonel snatched the words from his mouth and said, "Like the ghost in the taxi, I trust that your ghost, too, is very generous with money?"

The drowsiness disappeared from Professor Tanacha's eyes. He said, "How strange, how very strange! I see you can read people's thoughts."

"How much money have you made?"

Professor Tanacha lowered his voice and said, "A total of fifty rupees in five days. There was a ten rupee note in an envelope every day with 'Wish you good luck' written on the cover. What a thing to happen, Sir! Here are people trying to earn money by the sweat of their brow. They are even committing crimes and murders. And I get a ten rupee note in an envelope lying at my feet every morning out of the blue!"

"I suppose you didn't get any envelope this morning?"

Professor Tanacha shook his head sadly. I was staring at both of them foolishly. Then I saw that the Colonel was leaning back in his chair with his eyes shut, running his hands over his bald pate. He suddenly opened his eyes after a few seconds and said, "I hope nothing's been stolen from your room?"

"Stolen?" Professor Tanacha smiled faintly. "What is there to steal? I stay in a makeshift room on the terrace of a house in Mirzapur. There's a broken old bed – in fact, an apology for a bed. Underneath lies a suitcase containing some small props for showing magic. Apart from that, there is an earthen pitcher and a tumbler to drink water from. These are all my worldly possessions. What could a burglar possibly take?"

"You smoke opium, don't you?"

Professor Tanacha was taken aback. He smiled somewhat embarrassed and said, "What can I do... I suffer from insomnia!"

"You must be sleeping with your doors open?"

"It's so hot – it hasn't rained for days."

"Are you sure nothing's been stolen?"

"No!" Professor Tanacha shook his head violently.

The Colonel gave him a piercing look and said, "Perhaps it could be something trivial that you haven't missed as yet?"

At last, Shashthicharan brought some coffee. The Colonel asked, "Think about it while drinking your coffee. Think about it and tell me, Professor Tanacha!"

We sipped at out respective cups of coffee. We were enveloped by a grim and uneasy anxiety. A little later, the Colonel took his last sip of coffee, and as he was about to light a cheroot, Professor Tanacha suddenly stirred. Gulping down the remains of the milky coffee, he banged down the cup and stood up.

"Good heavens! Grandfather's amulet!" he cried out immediately. He pushed the curtain aside and disappeared. The curtain fluttered as if hit by a gust of wind.

The Colonel blew a ring of blue smoke, and smilingly said,

"What do you make of this, Jayanto?"

"A lot. I see you are the king of magicians. How did you know all this? You must know the gentleman."

"This is the first time I've met him, my dear!"

The Colonel got up from the sofa and walked towards the window. But there were no crows to shoo away. Peering down at the road below, he said, "Professor Tanacha has just got into a bus. Anyway, I can sense that you are somewhat surprised. You see, Jayanto, the important thing is observation. Besides, you know that observing people is one of my hobbies. This is not very difficult, even you can succeed if you try. For instance, you can make out that he is an opium addict by simply looking at his eyes. Moreover, he asked for extra milk in his coffee. Opium addicts are greatly fond of milk. You yourself wrote about the ghostly passenger of the taxi, who paid extra money to the driver so that he could return to the same place again at two o'clock in the morning. As soon as Professor Tanacha mentioned this, I knew something like that must have happened to him."

"How did you know that he did not get an envelope containing money today?"

The Colonel smiled. "If he had got the money today, he would not have come. Who wants to spread the word about getting money like this? He would have paused to think that the invisible donor might stop giving the money. He came to me only because it had stopped."

"But the theft?"

"There can only be one reason for giving money to an opium addict like him. If a needy man like him has money in his hands, he will increase his dose of opium and be knocked out. Taking that opportunity, the thief would have a lot of time to get the desired object in his hands. But I don't believe that he keeps the door open because of the heat. The door used to be left open because he would always be in a state of inebriation. This is the problem of all opium addicts, my boy! They will not let their craving for the narcotic drug be spoiled by anything – even if their house is burnt down in the process."

The Colonel suddenly frowned and walked a few steps forward. "Oh! The man has left his bag behind!"

I noticed the bag on the table. I asked, "What can be inside the bag of an opium addict?"

The Colonel opened the bag, looked inside and said, "Not having got any money today, Professor Tanacha was disgruntled and went for a bath in the Ganges. He came here on his way back. His *lungi* and towel are still wet. And… and… this… Hmm… A notebook! One should not look at other people's belongings. But this is a special case. I must try and know the gentleman better."

It was a thin and tattered notebook with a black cover. Its condition was like that of his card. I quickly glanced through the first page and saw Shri Tara Nath Chatterjee written in capital letters. "The Tanacha mystery is solved, Colonel! Please turn the page," I said.

The next page was filled with what were probably some magical invocations and chants, written in red ink. *Om wring cring phat phat... maray maray taray taray...* strange words and other chants like these. There were chants to tame, chants to kill, and chants to exorcise, followed by a detailed description of the magical powers of the roots of various trees. Then the Colonel opened another page and said, "Is this also a *mantra*? Or is it just a rhyme?"

When you are part of
That gross social class
Let your will abstain
Oh ghostly palm tree!

I started reciting this strange incantation or rhyme. After reciting it a few times, I had memorized it. The Colonel put away the notebook and said, "There is an uncanny rhythm in the lines. It can be memorized easily. Jayanto, the scribblings of a man whose amulet gets stolen like that must have some significance. I would rather sit down with all this in the afternoon. Right now, it is time for me to go up to my terrace. I have put an electronometer on my Mexican cactus in the morning. It is imperative for me to see if the wicked plant has responded to the graphic chart."

The Colonel got up. I understood that there was no scope for a chat at that point of time. The old man would now enter the world of strange creatures and insects, and his state would become like that of the opium addict Professor Tanacha. Even threats of violence cannot curb this obsession for nature study. I, therefore, got up to leave. I said, "See you, Colonel! Let me know on the phone how the mystery of Professor Tanacha is progressing. What a story it could make for the *Dainik Satyasebak* !"

The Colonel grinned mischievously and said, "May be Professor Tanacha wanted to be in league with evil spirits at one time. That may be a *mantra* to invoke those evil spirits. Concentrate on it and find out for yourself!"

I had to run around on some official errands for a couple of days after this incident. I would call the Colonel, whenever I found time, in between. There was no trace of Professor Tanacha. He did not come back even to collect his bag. After a week or so, the Colonel called me. He had gone to his rented room in a boarding house in Mirzapur to track Professor Tanacha down. He had found the door locked. The manager of the place had said, "He is a mad fellow. There is no certainty about when he's in and when he's out."

I told the Colonel over the phone, "Professor Tanacha has probably gone to that land of the *Hayagriva avataars* to recover his grandfather's amulet. Why don't you go in search of him?"

The Colonel said, "I don't have any time, my boy! It's almost the end of October. I am too busy trying to detect the reaction of dewdrops and fog on my Mexican cacti. Besides, the wings of the butterfly that I had brought from the jungle of Bhainsara have suddenly started changing colour. I am stuck in the maze of the mysteries of nature...." And the Colonel seasoned his talk with like remarks for another five minutes.

That very evening, I got a strange letter.

> Dear Reporter
> You are always on the lookout for thrilling happenings. Please come into the abode of the inauspicious goddess, next to the river, behind the Lohagara palace, on 2nd of November, at ten in the night. You will get some exciting news there and then.
> Yours truly,
> Ace of Spades.

Reading the letter, I laughed for a while. Many people write such facetious letters to those working in newspapers; some even threaten them with their lives. But I am immune to all this. I have often been led by such messages to rush to some spot, only to discover that the whole thing was a hoax, that someone had pulled a fast one on me!

But the peculiarity of this letter was that it was made up of words cut out and pasted from newspapers. It did not take me long to understand where he had got 'The Ace of Spades' from – the comic strip that appears at the bottom of page two of the *Dainik Satyasebak*. But even after going through files of the newspaper, I could not figure out from where he had fashioned 'Lohagara palace' and 'the abode of the inauspicious goddess'.

When I got out of the office on 31st October, I still thought of the incident as a prank. But after returning home, a pent-up restlessness stirred within me. I sat down with the letter once again. On the outside of the envelope, even my name and address were in print. That was an easy job. The name could have been cut out from my feature in the *Dainik Satyasebak*. As for the address, it is printed at the bottom of the last page. I could not read the postmark.

I did not have the heart to tell the Colonel about the incident, since I knew what he was like. Moreover, right then he was caught up in the 'mysteries' of nature! He could not be distracted from his butterfly's wing or the instrument attached to his cacti even if I were to burst a cracker.

Nevertheless, after a sleepless night, I desperately rang up the old man on 1st November. The call was received by his servant Shashthicharan. He asked, "Is it the *Dadababu* from the newspaper? *Babamashai* is not at home. In fact, he left for some place last night – let me think, Gargara , or was it Sonagara?…Hell! I know the name, but can't get myself to utter it."

"Was it Lohagara?"

"Yes! Yes! That's the place, Newspaper *Dadababu.*" He started giggling helplessly.

"He didn't say anything, did he?"

"When does he tell me anything? As soon as he thinks of any place, he gets up and goes there. It is always like that. But one thing, Newspaper *dada.*"

"Oh, tell me quickly!"

"A car came to fetch him from the Lohagara palace, you know!" Shashthicharan started laughing again.

"What is there to laugh at?"

"If you saw the car, you would also laugh, Newspaper *dada*!

"Must be a vintage car, isn't that so? The erstwhile rajas and zamindars are in a pathetic state. Okay, I'll hang up now."

"Please listen," Shashthi said anxiously. "I just remembered. *Babamashai* said something about you. Hell! I wish I could get the name straight... Yes, he asked you to get there immediately. You have to go."

Why had he not said so earlier? Furious, I banged the phone down. I stayed angry for a minute. The master and the servant were equally crazy. Why didn't the Colonel take me with him, or give me a ring before he left?

However, the mystery had deepened. The Ace of Spades had asked me to be at the temple of the inauspicious Goddess on the bank of the river, behind the Lohagara palace. On the other hand, people from the same Lohagara palace had sent a car to the detective-supremo. Surely, all this could not have been merely coincidental or a trick.

The more I thought about it, the more a dark veil of a

mystery seemed to obfuscate my mind. A white coloured card, the Ace of Spades, flashed across gaps in the veil. It all felt quite eerie to me.

But whoever this Ace of Spades might be, right now I needed to find out where this Lohagara was. I cursed the old Colonel many times. He could have at least left the address with Shashthicharan. For me to find Lohagara now would be like looking for a needle in a haystack!

I suddenly realized that the place couldn't be that unalluring since it has a palace.... Besides, it had the temple of the goddess of ill omens or whatever – which has a rare fame, you could even call it notoriety. I wanted to try to find the place. I must say I am usually lucky.... In the office library, I found the place in the guidebook of place-names. It was a small station of the Eastern Railways at the outer periphery of Bihar; a historical place with a temple worth visiting. The seventeenth century ancestor of the present royal family, Shivendra Narayan, was a most dreaded man. He perpetrated all kinds of atrocities on his subjects. He would not drink water without having performed a bloody rite everyday. He established the temple of *Alakshmi* and worshipped her. His descendants had tried in later times to destroy the idol and replace it with one of *Lakshmi*. But weird things kept happening. At last, even though the temple was demolished, nobody was able to remove that sculpted image of ill luck. Even now, the cruel eyes of the stone goddess stare at you from a throne on a raised platform in the rectangular ground. What kind of an imbecile would worship an *Alakshmi*?

Only I know how I reached Lohagara. The train seemed to move like a run-down car. It reached past eleven at night. There was not a soul on the platform. The station master was talking to somebody with a spectral lantern in his hand. What could I do but to ask him for shelter for the night? No other passenger had got down from the train. The surrounding areas were bathed in moonlight. But a fog had descended over the trees. The hillocks surrounding us seemed to be standing like huge elephants.

"Hallo, Jayanto."

I was startled to see the person talking to the station master, and immediately all my resentment, disappointment and tiredness vanished. My heart also melted. My aged friend had surely not come to the station at this time of the night to see rare specimens of nocturnal birds.

"I also checked the train that came earlier in the evening."

The detective-supremo placed a hand on my shoulder. "Don't be angry with this old man, my young friend! I had to hurry and come here as soon as I got the call from the Raja Bahadur. You work in a newspaper. You have so many kinds of assignments. You can't come away with me the moment I ask you to, can you?"

"I never asked you for any explanations. At this moment, there is only one thing I feel like asking for. That is a cup of strong and hot tea or coffee."

"You will get it," the detective consoled me. As soon as we reached outside the station, somebody spoke in a serious voice, "Has your reporter friend come, Colonel?"

A gentleman came out of the shadows. The Colonel said, "Jayanto has come, Jaygopalbabu. Didn't I tell you? Wherever in the world strange things happen, Jayanto pays a visit. I knew that he wouldn't be able to rest till he came."

The Colonel laughed loudly. But Jaygopalbabu did not laugh. I understood that he was a humourless kind of a person. He extended his hand and shook hands with me. "You are welcome to the Lohagara palace, Jayantobabu"

The Colonel said, "Jayanto, he is the manager of the royal estate – an extremely fearless person. Despite that, he too...", the Colonel stopped suddenly.

Jaygopalbabu said, "Please come this way, Colonel. Jayantobabu must be tired."

It seemed to me that the gentleman had come to the station with the Colonel rather unwillingly. Whatever be the reason, he wanted to get back to the palace quickly.

The small bazaar at the station was as silent as the night. A light was buring in only one tea stall. Some people were sitting there drowsily with tumblers of tea in their hands. My mind became restless for tea. But I had to get into the car because of the hurry that Jaygopalbabu seemed to be in. This must have been the car that was sent to Calcutta to bring back the Colonel.

Shashthicharan couldn't really be blamed for laughing at the car. It was a vintage car that was falling apart. And the road was also very rough. The car crossed some inhabited areas and took a turn after crossing a hillock. Then it started traversing a huge, empty field which was white with moonshine. The royal palace seemed to be quite far away.

Another mile on the road was very strenuous. After scaring some wild ducks next to a pond with the noise from the car, we reached the palace. When the car entered the gate, a shadow seemed to close the gate silently. Jaygopalbabu said to him, "Raghab! Hurry up and tell the *thakur* to make a pot of coffee."

The Colonel had been accommodated in a room next to the hall. Jaygopalbabu went away after saying "See you in the morning." A little later, Raghab came in and left some coffee. While drinking the strong coffee, I took out and showed the letter from the Ace of Spades.The Colonel responded with a few moments' silence. Then he said, "On this front, another mystery plot has thickened, because of which I hurried here. The Raja Bahadur Ajitendra believes that some catastrophe is going to befall the palace very soon. Some strange pounding and clanging sounds are heard at midnight. It seems as if some people are walking all around. It seems as if they are breaking some things. The Raja Bahadur claims to have seen the idol of the *Alakshmi* walking around in the garden. But stranger than that are the knocks on the door. On opening the door, however, you can't see anybody. And all this happens at night. Everything is normal during the day.

As soon as the Colonel stopped, one could hear loud, clattering sounds somewhere. Somebody seemed to throw a metallic thing far away. "See! I heard this sound even though I reached late last night..."

There was no doubt that I was startled by the sound. But my clever friend seemed to be even more startled than me. It made me feel like laughing a bit. I said, "So you have been living in a mysterious house for the last two days, I see! O great and wise detective, is it that you are ultimately coming round to believe in ghosts?"

The Colonel looked at my face and saïd, "You are still thinking of the matter as a joke, Jayanto! I can see by your face that you haven't got at all scared. But I am somehow really feeling kind of scared."

I was surprised. What could the great, intrepid and strong Colonel be scared of ? Surely it couldn't be a fear of ghosts. I asked, "Do you think that behind these ghostly happenings, there is some man whose pseudonym is The Ace of Spades?"

"I can't say. I can only guess that somebody wants to do something dreadful. This is all a preparation for that." Saying this, the Colonel lit a cheroot. Then he walked towards the window.

Somewhere above, one could hear the sound of what seemed like an enormous animal like an elephant walking around – *dhup, dhup, dhup*. "Frantically I asked, What sound is that?"

The Colonel did not reply. When the sound came from the terrace just over our room I really got paranoid with a fear of ghosts. Dhup dhup, dhup dhup... the entire terrace seemed to shake with the sound. This was certainly not the sound of human feet.

A little later, the sound seemed to move away. When it faded into the distance, the Colonel said, "Last night I ran up when I heard that sound. I was at the bottom of the staircase in the hall when I suddenly saw the rear legs of the elephant for a moment. Whatever it is, it is not a practical thing for elephants to roam around over a palace in the dead of the night."

Saying this, the Colonel shut both the windows. Then he said, "Go to sleep, Jayanto. Hmm, before that, you should eat something. See, your food is lying covered on the table."

After spending a night at the Lohagara palace, I know exactly what a nightmare is. The ringing of the grandfather clock in the hall seemed to become louder as the night progressed. It seemed to stop, to take some breath, and then rang again in a way that scared the hell out of me. At one time, somebody knocked on the door of the hall three times. Even if the Colonel had not forbidden me to do so, I would not have opened the door.

The two enormous windows were closed. That is why I could not sleep. I felt suffocated. At last, I got out of my mosquito net and opened them. But I did not have the heart to look out. If I suddenly saw the idol of the *Alakshmi* parading around in the garden, I would surely faint. The moonlight was flooding the room. But I was afraid to look at its silvery whiteness. I heard a fox cry out towards morning. A little later, in some room upstairs, somebody forcefully hurled a metallic object as if to break it in a fit of rage. Who was it?

Then somebody came down the stairway of the hall with noisy footsteps. Was it that ghostlike elephant? In fear, I took out my revolver, and kept sitting in my bed, fully alert. But that supernatural beast did not come to break the door of my room. I heard a dog howling. In the moonlight outside, an owl hooted and flew away. I must have dropped off soon after that.

I woke up to see that it was almost seven-thirty. The Colonel was not there. Possibly, he had gone for a walk. The door facing the hall was open. Somebody said from behind the curtain, "I've brought your tea, Sir!"

The hefty man called Raghab entered the room with a tray. He said modestly, "Please call me when you need me, Sir. My name is Raghab. I stay in the next room."

When we asked about Jaygopalbabu, Raghab said, "The manager is now in the dogs' room. He has this one obsession, Sir. He spends the whole day with his dogs."

After Raghab went away, I openend the door facing the south and went to the verandah on the other side. The surroundings were becoming clear in the daylight. The palace, situated in an open area outside the habitations, looked like a silent and haunted house. It occupied a huge area, and was bounded by high walls on all four sides. The garden, which must have been well cared for at one time, had transformed itself virtually into a jungle now. I could even see a black cannon inside the garden. I kept aside the cup of tea, and went down the stairs into the lawn. The grass was still bright with dewdrops. I started walking along a path going towards the east, running parallel to the south wall. The eastern gate was falling apart. The iron door had got rusted and broken. Getting out of there, I could see a river. So this was the river Loha. It had turned to the west in a semicircle. On this turn, the palace was situated on an elevated piece of land. I braved the wilderness to go ahead a little in order to find the temple of the *Alakshmi*. It was then that I saw somebody crouching next to the wall, obviously upto something.

The distance between the man and me was not more than fifty yards or so. I was startled to see him wearing a black coat. The next moment, he turned his face towards my side. Then I saw to my surprise that it was none other than Professor Tanacha!

He amazed me by quickly getting up and disappearing into the thick overgrowth. For one moment, I seemed to see a knife in his hand. If it had not gleamed in the sunshine, I might not have noticed it. I got very agitated and went after him, calling, "Professor Tanacha! Professor Tanacha! Listen, listen!"

There was no reply. The man had simply vanished. I was

standing there, quite stunned, when a brown-coloured cap suddenly appeared above the slope of the river on the left. "Here you are, Jayanto! I see you are awake very early. I thought you would not be up until nine." It was the aged nature-lover.

I said agitatedly, "Colonel, I just saw Professor Tanacha!"

The Colonel smiled, and with a wink said, "Hmm. Papaverassia family. Part of the poppy genus."

"What are you saying? I clearly saw Professor Tanacha with a knife there..."

"I understand." The Colonel removed an insect from his white beard. "My dear chap, are you from East Bengal or West Bengal?"

I got angry and said, "I am a pure West Bengali. But what are you raving about?"

"You are a West Bengali. Therefore you like eating *posto*. But do you know that that is the fruit of the white poppy?" Saying this, the Colonel held my hand and took me to the side of the wall. "See whose throat Professor Tanacha was slitting."

I gazed all round and saw that the place was filled with a plant of a pigmy size – only six or seven inches in height. Near the root of the plants, there were cut marks. I said, "I can't make sense of it. Will it help professor Tanacha in his magic?"

The Colonel laughed loudly. "These are opium plants, Jayanto! The sticky substance that accumulates at the slits is unadulterated opium. Poor Professor Tanacha was being provided money to buy opium by some generous-minded ghost. As soon as that stopped, he came with his begging bowl, knocking at the door of nature itself. However, the difference between you and him is that he eats the gum of the very plant of which you eat the seed."

"Calcutta and Lohagara are more than three hundred kilometres apart. How did he know that there are opium plants in the undergrowth here?"

"He has somehow got to know of it. How do I get to know which remote jungle houses a rare specimen of some bird?"

"Whatever you say, his behaviour is very mysterious. When he said that his grandfather's amulet had got stolen, he left his bag and disappeared. Then after so many days, I see him doing the rounds for his opium. Stranger still is his vanishing act on seeing me."

"Perhaps the gentleman felt very ashamed. That's most natural. That is why I did not go near him despite seeing him from afar." The Colonel pulled me by the hand and took a step. I asked, "Can you tell me where is the temple of the *Alakshmi*?"

"It's in the jungle behind. But when you see her, your body will go cold. A statuesque nightmare."

"Don't scare me – I'm not a little boy. I want to see the idol."

"No. Obey the instruction of the Ace of Spades, Jayanto.

He's asked you to go there exactly at ten tonight – not before that. This is a gentleman's contract, my boy. It should be honoured."

Keeping the river to our right, we kept going to the north on the bank. The high wall of the palace was to our left. After the gate, we could see a dilapidated outhouse. The Colonel said, "This was at one time the Raja Bahadur's boat-house. See, there's a boat. The boat must be incapable of going in the water any more..." Then he suddenly stopped. Someone was coming out of the wooden room one side of which had partly collapsed. Was it a *Saadhubaba*? But what a grotesque, monstrous visage the *saadhubaba* had!

Was it a *saadhubaba* or some madman? He came forward threateningly as soon as he saw us. "Who is it? Go away! I say go away quickly. The *Alakshmi* has awakened. She will chew the bones in your skull. Get out, get out!"

As soon as he took up a piece of stone, the Colonel said, "Things don't augur well, Jayanto. It is better to get away. I think he belongs to an abominable sect of *saadhus*. Their staple diet is human heads."

The stone he hurled came and fell short of us. We turned around and walked away as if to retreat. After entering from the gate, the Colonel giggled like a child, "So you see, Jayanto, what a formidable place this Lohagara is! Be very careful! I have reason to believe that your flesh is softer and tastier than my old, tough and fibrous flesh. These followers of the cult of

Shiva will salivate to see you. Of course, you know Professor Tanacha's *mantra* which can awaken evil spirits. You can try and chant it.

The Colonel started chanting:

> When you are a part of
> That gross social class
> Let your will abstain
> Oh ghostly palm tree!

We could see Jaygopalbabu a little distance away. A dog was running here and there in front of him. The dog came running to us. He sniffed the Colonel's and my trousers by turn, and then returned to his master. The Colonel said, "I see Jaygopalbabu keeps tracking dogs. Do you know what breed of dog this is? Labrador retriever. They look like *desi* dogs. Only their ears hang. They originate from Newfoundland. But they are found in Nagaland also. If a hunter shoots a bird, they go and find the bird, keeping track of the smell of gunpowder. But you need not have got so startled. These dogs are very fond of human beings. I have seen Labrador retrievers in the dog squad of the Lalbazar detective office. They assist in tracking down murderers."

Jaygopalbabu was coming towards us. I had the opportunity of seeing him properly in daylight. He was a ponderous man. He was wearing tight pants and a sports tee-shirt. His spectacle frame was made of nickel. When he was near us, a tall and slim dog ran towards us. When he whistled, the dog turned and sat down with its large tongue hanging out and started staring at us. This dog seemed as if coated in *ghee*. Its coat was almost like skin. Its tail was cut. The other dog seemed too scared to go near it. The Colonel shared his knowledge with me. "This is a Doberman Pincher. A German dog. Very aggressive. Be a bit careful about this one, Jayanto!"

Jaygopalbabu said, "Good morning Colonel. 'Morning, Jayantobabu."

The Colonel returned the greeting, "'Morning! I am very happy to see your dogs, Jaygopalbabu."

"I am not happy. Because the chaps are good for nothing," said Jaygopalbabu. "I leave them free at night. In spite of that, such weird things happen in the house. You have heard them with your own ears. In fact, my Alsatian was much more useful. At least it used to run after the ghostly beings. Poor chap! It died of a snake bite."

"What! Are there poisonous snakes around the palace?" I asked.

Jaygopalbabu said, "There are. Tell me where there aren't any snakes."

The Colonel said, "We saw a *saadhubaba* living there."

"*Saadhu*?" Jaygopalbabu knotted his eyebrows irritatedly and said, "That is the mad Janaai. He used to work in the palace at one time. You have seen Raghab. He is his first cousin. You might not believe it, but Janaai eats raw meat like a devil. I buried the Alsatian there. You see that gap there! Janaai retrieved its body from its grave in the night, and started biting into its flesh. As soon as light from a torch fell on his face, Janaai escaped!"

We approached the palace while we were talking. When we reached the verandah on the southern side, the Colonel said, "Jaygopalbabu, do you know anybody called Tara Nath Chatterjee?"

Jaygopalbabu's face became serious. "Hmm. The deputy of the Lohagara estate was Brajanathbabu, whom I have not seen. Tara is his grandson. Their family used to live inside the precincts of the palace at one time. Tarada's father Haranath was the accountant of the palace. Tarada was always a bohemian. He got obsessed with the idea of becoming a magician. Do you know him?"

"I was introduced to him once, in Calcutta, at a magic show."

"Was Tarada really able to perform magic? I don't believe it." Jaygopalbabu smiled a bit. "But yes! He knew a few card tricks. I once saw a card trick involving ten pairs of cards and some thought-reading. But that was quite a stunning trick. Suppose he asked you to select ten pairs from a packet. But Tarada would not be looking at those. He would say, 'Remember one pair of cards.' Suppose I remember the King of Spades and the three of hearts. You remember the Queen of Clubs and the Knave of diamonds. The pair that Jayantobabu remembers is the Knave of hearts and the Three of spades. Okay? Then he would display all the pairs at random in four rows. Tarada would say, 'The pairs that each of you has rememberd may be in one row, but they may be in two rows also. You just tell me, which row they are in.' Amazing, although each row has five cards, Tarada would inevitably find the right pair."

The Colonel was impressed, "Jolly good! But where does Tara Nath Babu stay now?"

"I heard he lives in Calcutta. He comes here only now and then. When he comes here, he stays either in my quarters or in Raghab's room. It is not fixed. The Raja Bahadur would chase him away if he saw him. Once, he stole something from the palace and fled. He's been forbidden to enter the house ever since then. Tell me, what can I do? I feel sorry for him if he comes here. I give him shelter. But you can well understand that the consequences would be disastrous if the Raja Bahadur got to know."

"I think I caught a glimpse of him on the banks of the river. Or my eyesight may have deceived me." The Colonel said this a little abstractedly.

Jaygopalbabu was a little surprised at the Colonel's words. "Really! I should have known if he had come. Anyway, let me arrange for your breakfast. Besides, the Raja Bahadur has said he wants to meet you at 9.30. Its almost nine."

Jaygopalbabu went out. I saw through the window that the two dogs were walking on either side of him like body guards.

After breakfast, we went upstairs to meet the Raja Bahadur Ajitendra Narayan. He was a short, rotund, heavy kind of a person. His face displayed an amiable smile. After being introduced to me, his eyes danced as he said, "I read the *Dainik Satyasebak* regularly. I really enjoyed your ' Ghostly Commuters in Nocturnal Taxi'. Now write something about the ghosts in this house."

I said, "It is indeed something to write about!"

"Why are you saying 'indeed'? Try and enter the room in the north-east corner. In front of your eyes, the chairs will move from one side of the table to the other. In the west, such happenings are sometimes attributed to spirits that are known by the name of 'poltergeist'."

"What are you saying? 'Poltergeist' is a very mysterious thing. Even scientists have not been able to solve this mystery."

The Colonel was sitting next to me. I don't know why, but he nudged me. The Raja Bahadur was giggling. He said, "So? I'm sure you want to see the doings of the ghosts with your own eyes?"

It suddenly came to my mind that we were sitting in front of a person who was not quite in his senses. The words of the Raja Bahadur, his manner, his laugh – none of them were those of a normal person. Noticing my reaction, the Colonel coughed a little and said, "Raja Bahadur! Is your headache better? I hope you get enough sleep."

The smile faded away from the Raja Bahadur's face. With a

contorted face, he said, "My illness will not be cured by the medicines given by Bhabesh the doctor. You came here last year in the winter. These things have been happening ever since then, and I have been swallowing Bhabesh's pills. At last I pleaded with Jaygopal to take me to Calcutta. He said it was no use spending so much effort in going there and that he would get a good doctor here. Its been a week since. Jaygopal said that the doctor will come. Imagine my plight!"

Jaygopalbabu lifted the curtain at the door, entered the room and said, "He is coming today, Raja Bahadur! I will send the car to the station at three o'clock. He has let me know by trunk call from Calcutta."

The Colonel asked, "Which doctor is this?"

Jaygopalbabu winked at the Colonel and seemed to indicate something as he said, "I don't know if you have heard his name. Doctor D.G. Dhol. He is a very renowned doctor. A brain specialist."

The Colonel became inexplicably serious. The Raja Bahadur absent-mindedly looked at the window and said, "It seems as if my brain has developed a hole in it, and that a sparrow has entered there. There is a chirping sound there all the time. No, I will not be alive for long."

The Colonel suddenly stood up. "Please rest, Raja Bahadur. We'll take our leave now."

The Raja Bahadur smiled sweetly. He rotated his eyes and said, "But tell me, what have you done about the problem because of which I sent for you in such a hurry? Please do something about the wretched ghost quickly! It has overstepped its limits!"

"Let's see what I can do." Saying this, the Colonel folded his hands in a *namaskaar* and went out. I also followed him. The Raja Bahadur reminded me of writing about all this in the *Dainik Satyasebak*.

When we returned downstairs, the Colonel said, "What did you think of the Raja Bahadur?"

"He seems to be off his rocker. But you hadn't told me about this!"

"No, I hadn't. It was necessary for me to know what you thought after meeting him face to face."

"Who is Doctor Dhol? Never heard of him."

"Neither have I. But Jaygopalbabu has privately told me that a psychiatrist called Doctor D.G. Dhol is being brought here from Calcutta. Let us see what happens ultimately…"

I am addicted to taking an afternoon nap. Moreover, I had not slept well at night. When was I woke the sun was almost setting. The Colonel had gone on the trail of some butterflies. He came back in the late evening. He described the characteristics of a few kinds of butterflies. Raghab brought in another round of tea. We heard from him that the doctor had arrived from Calcutta. He had been given a room opposite the hall. But it seems the Raja Bahadur had taken offence at the first sight of the doctor. Sometime later, however, Doctor Dhol personally came to meet us. A very pleasant man.

He said, "Where the hell have we landed ourselves? This place seems to be abnormal!"

The Colonel grinned and said, "But can you tell me why?"

Doctor Dhol was a short, plump man. His complexion was as ruddy as a ripe fruit. His hair was in a crew-cut. He had a pointed goat's beard which he stroked as he said in a low voice, "I feel that the people in this palace are not people at all. Have you seen their faces? They seem to be the faces of dead people. One feels eerie to see them gaze at you. Besides, look at the condition of the palace. Two miles away from the nearest town, this seems to be an abode of ghosts amidst silent and unpeopled surroundings."

The Colonel agreed and said, "You have hit the nail on the head, Doctor Dhol."

Enthused by this utterance, Doctor Dhol said, "Can you think of that ancient Raja Bahadur as a human being? He looks like a mummy from the grave. Yet he has a quite a temper. I was an idiot to come here. Things don't seem to augur well at all."

I asked, "What is the Raja Bahadur's ailment?"

Doctor Dhol said with an irritable expression, "I can diagnose that only if he lets me go near him. There are many kinds of mad people in the world. I have treated so many difficult, mad people. But the Raja Bahadur is consciously mad."

Saying this, Doctor Dhol turned to the Colonel and whispered, "I have heard that certain ghostly happenings take place here. It seems a private detective has been summoned from Calcutta for that. Are you the person?"

The Colonel laughed loudly and said, "Who did you hear this from, Doctor Dhol?"

"A man named Raghab told me." Doctor Dhol smiled a little. "I can then be a little anxiety-free , what do you say, Mister...er...sorry. I forget your name every time."

"Please address me as Colonel, Doctor Dhol."

Doctor Dhol sat up straight. His expression betrayed admiration. "Colonel! That means you were in military service?"

"I was. I am retired now."

"Even then! Hearing this, I have gained in mental strength", Doctor Dhol said happily. "If there is any trouble, when you are around, I have nothing to fear." Then he looked at me with a smile and said, "And this young man is a journalist. Glad to meet you. You can conquer the world with a pen in your hand. If we land in any trouble, you will write in detail about it. Then the government will be shaken out of their stupor. The bigwigs of the police will turn up at the Lohagara palace."

The Colonel caressed his bald pate and said, "Can you tell me what is likely to happen?"

Doctor Dhol said in a suppressed voice, "Anything! You just

name it, and it can happen. I don't think things in this house portend well."

"Like?"

Hearing the Colonel's query, Doctor Dhol said solemnly, "The managerbabu was saying that in the dynasty which the Raja Bahadur belongs to, each person is a notorious murderer. A murderous tendency is ingrained in their blood. It seems that the Raja Bahadur suddenly gets into a fit of rage and threatens whoever is in front of him with knives and swords. So someone can get murdered any time. Then suppose…"

"Yes? Go on, Doctor Dhol."

"The *thakurmashai* who cooks in the palace said that in the middle of the night, some Raja Bahadur belonging to a previous generation roams around the palace. The *thakur* can hear heavy footsteps each night."

"We have also heard them." The Colonel grinned knowingly at me.

Doctor Dhol seemed to get a little frightened. "Goodness gracious! What are you saying?"

"What else have you heard Doctor Dhol?"

"Some ancestor of the palace has buried some hidden treasure somewhere. Somebody seems to go looking for it at night."

"Who did you hear this from?"

"Raghab was telling me."

By that time, the moon had lit up the outside. The Colonel

got up and went and stood at the southern door. He said, "What a beautifully moonlit night!"

Doctor Dhol moved towards him and praised the moonlit night as he watched it. "Spectacular! But see what a tragedy it is, Colonel! Even as we want to enjoy such a beautiful gift of nature, we are being deprived of it."

"Why?"

Doctor Dhol smiled a little diffidently and said, "Doesn't one feel like roaming around on such a night!"

The Colonel said, "If you want to, please feel free to do so. Jayanto, why don't you take Doctor Dhol for a stroll in the moonlight? You can feel perfectly safe in going with my young friend to enjoy the moonlit night. Don't worry, Jayanto is a dare-devil of a fellow. Besides, he also has a revolver."

"Really?" Doctor Dhol looked at me disbelievingly.

Perforce I had to show him the revolver. Frankly speaking, I also felt like walking around in the autumnal moonlight rather than sit at home.

I went out with Doctor Dhol. On one side of us was a wide lawn and garden. I realized that the Colonel actually wanted to send Doctor Dhol out and carry out some secret investigation in the meanwhile.

The dew had started collecting on the grass. I could sense that despite praising the moonlit night, Doctor Dhol was engulfed in fear. He was warily looking at either side of him and cautiously putting his foot forward. I went ahead a little, turned and looked at the palace. It really seemed like an abode of ghosts. In the silvery moonlight, the grey house seemed to radiate an ethereal light.

Seeing me turn, Doctor Dhol suddenly caught hold of my shoulder and said, "What? what?"

"Nothing. Come."

"But we will not wander a round for long, Jayantobabu. I have to attend to my patient once again. Otherwise, the managerbabu will take offence."

Here and there, a tree or a bush stood like the black night. The grey fog seemed to swathe these dark bodies like a sheet. I went a little further near the length of the wall. Right then, a night-owl hovered over our heads screeching in its awful, croaky voice. Doctor Dhol caught hold of me. "What? What?"

"It's nothing to be afraid of, Doctor Dhol, it's merely an owl."

"Who knows, Mister! I have never heard an owl call."

Doctor Dhol then caught hold of my hand in a tight grip. After going forward a little, I saw somebody standing near the eastern gate, parallel to the wall. I did not say anything to Doctor Dhol because he would feel scared. The shadowy figure stood there, as black as coal. Was it Janaai the *pagla?*

But then a strange thing happened. The apparition vanished suddenly and imperceptibly. I stood transfixed. Doctor Dhol seemed to be speaking to himself again as he cried out, "What? What?"

"Nothing." I took out my torch from my pocket, switched it on, and searched the entire place thoroughly. Then I reasoned that on a moonlit night, to make such a mistake is only normal.

Doctor Dhol said, "It seems as if you are looking for something, Jayantobabu! What is it?"

Laughingly, I said, "People see a lot of things that are not there at night. But no, I did not see any such thing."

Doctor Dhol stopped and said, "Why at night? Mental patients see a lot of imaginary things even during the day. In our discipline, they are called hallucinations. Suppose, the patient suddenly cries out from his room, 'There is a man under the window!' He might even give you a description of what he is wearing. But it is all an optical illusion. I will give you a book. Read it and see. *The Philosophy of Perception* by Doctor Marlow Ponti. In that..."

Exactly at that point of time, some jackals howled loudly from the other side of the river. Doctor Dhol immediately clutched me in fright. In a shaky voice, he cried out, "What? What?"

"It's the cry of jackals."

"I hope they are real jackals! Who knows, I have never heard one before."

Extricating myself from his embrace, I said, "It may be a hallucination according to your branch of study. Come, let us go back."

Doctor Dhol was greatly relieved. "Whatever you say; there is a great excitement in being frightened. Besides, since you have a revolver, one can be frightened without having anything to worry about. Really mister, I had great fun."

One could hear dogs howling from the side of the palace. Listening to it, Doctor Dhol said, "The other menace is those two dogs. They are really ferocious dogs! They come to bite you the moment they see you. The manager Jaygopalbabu has this eccentric preoccupation. Those who rear dogs are an eyesore for me. What does he think? Will he be able to stop anything if an extremely spooky incident takes place? Are dogs not afraid of ghosts? They must be. What do you say?"

I said absent-mindedly, "They should be."

Suddenly I remembered that it was the 2nd of November. It was seven o'clock in the evening. Another two and a half hours later, beyond the eastern gate, in the temple next to the river, something was going to happen. The Ace of Spades had asked me to be present there at ten in the night. My insides not only trembled with excitement, but fear. And my body seemed to grow rigid.

I could see the Colonel in the southern verandah. When I went near, he said, "I hope Doctor Dhol's evening stroll has been exciting."

Doctor Dhol said, "Very exciting indeed. That is what I was telling Jayantobabu. If one has a revolver, it is fun to roam around at night. The incidents of the owl and the foxes were particularly wonderful."

The detective had, in the meanwhile, got Raghab to bring a pot of coffee for us. In the dewy cold of the November night, I was feeling a little stiff. We had the coffee in a leisurely manner. Then Doctor Dhol got up. "Many thanks, Colonel. I really spent my time most enjoyably. I hope I continue to do so. I will now take leave. I will have to attend to the Raja Bahadur in a while."

After Doctor Dhol left, I shut the door on the side of the hall. Then I asked softly, "Were you able to complete some investigation in the meantime?"

The Colonel winked as he said, "That's right, my child. Your guess is correct."

"Regarding Doctor Dhol, I presume?"

"Yes."

"What have you concluded?"

"His name is Doctor Dol Gobindo Dhol. There is nothing amiss. He lives in Sukia Street in Calcutta. His chamber is in Shyambazaar. But he is not a well-known psychiatrist."

"Anything else?"

The Colonel smiled. "No, my dear! There is nothing fraudulent about the man. He is a bit of a coward, that's all.

Jaygopalbabu has been able to hire him by tempting him with a very high fee. I would think that he would never have come to such a haunted place otherwise. I saw some letters from Jaygopalbabu in his bag. From those I was able to piece things together."

I looked at my watch and said, "It's almost seven forty-five. When will we go out?"

"Around nine forty-five. I have told Raghab that we want to finish dinner by nine as we are very tired after being out the whole day."

The Colonel stretched out his feet as he sat on the easychair near the corner. While he shut his eyes in a meditative pose, I opened a travel book and sat down. But somehow, I could not concentrate on the book. One could hear the horrible clanging of the grandfather clock from the adjacent hall.

Sometime later, there was a knock at the door of the hall. Then I could hear Jaygopalbabu's voice. On opening the door, Jaygopalbabu came in. "I came to disturb you at an odd time, Colonel."

The Colonel said, "No, not at all. Please come in."

Jaygopalbabu entered the room, looked around and said, "I hope you will not be inconvenienced."

"Not at all. We are very comfortable indeed."

"When you came to the palace last year, it was quite peaceful", said Jaygopalbabu with a smile. "These troubles have started over the last two or three months. But one must confess, with all the strange goings-on, nobody has been harmed so far. If no harm comes to us, provided God is willing, I will be greatly relieved."

"Why? Can you tell us what harm you are anticipating?"

Jaygopalbabu said with an anxious expression, "It is very difficult to spell out specifically, Colonel! But the weird sounds that we hear in the night... or those knocks at the door, and nobody can be seen on opening the door. I am getting very frightened by these. They seem to portend some dreadful impending event. By the by, Colonel, do you believe in spirits?"

The Colonel smiled. "I have had no opportunity to do so."

"Neither have I. But the history of this palace has not been a clean one. Numerous murders, tortures etc. have happened in the past. One of the ancestors of the present Raja Bahadur was reputed to be an extremely vindictive man. His spirit is still believed to wander around the palace. He used to rule in the seventeenth century. His name was Shivendra Narain. One of his misdeeds was establishing the idol of *Alakshmi*. People say that he had a desire to sacrifice men at the altar of the goddess. But for some reason, that wish was never fulfilled. Therefore his spirit is still roaming around, lusting for a human sacrifice."

The Colonel said, "Who knows! Human knowledge is very limited, Jaygopalbabu. Science has such an undiscovered world ahead of it."

Jaygopalbabu suddenly stood up and said, "I won't disturb

you any more. Be careful. The kind of things that are going on!" Saying that, he left.

In the sky, a heavy and solid-looking moon was watching with its big eyes. The bluish fog covering the moonlight had made everything acquire an eerie look. As we waited my anxiety worsened every minute. What exciting news was the Ace of Spades going to tell us? Who was he? Why did he call me to such a horrible place? I hoped he did not have any evil intention in mind. I was scared. But the Colonel was unperturbed. Raghab fed us by nine. The two of us went out on the pretext of going for a short walk. Somewhere in the distance, we heard the growling of Jaygopalbabu's dogs. But even after crossing the eastern gate, the dogs did not come near us. The river was shining in the moonlight. On the other side of the river, a bird called twice and stopped. Then a band of jackals started calling some way ahead. In the meanwhile, a lot of dew had collected on the grass and hedges. My mind had started becoming restless. I touched the small revolver in my pocket.

We could see an empty space before us. The Colonel suddenly stopped short and whispered to me, "Sit down. There are still two minutes more to ten o'clock." Both of us sat down under cover of the hedge. An owl hooted and flew away. On the vacant plot, I could see a huge, rectangular, raised platform. Was it the statue of the *Alakshmi* I could see on top of that?

I sat with bated breath. Time did not seem to move. A little while later, I suddenly saw somebody get up on the platform with cautious footsteps. Immediately, I heard a muffled scream. Simultaneously, I heard the sound of a scuffle. The Colonel turned on his torch and ran towards the place. I was behind him. In the light of the torch, I first saw the black statue. Had it come alive at this moment? Its appearance was ferocious and awesome. And somebody was lying on its lap. The Colonel climbed up onto the platform in one leap and went near the person. Then, in a shocked voice, he said, "Damn it! This is Professor Tanacha!"

This dreadful incident happened within the span of half a minute. I was greatly regretful of the fact that we could not save Professor Tanacha. The Colonel said in a voice that had taken his breath away, "I did not think this would happen. I never imagined that such a thing could happen."

I was standing stupefied. I had completely forgotten that I had a torch in my hand and a loaded revolver in my pocket. At last I switched on my torch and saw Profesor Tanacha properly. The gentleman was lying on his chest in the lap of the ferocious-looking female form seated on the throne. He was wearing the same black coat and grey baggy pants. The lower part of his body was hanging. Terror was written over his face. His eyes were shut. Fresh blood was flowing from his nostrils. Then I flashed the light on the goddess. I shuddered to see that her two hands were poised in the manner of strangling somebody. Her two stony eyes were flashing with cruel malice.

On her lips, there was a wicked smile of blood-thirsty revenge. My numbed finger moved away from the switch of the torch. The light went out.

In the courtyard surrounding the platform, the Colonel was looking for signs of the murderer in the light of his own torch. I asked, "Colonel, is the murderer just a spirit? We were sitting with all our attention focused on this side. Yet we could only see Professor Tanacha – not his murderer."

The detective did not reply. He came near Professor Tanacha, knelt down and started going over his clothes. He got a dirty handkerchief, a two-rupee note and some change in the pocket of his pants. He put those in the pocket and put his hand in his shirt pocket extracting a folded envelope. He put it inside his own pocket. Then he looked on all sides and said, "The police must be informed immediately. Jayanto, I am staying here. You go back to the palace and tell Jaygopalbabu everything."

I? I got totally unnerved and said, "After what has happened, for me to go alone through this jungle to the palace... and on top of that, to face those monstrous dogs! Whatever you say Colonel, this is impossible for me."

The Colonel said, "Then you stay here. I will go and inform them."

I got even more alarmed and said, "That is even more impossible. To stay in this deadly place and guard the dead body! Heavens! Besides, don't you see the idol seems to have come alive? I am tempted to believe that the goddess is the heroine behind this dramatic manslaughter!"

The Colonel said grumpily, "Okay. Come, let us both go."

Just as we got down from the platform, somebody laughed and called out suddenly in a horrible, shrill voice. "O run away! Escape! The *Alakshmi* has come alive. You are doomed to die. Run away!" In the torch light, I saw Janaai the *pagla* standing at a distance with his teeth bared. Then there was a pelting of bricks all around us. We chased the *pagla*. He laughed nastily and ran away.

The full moon was shining, as if with eyes to see us with, over the river. We could hear the sound of the river, and see the moon reflected in the water. On the other side of the river, the jackals started calling. The Colonel went up to the gate of the palace and said, "There was no need to be afraid of the dogs, Jayanto! Whether it is because of the fear of snakes or some other reason, Jaygopalbabu possibly does not let them go out of the palace at night. The growls that you heard while coming was because they are tracking dogs. Their sense of smell is very powerful. They could sense our movements. Listen again, they are growling."

As we neared the palace we heard somebody shouting upstairs. The Colonel said, "It seems that the Raja Bahadur is threatening somebody."

We opened the door to enter our room. The Colonel opened the door towards the hall and called Raghab. There was no reply. We heard the Raja Bahadur screaming:

"Get out! You may be a doctor, but don't come near me. I will murder you. I feel murderous all the time. You dare come close to me again! Go. Get out!"

We realized that the Raja Bahadur was threatening Doctor Dhol. A little later, the thundering stopped. The Colonel said, "Amazing! Raghab is supposed to be sleeping in the hall. I see his bed is empty."

The Colonel was trying to go up when the bigger dog appeared at the head of the stairs and arrested his movement. He seemed as if about to pounce. The Colonel walked back. Seeing the reddish dog, which had been shorn of all its fur and bereft of its tail, my body froze. A little later, its companion, the dog with the floppy ears, also appeared at the head of the stairs, yawned, straightened its legs and sat down.

But it was necessary to inform the police! The Colonel gave up and came back to the room. I had lifted the curtain and was watching what was happening. I shut the door immediately. The Colonel said, "Don't the dogs show any hostility to Doctor Dhol?

"A very obvious question, Jayanto!" I racked my brains and anwered, "He must have to attend to the Raja Bahadur from time to time. Perhaps that is why Jaygopalbabu has trained both of them not to obstruct him."

After about five minutes, when the Colonel was walking to and fro very restlessly, Doctor Dhol's voice could be heard in the hall. He was calling Raghab. The Colonel hurried to open the door and called him in. Doctor Dhol entered the room and said with an angry expression, "Strange case, mister! The Raja Bahadur is actually suffering from schizophrenia. He is one thing in the day, and its total contrast in the night. Doctor Jekyll and Mister Hyde."

"But when you went upstairs and came back, did the dogs not chase you?"

Doctor Dhol at first got a little shocked at this unreasonable question. Then he giggled and said, "Didn't they! The rascals are ready to pounce on me whenever they see me. The *thakurmashai* took me to the Raja Bahadur's room from the staircase at the back. I came down that very way. The dogs don't respect the *thakurmashai* much either. Aren't you aware that in the night, no living creature in the palace dares come out of his room? There are these ghostly onslaughts, and on top of that, there are these two formidable dogs."

"But I need to go up once. I have seen a phone in the Raja Bahadur's room. It is imperative to phone the police."

Doctor Dhol was surprised. "Police? Why?"

"On the bank of the river, there is a dead body lying on the platform of the *Alakshmi*."

"Good heavens! Then something terrible has really happened! Who... who got murdered, Colonel?"

The Colonel did not deign to reply, but said, "Jaygopalbabu's room also possibly has a phone. You wait a little. Don't go away, Doctor Dhol. I have something important to talk to you about."

After the Colonel left, Doctor Dhol asked, "What really is the matter, Jayantobabau?"

I said, "We weren't being able to go to sleep. So we went out. When we reached the temple of the *Alakshmi*, we saw a dead body lying there. Its nose was bleeding."

"What are you saying! I am scared out of my wits, Mister! If only I knew earlier...Oh!"

"If you knew what?"

Doctor Dhol seemed to be surprised at my question. "Don't you understand? Nocturnal knocks at the door, the sound of clanging utensils, heavy footsteps! To top it all, these wicked dogs – and a schizophrenic patient!"

"What is the matter with the Raja Bahadur?"

"Exactly what I said. It's a case of Dr. Jekyll and Mr. Hyde. God and Satan inside the same man – a split personality. These patients do not realize themselves what they do in the night. There was a gentleman who used to bury his coat in the garden in the night. In the morning, he used to scold his servants because he couldn't find it."

Listening to Doctor Dhol, it was arguable that the Raja Bahadur had murdered Professor Tanacha and come back, and seeing his condition, the cook of the palace had summoned the doctor. I kept looking at Doctor Dhol absent-mindedly.

Or was Doctor Dhol also part of this conspiracy? I could not understand anything. Before I realized it, the words escaped from my mouth – "Doctor Dhol, do you think it is possible for the Raja Bahadur to go outside the palace and murder anybody?"

Doctor Dhol sat straight and said, "Your question is logical. These patients cannot walk in the daytime. But as soon as it is night, they seem to be rejuvenated by a certain kind of strength."

"Did you put your patient to sleep and come away?"

"What else? I had to give him an injection forcibly to put him to sleep."

I looked sharply at Doctor Dhol, and was about to ask him more questions, when he stood up. "I am not going to stay in this house of ghosts any more, Mister. Let the patient go to hell. I do not need money. I will leave tomorrow."

As Doctor Dhol left I became even more suspicious. I heard the door of his room close a little while later. I also closed the door. I wondered why the Colonel was taking so long. I sat on the chair and started imagining weird possibilities. The caretaker of this palace, Haranath Chatterjee, was the grandfather of Professor Tanacha. The grandfather's amulet was stolen from his house in Calcutta. After that, Professor Tanacha left his bag and disappeared. I came to Lohagara after getting an anonymous letter from somebody called the Ace of Spades. After coming here, I discovered Professor Tanancha. And then

I saw his dead body on the lap of the *Alakshmi*. On the other hand, there is this onslaught of spirits in the palace. The Raja Bahadur seems to be suffering from schizophrenia. I could not make head or tail of it all. And then there was this strange rhyme or chant in Professor Tanacha's notebook:

When you are a part of
That gross social class
Let your will abstain
Oh you ghostly palm tree!

This was a maze indeed!

Knock-knock-knock.

I got startled. Somebody was knocking at the door on the side of the hall. Again. Knock-knock-knock.

I suddenly got furious at myself. I had earlier got into so many dangerous situations as the assistant of the ingenious Colonel. How many times have I escaped death narrowly! Imagine getting frightened by the call of ghosts in this Lohagara palace! I took out my revolver and torch and opened the door in one swift jerk.

Amazing! There was nobody there. The dim light of the hall was on. Still, I put on my torch. Then there was a sound upstairs: *dhup-dhup-dhup*! As soon as I showed the torch light, I saw the rear legs of an elephant, and the weird elephant was making the verandah upstairs shake as it walked. The sound rose, *dhup-dhup-dhup-dhup*!The two dark, fat legs disappeared into the verandah upstairs.

I kept the revolver ready and had just taken a step towards the staircase when the ferocious dog with the greasy, hairless, tall, slim mien – Doberman pincher, bared its teeth and stood barring the way at the head of the stairs. The next moment, somebody threw something with a bang.

I retreated immediately to the room and bolted its door. I started shivering. All my courage vanished. I retired limply to my bed like a punctured balloon. But what was the Colonel doing for so long? I hoped he had not got into a perilous situation. I lit a cigarette and gave vent to my anxiety. My nerves were somewhat soothed. Then I saw that there was a folded paper on my bed. I got a shock when I opened it.

It was a letter written on a dirty paper with a ball-point pen. When we had gone out to the temple, somebody had either thrown it in from the window or the door.

> So, greatest of journalists? Tell me if I kept my word! Since you are a journalist, you must know that all fresh news is followed up, or has a sequel to it. Tomorrow, the 3rd of November, around two in the night, you will get it if you stand in front of the north-east room on the first floor of the palace.
>
> Yours truly
>
> The Ace of Spades.

Whatever little courage I had left evaporated then. Who

was this Ace of Spades? I saw that he had made a dummy of me and had got maddeningly involved in a terrific game with the greatest of all detectives. The words of the first letter had come true. Now who knew what dreadful event the second letter portended? I hoped I was not going to be the victim of this follow-up. He knew very well that I was the Colonel's favourite companion. The Colonel loved me more than a son. Did he want to take some revenge on the Colonel by hurting me?

It was quite possible. In the past, the Colonel had caught and handed over many dangerous murderers and criminals to the police. This Ace of Spades was probably one of them. Moreover, he seemed to have some connection with the Lohagara palace. He had therefore laid his net of revenge in this palace...

I sat down with the letter in my hand. Why was the Colonel not coming? I did not have the courage to look out of the window. What if the idol of the demon-goddess came to take a breath of fresh air in the palace garden? I could hear a jackal calling in the distance. Even the owl seemed to be restlessly wandering around that night and prophesying some bad luck – *craw-craw-craw*! The clock in the hall was making a horrible '*dhong-dhong*' sound all the time. Then the owl hooled loudly in its booming voice. The whole house seemed to shake with that sound.

Sometime later, I heard the Colonel calling at the southern

door. "Jayanto, you aren't asleep, are you?"

All my fear vanished at once. I eagerly opened the door and asked, "Why are you so late?"

"Jaygopalbabu had gone to sleep. He lives outside the palace, to the north, in a one-storeyed house. I had to call him several times in order to wake him up. He phoned the police. The police came after half an hour. Then we went out through the eastern gate and went to the temple of the *Alakshmi*. Then…"

When the Colonel stopped, I asked, "Then?"

"Amazing! There is no trace of the dead body. The police inspector got very angry and went back."

"Do you mean to say you saw no dead body?"

The Colonel smiled. "Jaygopalbabu said that this must have been done by Janaai the *Pagla*. He claims to have seen Janaai eating a dead body. He has probably hidden the body somewhere so that he can eat it at an opportune moment. However, we went to the boat-house and looked for Janaai. We found neither him nor the dead body."

Without any further delay, I showed the Colonel the letter of the Ace of Spades. Then I told him in detail about the knock on the door, the view of the elephant's legs etc. The Colonel shut his eyes, and swinging to and fro, said, "I see, but go to sleep, my dear friend. Your mind will get boggled if you think too much."

Nothing else happened that night but I did not sleep well.

Whenever I pricked up my ears, I heard the Colonel snoring. Finally, I must have slept a bit. When I woke up, my aged friend had completed his morning stroll. He was sitting at the table with his tea. Seeing me open my eyes, he addressed me in his habitual manner, "Good morning, Jayanto! I hope you have had a good sleep."

Sometime later, Raghab came in with the breakfast tray. The Colonel asked, "Where were you yesterday, Raghab?"

Raghab got a bit startled and said, "Sir, I went to see a performance of dance-drama which has come from Calcutta."

"Good. What is the managerbabu doing?"

"He is in the field, training his dogs. He has this obsession, you know."

"Tell me Raghab, Janaai is your mother's sister's son, is he not?"

Raghab's face became serious. "Yes, sir. My cousin. It was he who brought me to this palace. Janaaida belongs to the Raja Bahadur's father's generation. He is reduced to this state because of bad luck. I feel very sorry to see him."

"Why did Janaai go mad, Raghab?"

Raghab lowered his face and said, "If the managerbabu gets to know, he will beat me also, Sir."

"You can tell me without any fear," the Colonel said to assuage him. "It will not reach the managerbabu's hearing."

Raghab looked around nervously and lowered his voice, "I

heard all of it much later. I have not seen it with my own eyes, Sir! It seems Janaaida had entered the managerbabu's room at night – why he did so I cannot tell you, sir! The managerbabu had a dog, not one of the two he has now, but another one. The dog only 'bit' him, but the managerbabu 'beat' him black and blue. After getting beaten up, Janaaida left the palace and went off. Then he stayed incognito for a while. Some days back, I suddenly saw him standing in front of a boat-house on the bank of the river. His hair and beard had grown like that of a *saadhu*. He just couldn't recognize me. Actually, Janaaida went mad because of that very beating he got."

"How long back was it when Janaai got this beating?"

"It's almost two-three months ago."

"You must have seen Tara Nath Chatterjee in this house, the grandson of the caretaker?"

Raghab smiled. "Oh the magicbabu? He used to live in Calcutta. Whenever he would come here, which was seldom, he would stay in our room. Sometimes, he would stay in the managerbabu's house. According to the orders of the Raja Bahadur, he was not allowed to come to this house. But as per the managerbabu's instructions, we would let him stay here. Poor chap, he was a really good man. He got killed senseleasly because of his lack of intelligence."

"When did you last see him?" Raghab was somewhat startled at the Colonel's question. He gulped and said, "Yesterday evening I think I got a glimpse of him on the bank of the river.

It could have been an illusion. But he also had that addiction, Sir."

"What addiction?"

"Searching in the wilderness for opium plants."

"Only opium plants? Or something else?"

Raghab stared with a pale face. Then he suddenly became restless and said, "The managerbabu will scold me, Sir! It is very late. I better go."

The Colonel smiled and said, "Hm! You are very scared of the managerbabu, I know. But I am trying to dispel your fears, Raghab. Do not be afraid. Say, what else did the magicbabu look for?"

Raghab made a pathetic face, "I really don't know, Sir. The magicbabu was a crazy fellow. He had so many fads."

"Who do you think could have murdered him?"

Raghab put on a panic-stricken expression and said, "The *Alakshmi* is a very powerful goddess, Sir! Nobody goes near her even during day-time, let alone at night."

"Hm, are you suggesting that she is a live goddess?"

"Yes Sir!"

"Does your Janaaida really eat dead bodies?"

Raghab became even more serious and said, "The poor chap is mad. That managerbabu's dog died of a snake bite. Janaaida is supposed to have eaten its carcass also. Now we hear that the dead body of the magicbabu cannot be found. You see he must have hidden it."

"Okay, you may leave now, Raghab."

After breakfast, the Colonel said, "Come on. Let us go for a stroll amidst nature today. Nature helps us to recuperate and clear the cobwebs inside our heads."

Like the previous day, I saw Jaygopalbabu training his two dogs. But they did not rush towards us. After crossing the gate, we first went to the boat-house. There was no sign of Janaai *Pagla*. We turned around, and walking along the river, reached the temple of the *Alakshmi*. The image of the goddess did not seem as ferocious in the daylight. In fact, I could not help but praise the ancient sculptor who had carved it. A black female form on a throne made of black stone! The figure was a little rough. When I reached the platform and saw the statue in some detail, I saw that something had been inserted through a crack in the throne near its back. A black thread was attached to it. As soon as I pulled at the thread, a card came out. "The Ace of Spades!" I said excitedly. "Colonel! Colonel! See."

The Colonel was scrambling around in the undergrowth at a distance. Turning around, he saw the card in my hand and said, "Do you see, my boy? Our mysterious hero wanted to make the murder more glamorous by tying the card to the dead body of Professor Tanacha, but he did not get time. However, I seem to have discovered something more interesting here."

I put the card in my pocket and got down from the

platform. When I reached the Colonel, I saw a small bottle of nail polish in his hand. Surprised, I said, "Does the goddess wear nail polish?"

The Colonel laughed loudly. "How stupid! How stupid! The man has become senile."

"Who is stupid? Who has become senile?"

The Colonel said amidst peals of laughter, "Who else? Colonel Niladri Sarkar."

Whoever else might believe that Colonel Niladri Sarkar has become senile before the age of seventy-two, I certainly will not. "Please tell me what the matter is."

The Colonel suddenly pulled me down and we crouched in the bushes. I got very startled at this kind of behaviour of his. As soon as his eyes met mine, he put his finger on his lips indicating I should be quiet. Then he started crawling towards something signalling me to follow him. The earth was hard and full of stones and the plants were very thorny. I could not keep track of the number of places my body got scratched and bruised.

Then he suddenly stood up. "All clear! Get up, he said!"

I stood up. I looked around and asked, "What is the matter?"

"Professor Tanacha's murderer was probably coming to look for something. But careful as we were we, he saw us as we sat down and turned his back on us. But its amazing, Jayanto! Why have I become such a fool after coming to Lohagara?

Why has senility overwhelmed me so much before my time?"

Saying this, the great detective started shaking the dust off his clothes. He did the same to his cap, and then picked out a few dry leaves and a miniscule coloured insect from his white beard."

I could not understand why the Colonel called himself a fool and a victim of premature senility even after questioning him in detail. He roamed about here and there for sometime in the manner of tracking dogs which run on the path of the murderer on the lead of a scent. His eyes were glued downwards. He went round the platform of the goddess a few times. Then he stood straight and lit his cheroot.

I gave up and stood under a tree. In the hedge in front of me, bunches of wild flowers in blossom spread their fragrance all around. Below it, the full river roared along. The width of the river was not more than about thirty meters. The *kash* bushes in the woods on the other side were white with blossoms. Beyond them, there were undulating fields of paddy and a hillock here and there. Since according to the Colonel, one's head is supposed to clear up in the midst of nature, I hoped that even I would be able to unravel the mystery.

I tried to think. The nailpolish was indeed a mystery. Such a thing lying in the undergrowth on the bank of a river was not something that happened usually.

Or did it? At a distance, I could see a slum of the tribal

people. An *adivasi* girl must have gone this way to the Lohagara bazaar and bought herself a nailpolish that she fancied. While returning, she must have dropped it here.

Being quite satisfied in my mind over this solution, I said 'Eureka!' Then I turned around to see that the crazy old gentleman had disappeared. Looking on all sides, I could not find him. Then I got up on the raised platform of the *Alakshmi*. His cap was barely visible. Sitting on his knees, I thought, he must be watching some rare species of bird with his binoculars to his eyes. I realised that he would not be available for half the day.

I got down from the platform and walked towards the boat-house. If Janaai *Pagla* had really hidden the corpse of Professor Tanacha, he must have eaten up a portion of it for breakfast. Since there was no sign of the police within striking distance Janaai? could go back to his den, rid of all anxiety, and make up for his lost sleep.

Whatever I conjectured turned out to be right. I could see Janaai the *Pagla*'s legs inside the boat-house. Then I saw his whole body. I stood on the grass in the shelter of a broken boat, watching him. Janaai was swinging his legs. His eyes were shut. He was not sleeping. I had read somewhere that sleep cures madness. That is why mad people do not sleep.

As I took courage in my hands and coughed a little, Janaai sat up with a start. He even took up a broken brick from the floor of the boathouse. Then I took out the revolver from my pocket and said, "Be careful, Janaai. I will aim this at you."

Janaai dropped the brick and screamed incoherently. "Oh God! I will die. I'm telling you I will die! Hai ...! Hai!"

I went into the boat-house and asked, "Where is the corpse of Magicbabu?"

Janaai looked at the revolver with trepidation, "It has escaped, I swear on your name."

"Escaped? Can corpses ever escape? You must have hidden it so that you can eat it."

"Come on, what are you saying? Magicbabu takes opium. His corpse is bitter."

"The corpse of Jaygopalbabu's dog must have been sweet."

Janaai the *Pagla* extended his hand and said, "Will you give me a cigarette? Please..."

I put the revolver in my pocket and gave him a cigarette. After I lit it with my matchstick, Janaai took a few deep puffs. Then he started coughing. I said again, "Janaai! Where did Magicbabu's corpse disappear?"

He stubbed out the cigarette, inserted it inside his tangled hair, "I swear by the *Alakshmi*, it fled. It fled just as I went to get hold of it."

"Don't behave madly, Janaai. Then I'll really shoot you." I had just put my hand in my pocket when Janaai knocked me down and catapulted away. Removing the dust from my body, I ran out of the boathouse, but I could not see him any more.

I met the great detective near the gate. I said, "Did your bird also escape like Professor Tanacha's corpse?"

The Colonel laughed a little. "In exactly the same manner as I saw Janaai the *Pagla* fleeing. But I did not scare it away."

"How did you see that I was scaring him?"

The Colonel showed me his binoculars and said, "This instrument for seeing distant objects and people makes things that are happening far away as clear as daylight, my dear! However, I saw that Janaai was being very hospitable to you."

The Colonel laughed heartily when he heard the account of Profesor Tanacha's corpse running away. Then he said, "Come! The sun is scorching. Let us get back."

On reaching the palace, the Colonel called Raghab. It was Raghab's duty to do small errands for us. That is why he was present in the hall. The Colonel said, "Raghab! Doesn't anybody play cards in the palace?"

Raghab said, "I have seen the Raja Bahadur play. But he plays alone."

"That means he plays 'patience'. He stroked his beard and said, "Hmm, doesn't anybody else play? What about the Managerbabu?"

"No, sir. He only has his dogs to play with."

"Can you get hold of a pack of cards?"

Raghab scratched his head and said, "Then I'll have to buy it from the market. Let me tell the managerbabu."

"No. Can't we get the Raja Bahadur's pack of cards?"

"If I mention that you want it, it can't be that he won't lend it. I'll get it just now."

After Raghab left, I said suspiciously, "What will you do with cards? I have never seen you play cards."

The Colonel smiled. "I'll show you some magic, Jayanto! I'll mesmerize you with my trick of thought-reading."

After a while, Raghab smilingly entered the room with a pack of cards. "The Raja Bahadur was in the *puja* room and I seized that opportunity to bring it. If he gets to know, I've had it." The Colonel reassured him that no such exigency would arise.

After Raghab left, the Colonel sat on his bed and, spreading the cards out in great disarray, started playing with the cards as if he were a child. He would spread them out, and then pick them up and shuffle them. He would again scatter them, and then rearrange them. Looking at this for a while, I got bored. So I shut my eyes and started puffing at a cigarette. At one point, Doctor Dhol said, "May I come in?" and entered the room. Seeing the Colonel play with cards, he asked, "Are you playing patience, Colonel *saheb*?"

Smiling winkingly, the Colonel said, "Come Doctor Dhol! I will show you some magic."

"Very good, very good. Show us. I thought I would go back today, but could not. Let me spend my time watching some magic."

"Come here. Jayanto, you also come and sit here."

I have often seen this kind of crazy behaviour in this childlike old man. When we drew near, he said, "Doctor Dhol! I will not touch anything. I will turn round and sit. Nor will I see anything. Please select ten pairs of cards between the two of you. Remove the rest of the cards. Among these ten pairs, you should mentally select one pair and Jayanto should select one pair. Remember which pairs you have selected. Then put the twenty cards together."

"This is Professor Tanacha's magic. Jayagopalbabu was telling us about it," I could not resist saying.

Doctor Dhol picked out twenty cards and made them into ten pairs. He said, "Hmm, I have selected one pair. Jayantobabu, please select one."

I selected the Queen of Spades and the Three of diamonds. Doctor Dhol put all the ten pairs of cards together and gave them to the Colonel. The Colonel had turned around by now. He said, "Finished? Okay, abracadabra, here it goes!"

Saying this, he stroked the cards and started chanting:

> When you are part of
> That gross social class
> Let your will abstain
> Oh ghostly palm tree!

I listened, dazed.

The Colonel kept five cards in a row and arranged the rest

in four rows. Then he said, "Doctor Dhol, is your pair of cards in one row or in two different rows?"

"One is in the second row, the other is in the third row."

The Colonel picked out the Knave of Hearts from the first row and the Ten of Diamonds from the third row and said, "Right?"

Doctor Dhol said with amazement, "Wow! This is quite weird!"

"My pair is in the second row," I said.

The Colonel picked out the Queen of Spades and the Three of Diamonds from the last row and asked, "Right?"

"Yes. But..."

"There is no 'but' here, darling! This is a matter of charms and spells." The Colonel put the cards away and lit his cheroot.

Doctor Dhol said, "I see you are a very talented person. I was hearing about many feats of yours from Jaygopalbau. But he had not said anything about magic."

"Then shall I show you some more magic?"

"Certainly, certainly!" Doctor Dhol said eagerly.

As he collected all the cards. "There is a whole pack of playing cards here," the Colonel said. "You know that a pack of cards contains fifty-two cards, leaving aside the jokers. Okay?"

"Yes, I know."

The Colonel gave the cards to Doctor Dhol and said, "I have made a card disappear from this pack. Please see which one that is."

Doctor Dhol started looking at the cards minutely. I was looking at the Colonel. There was an enigmatic smile on his face. After scrutinizing the cards, Doctor Dhol said, "I don't see the Ace of Spades! Have you hidden it?"

The Colonel extended his hand and said, "Jayanto, you can see that I have transferred it to your pocket by the force of my spell. Give it to me."

I was startled. But I did not understand anything. I felt in my pocket and took out a card. It was the Ace of Spades. Amazing! It belonged to the same pack, made by the same company. Then was it the Raja Bahadur who, as in the story of Dr. Jekyll and Mr. Hyde, became his own anti-self at night? Did it mean that he was the murderer of Professor Tanacha?

I shuddered. The Colonel said laughingly, "See Doctor Dhol? See what a fool I have made of Jayanto!"

Doctor Dhol said appreciatively, "Really! You are really very skilled! There is no match for you."

The Colonel put the pack of cards a side and said, "Tara Nath Chaterjee – meaning Professor Tanacha, had invented the first trick, do you know Doctor Dhol? However, the second is my invention. The sad thing is that not only was Professor Tanacha murdered, but his dead body was also quickly hidden."

Doctor Dhol frowned and said, "Did you get any clues?"

"Yes. A bottle of nail polish. See."

Doctor Dhol turned the bottle around in his hands for some time, and was startled as he opened its cap. "Goodness! This is liquid chloroform. Anybody will faint on holding it close to one's nose." Saying this, he tightened the cap. A strong, sweet smell spread all around for a few seconds.

The Colonel said seriously, "Hmm, chloroform. Mixed with nailpolish. Poor innocent Professor Tanacha! He had absolutely no idea.... Tell me Doctor Dhol, how long have you known Jaygopalbabu?"

"I did not know him at all. It was he who saw the advertisement of my clinic in the newspaper and got in touch with me by trunk call. I was pressed for time. In the end, he hurried me. He sent me some money as advance also. Then I decided to come." Doctor Dhol said with a puzzled expression on his face, "But please tell me why you are asking this question. Do you have any suspicions about me?"

The Colonel raised his hand and said, "No. I just want to know."

"I don't know why, but from what I have heard about you, mister, I feel very scared." Doctor Dhol smiled a little drily.

The Colonel said in a hushed voice, "I need a little help from you, Doctor Dhol. I hope I will get it."

"Of course you will get it. Tell me what I have to do."

"Jaygopalbabu has two dogs. One is reasonably quiet, and fond of human beings. There is no problem regarding that one. The other dog, which is tall and slim, I mean the

Doberman pincher ..."

"Oh God! That one is a wicked rascal. He keeps showing me his teeth from a distance!"

"Doctor Dhol, it is human intelligence which has made man the master of all creatures. You are a skilful person. You have somehow to give an injection to the second dog and put it to sleep."

Doctor Dhol was startled. He scratched his nose and said, "Heavens! But that is very risky."

"I will assist you, Doctor Dhol! But please take care that Jaygopalbabu does not get to know."

"You need not tell me that," Doctor Dhol said anxiously. "But the point is, what if it bites me suddenly? One can't say what dangerous viruses the saliva of a dog is full of."

The Colonel said emphatically, "Please remember Doctor Dhol, the solving of this mystery depends entirely on putting that dog to sleep."

Doctor Dhol reluctantly made a face as if in agreement, nodded his head and said, "Okay."

At this moment, Raghab lifted the curtain and said, "Sir, the Raja Bahadur is calling both of you."

Doctor Dhol went to his own room. We both went to the Raja Bahadur. After his *puja*, the Raja Bahadur was leaning on his bolster. He smiled and said, "Come in, Colonel. Come in, Journalistbabu."

The Colonel gave him the pack of cards and said, "Your cards, Raja Bahadur. I hope you will forgive me for this unauthorized intrusion on your privacy."

"I can forgive you on the condition that you trace the lost card."

"I have done so."

"Then I have forgiven you."

"I have another small question, Raja Bahadur."

"If it is worth answering, I will answer it. Otherwise, I will not."

"Jaygopalbabu beat up Janaai so badly on his head that he went mad. Why did he beat him?"

"Janaai injected his Alsatian with a poisonous substance and killed him."

The Colonel smiled faintly. "I am not asking any more questions. But it was probably you who ordered Janaai to do so secretly. Raja Bahadur, I know you are scared of Jaygopalbabu, yet there was no need for such fear. Even now there isn't."

The Raja Bahadur whispered agitatedly, "There is. He has brought the doctor. He is trying to forcibly put me to sleep because he has seen that I have summoned you. I have found out about all his fraud."

The Colonel shut his eyes, caressed his bald pate and said, "Hmm, knocks on many doors, the sound of metal utensils being thrown in the North-east room, walking with heavy feet..."

The Raja Bahadur agreed and said, "*Dhup-dhup-dhup-dhup*...as if a two-legged elephant is walking there."

"If my plan is successful tonight, then nobody will knock on any door or throw metal plates."

"And can't that two-legged elephant be tied up?" The Raja Bahadur giggled.

"I will try." Saying so, the Colonel stood up. "Now we will take leave of you. Please be careful."

The Raja Bahadur looked at me and said in a humorous vein, "What do you say, Mr. Journalist? What a red-hot mystery it is! I hope you are taking notes. Please write about it in the *Dainik Satyasebak* at an appropriate time."

I nodded my head as if in agreement with him and followed the Colonel. After reaching our room, I said to the Colonel, "Heavens! My head is reeling. Nothing is registering there."

"Tell me what you are unable to understand, my dear child."

"Which one shall I tell you about? For instance, Professor Tanacha's thought-reading and that incantation."

The Colonel smiled. "Oh, that is one of the threads I have been following up from the card trick I showed you. After Jaygopalbabu mentioned a card trick with ten pairs of cards, I racked my brains to unravel the mystery. Note that the incantation has only ten pairs of unbroken sounds. The first letter of each of those syllables appears twice in the whole chant. That makes it twenty. Suppose you choose a pair comprising the Ace of Spades and the Ace of Diamonds. I keep the first card at the top of the first line. I put the second of that pair in the middle position of the third line, because that syllable begins with the same letter in the rhyme. There I keep the second card of your chosen pair. As soon as you say your cards are in the first and third line, I get to know which cards you had chosen." The Colonel wrote out the arrangement on a piece of paper:

When	You	Are	Part	Of
That	Gross	So	Cial	Class
Let	Your	Will	Ab	Stain
Oh	Ghost	Ly	Palm	Tree

Then it was pure magic! Damn it! I thought it was a code for finding some hidden treasure…

After lunch, I saw the veteran reading a tattered book with great concentration. *Kulkarika: The History of the Royal family at Louhagarh:* Compiled by the Maharaj Asitendra Narayan Dev Sharma.

The Colonel remained absorbed in the book till evening. In the earlier part of the evening, Doctor Dhol and I had gone to see the ducks in the lake on the western side. When we entered the palace gate, we saw Jaygopalbabu threatening Raghab, "I will get you devoured by my dogs. Haven't you learnt after seeing Janaai?" Once inside, when Raghab came to give us tea, he looked sullen. The Colonel was still reading his book. When the clock in the hall struck seven, he shut his book and said, "Today is the 3rd of November. Tonight, at two o'clock, Professor Tanacha's soul will return. There is likely to be a wrestling match. The caretaker Brajanath's amulet will be retrieved. How many items did that make, Jayanto? Hmm- there is another one. I won't tell you that. Be prepared! Of course, you have an invitation..."

It was ten o'clock by the time I finished dinner. Jaygopalbabu sat and chatted with us for a long while in our room. Then he yawned, bid good night and went to bed. Doctor Dhol had possibly given the Raja Bahadur a soporific injection because we could not hear the Raja Bahadur's shouts from upstairs. At eleven-thirty, I was startled to hear a knock on the door of the hall. The Colonel whispered, "Open the door, Jayanto!" He was smoking a cheroot sitting near the table lamp. As I opened the door with trepidation, with the revolver in my hand, Doctor Dhol entered. He was anxious.

"What news?" the Colonel asked.

"Very good. But I could not have done it without Raghab's help," he said in a hushed whisper. If you had not suggested it, I would not have had the courage to ask for his help. I realised that because of the condition his cousin has been reduced to, he is very annoyed with the managerbabu. He has not had the opportunity to express it all this time.

"Hmm. Where is the dog sleeping now?"

"On the steps of the hall."

"The other one?"

"Sitting near his head, and sniffing the body of his comrade from time to time." Doctor Dhol laughed silently. "I am feeling very elated, Colonel! I have never achieved such a formidable feat in my life. But it is also true that I could never have done it without your brainwave and your inspiration to guide me. Never."

"What is the news of the Raja Bahadur?"

"Since it was Jaygopalbabu's order to attend to the patient's need, there was no way I could avoid it. But in accordance with your instructions, I have given him an injection to activate his nerves instead of a tranquilizing dose. Actually, it is because of the stress caused to his nerves that he suffers from insomnia and restlessness. This is how schizophrenia develops. It is only the first step."

The Colonel said solemnly, "Jaygopalbabu wanted it to be established by you that if Professor Tanacha is killed, the responsibility for the murder would be the Raja Bahadur's because he is not in his senses at night. He does not know what he is doing. Therefore…"

"Right, cent per cent right. If you had not indicated anything to the contrary, I would have got carried away and accused the

Raja Bahadur."

The Colonel shut his eyes, swung to and fro and said, "The Raja Bahadur is over seventy years old. He is a widower, and childless. In this big house, there are no longer as many people as there used to be. An eerie emptiness echoes through the house. In this ambience, if the *Alakshmi* embarks on some ghostly misdeeds, he is bound to get overwhelmed by a nervous disorder. But he is also an intelligent man. That is why he was able to understand the basics. He wasn't afraid. Jaygopalbabu, therefore, desperately wanted to put him to sleep at night with your consent and help so that he could look for Brajanath's amulet."

I could not stay quiet. "But the amulet was with Professor Tanacha. It was stolen from his room."

The Colonel said, "Try and remember, Jayanto. In Calcutta, as soon as I raised the question of theft, Professor Tanacha cried out like a mad man, 'Heavens! Grandfather's amulet!' and ran out. Although he never said it, he ran out to see if his grandfather's amulet had been stolen."

I looked like a fool and said, "What is in the amulet that there is so much furore over it?"

The Colonel said slowly and emphatically, "The great king of the seventeenth century, Shivendra Narayan, not only established the idol of *Alakshmi*, but also got some jewellery made for her. Most of it was made of diamonds, and worth lakhs of rupees. After his death, his son Narendra Narayan took it and brought it to the palace. But as soon as he did this, many mishaps started occurring. This is the superstitious belief of the people. At last, the jewels were buried somewhere. The caretaker Brajanath Chatterjee had got to know of this. But he did not have the courage to retrieve it. He wrote its whereabouts on a piece of paper which he put inside the amulet. At the time of his death, he wrote that if any of his successors have the courage, they should open the amulet and see. Superstition is a very complicated disease, eh, Jayanto? His grandson Professor Tanacha understood the seriousness of this, but he, too, did not have the courage to go beyond a certain limit. Anyway, there is some indication about this in the book *Kulkarika*. The Raja Bahadur told me everything openly. Jaygopalbabu had become desperate in his hunt for the amulet. Not finding it in Professor Tanacha's Mirzapur lodgings, he laid a trap. He told Professor Tanacha to be present near the idol of the goddess on 2nd October. He tempted him by saying that if he acted according to the instruction, he would get money."

"How did you get to know?"

"There was a letter from Jaygopalbabu in Professor Tanacha's chest pocket."

"Yes, I remember. You had taken out an envelope from his pocket."

"Jaygopalbabu did not know that we would be waiting in the wings exactly at that time. That is why he could not do the rest of his work in a hurry. But we made a mistake. We both came away. However, his bottle of nail polish fell down while he was running away. He never found it again. Even as he was looking for it, he spotted us and ran away."

My head was reeling. I said, "But we only saw Professor Tanacha in the temple of the goddess that night. If Jaygopalbabu had been there, would we not have spotted him by the torch light?"

"Jayanto, on a moonlit night, if somebody is sitting on the lap of the goddess, it is difficult to make out. Even Professor Tanacha had not realized it." The Colonel sat up straight. His cheroot had got extinguished. He lit it again. Outside, in the foggy moonlight, that ill-omened owl screeched as it flew over us. Then a jackal started calling from across the river. An unknown fear made a shiver go through my spine.

"Then who is the Ace of Spades?" I asked.

The Colonel smiled mischievously as he said, "That you will get to know tonight, Jayanto. Don't be impatient."

Then he suddenly got up and walked out of the door of the hall. A little later, he returned with a pair of enormous gum boots. I have never seen gumboots of such a huge size. Were they made for human feet, or for those of a demon?

Surprised out of my wits, I stuttered, "Goodness! Are these a giant's gumboots?"

Doctor Dhol was staring, stupefied. He also shivered and

said, "These are the gumboots that the bodiless spirit of the palace wears while roaming around all night. Whatever you say Colonel, even the ghosts and spirits of the palace are mental patients. Otherwise, who has ever heard of ghosts wearing gumboots and going around with heavy steps?"

The Colonel said, "It is *not* a ghost, Doctor Dhol. A human being wears them. A man has to wear these gumboots made by special order and roam about in the night like an elephant-ghost, according to his master's instructions."

Doctor Dhol and I said together, "Who is that person?"

"Who else but Raghab," said the Colonel as he smiled. "Today, he deliberately kept them under the stairs so that we would notice them. Raghab is not prepared to listen to that master's order any more. He has got rid of his fear upon seeing us."

The one and a half hours did not seem to pass. I saw Doctor Dhol's head nodding in drowsiness, seated on his chair. The Colonel had his eyes shut in a meditative pose. The table lamp had been turned off. As soon as the clock in the hall struck two with an awful chime, the Colonel stood up and said, "Jayanto, come. Doctor Dhol, please come. The path is clear tonight."

Doctor Dhol rubbed his eyes to wake up. We opened the door softly and got out. There was no light in the hall. In the verandah upstairs, a dim bulb was on. On the staircase, the huge dog was snoring in his sleep. We stepped over him to go upstairs. Then we saw that Jaygopalbabu's other dog was standing in front of the Raja Bahadur's door, and was scratching at the door with one paw. The Colonel whispered, "Do you see how he has been trained? The Doberman pincher would guard him. There was no way that anybody could come into the inner recesses of the house and catch him. Before doing that, the Doberman would go for that intruder. The Alsatian was also trained to knock on doors. After knocking, it would soundlessly hide for cover. See, that Labrador retriever has also disappeared! Come. Let's see what he is going to do."

The verandah turns off to the eastern side. There were huge pillars there. I saw the dog push a door to get into a room. Then there was the sound of falling utensils. The Colonel said, "That is the kitchen. He will throw the plate and immediately pick it up and keep it in its place. See, how he is coming out from there as if he is totally innocent."

The dog saw us and came running towards us. I was scared to see it coming. Doctor Dhol immediately hid behind me. But the dog only sniffed at our legs and went to the other side. We reached the north-eastern corner through the verandah. The Colonel pulled Doctor Dhol to himself and listened, standing behind the pillar. I went and stood outside the last room with great anxiety. I put my hand in my pocket and kept the handle of my revolver pressed firmly. Then I lifted the curtain and saw that the door was closed. Some people were talking in low voices in the room. A little later, I understood that some argument was going on. I kept my ear pressed close to the gap on the side of the door. I could hear the conversation that was going on inside the room quite clearly.

"You are the one who has always disclosed everything to the Raja Bahadur. You have even told him that I asked you to come to the abode of the *Alakshmi*. Otherwise, why would the Raja Bahadur send those two cunning men there at that time? How would he know about it, tell me?"

"Right thing I did. Why did you want to steal my amulet? Answer me."

"You must have kept it with the Raja Bahadur. If..."

"Good thing I did."

I got startled. What was this! This was Professor Tanacha's voice. I remembered, Janaai the *Pagla* had said, 'The dead body has escaped!' If I believed what I heard, Professor Tanacha's corpse had really escaped. But if it was really a corpse, then how was it speaking? I listened, nonplussed...

"Then there is nothing I can do to save you, Tarada. Let me offer you as food for Don. You must have seen Don! What a gaping, big mouth he has!"

"Oh, come on. I might have given you the amulet, but now I won't."

"You will get five hundred rupees, Tarada."

"I would have given it to you for nothing. You asked me to go to the Goddess' seat. I went there. But why did you make me unconscious? Despite that, I didn't die. But you tied up my hands and feet and brought me to this room in an unconscious state. You gave me good things to eat. That is why I quietly hid here. But what about my opium pills? I haven't had one till two in the morning. Now you are demanding the amulet. Oh, what an angel you are!"

"Tarada, I tell you I am now desperate. Do you see this in my hand?"

"Goodness! You are showing me a kn-knife! I warn you I am going to shout now."

"This knife will enter your heart before you can shout. You see how sharp it is?"

"Oh what an idiot I am! I walked into your trap for pure greed of money. Why don't I die?"

"Leave all this self-indulgence. The Raja Bahadur has been put to sleep with an injection. Get up, Tarada. Go to his room and take out the amulet from wherever it is. Come on! It is getting late."

"You go find it. What do I know about where he has kept it? Besides, his door is bolted from the inside."

"The front door is closed. The door on the other side is just shut."

"Ha ha ha! I see you have some brains, Gopal. You have even tamed that fellow Raghab."

"Get up. It's getting very late."

"Okay. I'll go. But you have said you will give me five hundred rupees. I want it immediately, by hand."

"See these five hundred-rupee notes! Can you see?"

"I hope they are not fake notes! I can't believe you, after the way you are making me suffer."

"Oh, come. It's getting late."

Hearing some footsteps, I came out. The Colonel was beckoning from behind a pillar. I went and crouched near them. The first person to come out when the door opened was Jaygopalbabu; behind him was Professor Tanacha. I clearly saw the trace of blood – no, nail polish – under his nose. After they had gone around the verandah towards the Raja Bahadur's room, we got up without making a sound. The two could not be seen. They were probably in some room adjacent to the Raja Bahadur's, from which they were going to enter his room.

As we approached the Raja Bahadur's room, the Raja Bahadur came out smilingly from the room. He was wearing his night-suit. He whispered, "Be ready. When they get inside the room, they will not be able to see me. They'll get confounded."

We waited in the wings again. A light went on in the room. Then we could hear them talk from inside the room.

"Oh! Where is the Raja Bahadur?"

"He must be in the bathroom."

"Impossible. You must have spilled the beans to him about

my coming at two o'clock. That is why the Raja Bahadur is sleeping in the next room. Anyway, whatever you have done is done. Take out the amulet."

"He had kept the amulet under his pillow the other day. No...I see it's not there."

The Raja Bahadur smiled silently and took out a huge amulet tied with a red string and showed it to us. We could hear their conversation from inside again. "Do you think you'll hoodwink me? Find it. Otherwise..."

"Oh god! I'll die ! I'll die! Hey! What are you doing? Raja Bahadur! Save me! Save me!"

The Raja Bahadur rushed into the room first. We followed. In the bright light, the two figures became still, like a sketch drawn with chalk on a blackboard, and their eyes widened in amazement. Then Professor Tanacha shot forward and came and stood behind us as though released from a catapult. The Raja Bahadur dangled the amulet in front of Jaygopalbabu's face, made a face at him and said, "So you want the amulet? A-M-U-L-E-T ? You are sacked. I should have taken you by the shoulder and thrown you out long ago. I didn't have the courage, that's all. Go on, get out of the palace."

Jaygopal suddenly brandished his knife and pounced on Doctor Dhol, screaming "You traitor!" I shut my eyes in fear. Then hearing a struggle, I opened my eyes to see that Jaygopalbabu was on the floor and my aged friend was sitting on his chest and squeezing his knife-wielding hand. As soon as the knife fell to the floor, the Raja Bahadur picked it up. He examined it and said, "He has sharpened it, you know, mister? Hmm. It must be the knife which had disappeared conveniently from the armoury. Wait, let me phone the police station and call the police."

The Raja Bahadur went near the bed, picked up the phone and started dialing. The Colonel freed Jaygopalbabu and stood up. Jaygopalbabu was breathing heavily. The great detective's old bones must be weighing a quintal. Doctor Dhol shivered and said, "Goodness! This guy is murderous. if the Colonel had not quickly captured the knife...God! I can't think of it. I really can't think of it. Oh Colonel! I see that it is this gentleman who is suffering from schizophrenia. He is Doctor Jekyll and Mister Hyde!"

The Raja Bahadur hung up the telephone and said, "Come on, Mister, you were going to afflict me with the Jekyll-Hyde disease."

The Colonel said in a firm voice, "Jaygopalbabu! Don't even try to run away. Then he took out his small yet powerful revolver from his pocket and held it to his nose. "Sit and wait like a good boy. Raja Bahadur! What did the police say?"

"They said they are coming within five minutes or so."

Professor Tanacha had been gaping so far. Now he said, "Do you think that this damned Gopal would have murdered me also?"

The Colonel smiled a bit and said, "Yes, if he did not get

the amulet, he certainly would have. You know all about his misdeeds. Keeping you alive after all this would entail a great risk for Jaygopalbabu's stay in the palace."

Professor Tanacha gulped and said in an intimidated voice, "Heavens! Then I made a mistake in agreeing to his scheme. Hearing about the possibility of the amulet getting stolen, I had thought that if I found the amulet still intact I would go and keep it in some safe place. When I went back to my lodgings, I saw that it had not been stolen. The thief had not found it. That day itself, I came away from Calcutta. Immediately, I went and kept it in the custody of the Raja Bahadur and went back to Calcutta. After two days, I got a letter from this wretched Jaygopal."

The Colonel said, "Yes, the letter was in your pocket. See, now it is with me."

Seeing the envelope, Professor Tanacha said, "Sir, you are really very shrew…" He bit his tongue in shame and stopped.

The Colonel laughed. "Everybody calls me the shrewd master. Professor Tanacha! You don't have to be ashamed of saying it."

Professor Tanacha said, "I had no inkling that Jaygopal was going to make me unconscious, bring me to that room and keep me there!"

The Raja Bahadur made a face at him and said, "Oh my innocent! Idiot! Opium-addict!"

"Come on, after getting the letter, I came and informed

you again. How was I to blame?" Professor Tanacha said with a pathetic face.

The Raja Bahadur showed annoyance and said, "I had told you that before you go near the *Alakshmi*'s temple, you should hang an Ace of Spades round your neck with a black thread. Why did you drop it? If the Colonel had not found it, would the Ace not have got lost?"

"When I got on to the platform of the goddess and was about to hang it, I suddenly felt something on my nose…". Looking at a huge mirror, Professor Tanacha stopped. "Hell! Do you see what Jaygopal put under my nose? Shame-shame-shame!" He took out his handkerchief and started rubbing the spot.

The Raja Bahadur snarled and said, "Don't really make it bleed by rubbing it. Under these circumstances, any bloodshed would spell trouble. Whatever happens, I will be answerable for it."

The Colonel said, "That is exactly what was going to happen, Raja Bahadur. Jaygopalbabu would have murdered Profesor Tanacha in this room. It would have been easy to accuse you of it. Doctor Dhol would not have understood the inner story, and in court, would bear witness to the claim that the murderer is a patient of schizophrenia. These patients are not aware themselves of what they do in the night. Therefore, it would have been established that you had committed a murder unknowingly. Moreover, being annoyed with Doctor Dhol, you had even said that you were feeling murderous. Doctor

Dhol would also have reported that in court."

The Raja Bahadur giggled. He asked Doctor Dhol, "Would you have said it, Mister?"

Doctor Dhol only smiled somewhat embarrassedly. I was silently listening to their conversation. At last my brain seemed to clear up. I couldn't help saying, "Colonel, I have understood who the Ace of Spades is."

The Colonel said, "You should have understood long ago, after seeing the kind of language that the second letter used. The Raja Bahadur's style of speaking is evident in every line of it."

Dumbfounded, I said, "Only one riddle remains. How did the Raja Bahadur know that there would be such a drama in that room at two in the night?"

Hearing my question, the Raja Bahadur said with a twinkle in his eye, "You see, Mister, Raghab knew all about Jaygopal's plans. He had asked Raghab to pick up the unconscious Taranath from the abode of the *Alakshmi*, and keep him in the ghostly room full of old furniture. He had tempted Raghab with money. The deal was that Raghab would get half the money earned by selling the jewels of the goddess, on condition that Raghab would help him and be with him when he would barge into my room at one-thirty or two in the night. Jaygopal has struck Raghab's poor cousin Janaai in a way that he has gone mad. Raghab knows I am an old man, and quite helpless before that rogue. Wouldn't Raghab feel angry inside in being an accomplice in all this? So he told me everything. Instead of his having to open the door for them, I kept the bolt of this room open to keep the poor fellow out of suspicion. He is a poor chap. Why trap him uselessly? Instead, I thought I should catch the scoundrel red-handed. That is why I sent the car to fetch the Colonel. And…" He turned towards me and said, "I had wanted to entertain this gentleman who is a journalist. What do you think, Mister? Isn't it all very thrilling? I hope you will write about it in the *Dainik Satyasebak*."

At this point of time, taking advantage of everybody's preoccupation, Jaygopalbabu suddenly pushed the Colonel stood up and bolted towards the door. The Raja Bahadur screamed, "Catch him! Catch him!"

The Colonel said, "I don't think we will be able to catch him tonight, Raja Bahadur. Besides, it is better to leave the job of finding and arresting him to the police."

The Raja Bahadur calmed down and suddenly giggled. "Then let us have a round of hot coffee, what do you say? Oh I haven't had coffee for ages. Today I will enjoy a cup of coffee with you. What do you say, Doctor Dhol? Will it harm me if I have just one cup?"

Doctor Dhol said, "Of course you can have it. Jaygopalbabu would not let you have any coffee because he wanted to put you to sleep."

The Raja Bahadur almost danced with excitement. He frowned at Raghab and said, "You wretch! Why are you gaping like that? Go and wake up the *Thakurmashai*. Go and see whether he has become a follower of Tara Nath here and is lying doped on opium."

Raghab went away.

Swinging the huge and shapeless amulet on its string, the Raja Bahadur said, "This inauspicious amulet is at the root of all the happenings. Tomorrow it has to be thrown in the river, okay Colonel?"

The Colonel said, "Very well. But I want to see the amulet once, Raja Bahadur."

Taking the amulet from the Raja Bahadur, the Colonel examined it minutely and said, "Professor Tanacha, did you ever open the amulet? It seems that the adhesive that is keeping it together is not very old."

Professor Tanacha did not pay any heed to this and said, "I am feeling very sleepy, Raja Bahadur. Where will I sleep?"

The Raja Bahadur snarled, "Sleep on my head, you damned opium-addict!"

Professor Tanacha lay flat on the divan in the corner, and shutting his eyes, started to swing his legs. The Colonel said, "Profesor Tanacha, the amulet was with you. That is why nobody except you opened it. The whereabouts of the goddess' diamond necklace is supposed to be contained inside this. You had thought that you would sell the amulet once you got the jewellery. But..."

Snatching the Colonel's words, Professor Tanacha said as he swung his legs, "It's a deadly, enchanted amulet, Sir! It will curse you if you open it. Don't you see I have been cursed? I have been completely overtaken by the stars of misfortune. The curse of the *Alakshmi* is not a matter of joke."

The Colonel asked the Raja Bahadur, "Could you give me a pair of forceps?"

"Of course." Saying this, the Raja Bahadur took out a pair of small forceps. He smiled broadly and said, "The forceps were bought by that scoundrel Jaygopal. Do you see these big hairs inside my nose? I use these forceps in the afternoon to pick out those hairs."

The Colonel was cleaning the face of the amulet with the forceps. While he was still prostrate, and with his eyes shut, Professor Tanacha said, "I have the same problem. But Raja Bahadur, doesn't it make you sneeze?"

"Yes. As soon as I see forceps, I feel like sneezing." The Raja Bahadur sneezed a few times.

The Colonel cleaned the neck of the amulet and took out a piece of twisted golden substance. At that point, Raghab brought in a tray of coffee.

While we were drinking coffee, we leaned over the table and looked at the yellow substance. It was a cotton-like paper of olden times. It was in a tattered condition. The Colonel unfolded it carefully and laid it on the bed.

The four sides of the paper were painted with a lovely, red

border. It was torn in places. In some places, the paper was also damaged. But seeing what was written on it in red ink, I was amazed and almost screamed, "Isn't it the card trick!"

That the same lines that were the source of the magic trick with cards were written there!

When you are part of
That gross social class
Let your will abstain
You ghostly palm tree

The Colonel's face also lit up with wonder. He said, "Then this is not only the source of a card trick, but also the indication for locating the hidden treasure!"

Professor Tanacha was giggling. He sang the rhyme to a tune and said, "I have looked all over on the bank of the river. I haven't been able to find it, Sir!"

The Colonel asked, "Why on the bank of the river, Professor Tanacha?"

Professor Tanacha replied with his eyes shut, "Would anybody dare to leave the jewels of the *Alakshmi* within striking distance of the palace? The belongings of the goddess must be somewhere near her seat. According to my ordinary intelligence, I understand only this much."

"But this rhyme is the basis of the card trick!"

"That is the riddle, Sir." Professor Tanacha started laughing again. His legs again started to sway over the divan.

Seeing that, the Raja Bahadur yelled, threatening to slap him simultaneously. "Quit dancing, you wretch. I'll cut off your legs, I tell you."

Then Professor Tanacha lay down straight like a corpse. His legs also stretched and stopped swinging. In the distance, the horrid sound of the grandfather clock downstairs in the hall made the whole house shake. It was three in the morning...

I woke up from sleep late in the morning. But I woke up to see that the elderly nature-lover had disappeared for a morning walk somewhere. I heard from Doctor Dhol that in the wee hours of the morning, the inspector from the Lohagara police station, Bhaja Gobindobabu, had come with his team. Not finding the criminal, he had said very angrily that only the other night he had been made to go back and forth unnecessarily in the name of a dead body near the seat of the *Alakshmi*. He had now once again faced frustration in the name of apprehending a criminal. He would not let the Colonel get away so easily this time. How dare he disturb his sleep on two occasions over a wild goose chase!

Doctor Dhol said, "Come on, Jayantobabu! My body is aching. Let us go and do some jogging for a while."

We both set out. Inside the palace, on the north-eastern lawns, I saw the Raja Bahadur standing, and Jaygopalbabu's two dogs playing with him by making him the dummy. The Raja Bahadur was smiling like a child...

Doctor Dhol got alarmed and said, "Oh no! The fellows will get enraged as soon as they see me. What I did to them last night! Let us quickly make ourselves scarce, Jayantobabu!"

Doctor Dhol crossed the eastern gate with the speed of a sling shot as if he were in the middle of his running regimen. Perforce, I also followed him.

Pantingly, Doctor Dhol said, "I hope they have not followed us."

I reassured him and said, "No. They did not see us. They are quite engrossed with their new master."

Doctor Dhol suddenly stopped, stood and said, "Enough. Jogging at this age is very strenuous. Besides…" Saying that, he looked here and there in a peculiar manner.

I asked, "What is it, Doctor Dhol?"

Doctor Dhol whispered, "There is supposed to be the headquarters of a *saadhu* of a weird sect who has power over evil spirits here. It seems he eats corpses. Have you seen his den?"

"I have seen it. He is not a sage, but an unadulterated mad man. Your patient, what else!"

Thus talking, we went ahead towards the temple. After hearing the story of Janaai the *Pagla*, Doctor Dhol said, "I will tell Raghab. He will send his cousin to me in Calcutta. I will arrange for him to be admitted in a good mental hospital."

Walking through the wilderness, when we reached the

Alakshmi's temple, we saw the veteran Niladri Sarkar leaning against the throne of the goddess. He was wearing a cap. Next to him was a small net to catch butterflies. And inside the net, a multi-coloured butterfly was dozing quietly.

But what struck the eye was the sight of the Colonel absorbed in reading a huge book all by himself. I could not understand how he could sit in such a relaxed manner near the throne of the goddess and read such a book.

Doctor Dhol saw the idol with fear, and said, "Ought I to pay my obeisance? Should I kneel at the feet of the goddess?"

The Colonel lifted his eyes, smiled a little, and said, "If you feel any reverence for her, then do so by all means, Doctor Dhol."

Doctor Dhol grimaced and said, "No Mister. I don't feel any respect. What a ferocious look! She looks as if she will come and strangle us."

I got up on the platform and said, "Hallo, old man. What is the meaning of coming here to read a book?"

The Colonel said, "*The History of the Lohagara Dynasty* – it is that book. The more I read, the more exciting I find it. Everybody in this dynasty seems to be obsessed with something or the other. The present Raja Bahadur's grandfather was Prasitendra Narayan. His obsession was peculiar. He used to proclaim himself as an incarnation of god. Even in this modern age he called himself the *Kalki avataar*. He used to wear white and ride on a white horse. His father Harashitendra Narayan, seeing his ways, turned him out of the house. At that time, Prasitendra built an *ashram* here on the bank of the Loha river. He named the *ashram Kalki Samaj*. But he did not get too many followers, except for Professor Tanacha's grandfather Braja Nath. Even so, Braja Nath would clandestinely come to pay his obeisance to the *Kalki avataar* at an unearthly hour of night."

"Braja Nath was a caretaker. It was he who discovered the jewels of the *Alakshmi*, isn't it?"

"Yes. But god knows where that *ashram* really was. I don't see any signs of it on the bank of the river."

Just then the Raja Bahadur emerged from the eastern gate. With him were the two dogs. Doctor Dhol, who had so far been standing under the platform now leapt onto it and went behind the throne of the goddess. The Colonel stood up and called, "Raja Bahadur! Raja Bahadur!"

The Raja Bahadur shook his head from there and said, "I won't go there."

The Colonel smiled a little and got down from the platform. Putting the book under his arm and the butterfly net over his shoulder, he took a step forward. I also went with him. But Doctor Dhol indicated with his eyes that he would not go.

When we went near, the Raja Bahadur said, "I don't go to such ill-starred places. I had given up coming to the bank of the river for such a long time. Being escorted by Jaygopal's dogs has given me fresh courage, so I have come now."

The two dogs sat on either side of him on their haunches. The Colonel remarked, "I see you have been able to tame them."

"Haven't I? Don't they have any intelligence? Whose bounty have they been fed on for so long? And Jaygopal had bought them with my money. Do you see? It was all my generosity – and the wretch used to try and scare me with ghosts." The Raja Bahadur brandished his stick in a threatening gesture. "Where will he escape? If I get him, I'll beat him till his bones break. Then I will send him to the care of Bhaju the inspector. Then he'll know."

Looking around, the Colonel asked, "Raja Bahadur, do you know where your grandfather's *ashram* was?"

The Raja Bahadur frowned and said, "Are you talking about the *Kalki Samaj*?"

"Exactly."

The Raja Bahadur giggled and said, "My grandfather was one hundred per cent mad. The dam in the river that you see there was washed away in last year's rains. It took almost a year for the river to devour this space and come so near. The *ashram* must have sunk in all this."

"I see. Raja Bahadur, was there a palm tree in the ashram?"

"Yes. There were two on either side of the gate. There were some inside also. They were huge palm trees."

"Did any lightning strike any of the palm trees?"

The Raja Bahadur stared in amazement. Then he smiled a bit, and said "Did you come to Lohagara during my grandfather's lifetime? At that time, mister, you couldn't have been more than a mere child."

The Colonel said, "You are right, Raja Bahadur."

"Then how did you know that lightning struck some palm tree?"

"It is my guess."

"I have heard a lot of your clever detection. I have seen it this time also. But I see you are a clairvoyant, Colonel. Ah!" The Raja Bahadur started laughing helplessly.

"So there was a palm that was burnt when it was struck by lightning?"

"Yes. There was one. That was right inside. On the ground floor of the *ashram* building, it was towards the north-eastern corner. That was the tallest palm tree. My grandfather was quite friendly with a *saheb*. He had got a few saplings of palms from the Mexican desert."

"Then there is no hope of recovering the jewels of the goddess. They must have sunk in the river."

The Raja Bahadur was startled to hear the words of the Colonel. So was I. The Raja Bahadur asked, "What does that mean?"

The Colonel smiled. The diamond jewellery of the *Alakshmi* was buried under that tree which got burnt by the lightning."

"How did you know?"

"From the rhyme written in the paper that was inside the amulet."

"What are you saying?" The Raja Bahadur stared blankly.

At this juncture, I saw Professor Tanacha emerging like a tiger from a bush behind us. Possibly, the gentleman was collecting opium from some wild poppy plant. He was also listening to us with his ears pricked. He screamed, "Have the jewels of the goddess got sunk in the river? Shame, shame! I had feared as much!"

The Raja Bahadur raised his stick and said, "Shut up! I'll set the dogs on you if you start your death-lament, you wretched opium addict!" Professor Tanacha got unnerved and stepped back immediately.

The Colonel said, "The rhyme clearly says:

When you are part of
That gross social class
Let your will abstain
Oh ghostly palm tree!

... Now notice the words. If you translate it into prose, it reads: When you are a member of the social class of the *Kalki Samaj*, that is, the *ashram*... Then it makes an appeal for abstinence, because the desire to possess the jewels of the goddess is evil. Therefore, one should do away with such desires. Now see, in the last line, there is a clear hint that the jewels are buried under a palm tree. But which one? The palm tree is 'ghostly' because it has been burnt, and the exclamation suggests that the jewels have been hidden under that particular tree."

Professor Tanacha beat his head and said, "I knew that it was not pure magic – the real fun is in that rhyme. Yet I could not guess at all. The lightning did not strike the palm tree – it struck my forehead. Shame! Shame! Such a priceless thing! If I got it, I would have been a millionaire by now!"

The Raja Bahadur rushed towards him. "Would you have been a millionaire, or an opium king? You would have bought mountains of opium. It is better as it is."

Professor Tanacha sadly entered the gate and went into the grounds of the palace. I realized that the poor chap really felt cheated.

The dogs had been getting restless for some time. Now they suddenly ran towards the boathouse. The Raja Bahadur lifted his stick and, calling out their names, also went towards it. Then I saw Janaai the *Pagla* come out of the boathouse and fall headlong into the river. Swimming desperately, he reached the other bank. Climbing onto it he started cursing everybody, even as he gesticulated with his hands in a sort of a wild dance. On this bank, the Raja Bahadur stood in front of the boathouse and used his stick as a rejoinder in order to threaten him.

The dogs had entered the boathouse. The Colonel frowned as he inspected all this. He said, "Come with me, Jayanto! What are the two dogs doing there?"

As soon as we got to the boathouse, we stood aghast. Jaygopalbabu was lying there, wedged in a broken boat, tied hand and foot. The dogs were sniffing at him.

Turning around, the Raja Bahadur saw the sight and said, "What's this? Isn't it Jaygopal?"

The Colonel untied the ropes with which he was tied. Jaygopal Babu's appearance was now different. His eyes and face were swollen. His pants and shirt were in tatters. The Colonel said, ""What is the matter, Jaygopalbabu? After escaping from the palace at night, you must have fallen into the clutches of Janaai the *Pagla*."

Jaygopalbabu seemed to be talking to himself as he muttered under his breath, "Yes."

The Raja Bahadur blinked and said, "I feel very sorry to see your condition. I brought you up like my own son from the time you were so high. I don't have children. I had thought that in my will I would leave whatever I have to you. And you incited ghosts to attack me in pure greed for the jewels of the *Alakshmi*!" Jaygopalbabu got up, and catching hold of the two feet of the Raja Bahadur, said, "I have learnt my lesson. Please forgive me. I will never do such a thing again."

The Raja Bahadur wiped his eyes and said, "I do. Get up. Come to the house. How you must have suffered all night! He kept his hand on Jaygopalbabu's shoulder, went towards him and said, "Don't ever touch a knife again. This knife in our collection of weapons is very unlucky. Just by taking it in my hand, I feel, well, kind of murderous. Say Gopal, did Janaai beat you a lot?"

Jaygopal said like an overgrown baby, "Yes. He suddenly threw a stone at me. And as soon as I fell unconscious, the fellow caught me. He then carried me in his arms to the boat-house and used the old ropes to..."

The Raja Bahadur said, "Keep quiet. Don't talk any more."

While going inside the gate, I looked for Doctor Dhol. I saw him on the platform of the goddess, beckoning to Janaai the *Pagla* who was standing on the other bank. I realized that the psychiatrist had at last found a real patient. He did not want to let him go. What had got into his head was that he would explain everything to him, and get him to agree to go to Calcutta for treatment...

The Riddle of Thirty-two

The private detective K.K. Haldar, our favourite 'Haldarmashai,' was reading the newspaper. He folded the paper all of a sudden, took a pinch of snuff, and said, "Jayantobabu is a reporter. My question, therefore, is directed to him."

"Fire away, Haldarmashai," I said.

The well-known detective grinned, "I see the advertisements in your newspaper– some headings say 'Lost', while others say 'Missing'. Why? They mean the same, don't they?"

"This depends on the whim of the people in the advertisement section – they work on the headings."

The Colonel was reading an English newspaper, reclining on an easychair. The blue smoke from the half-bitten stump of his cheroot was circling over his head to disappear into nothingness. He folded the newspaper and said, "Typical! Jayanto's answer can never satisfy Haldarmashai."

Haldarmashai nodded. "You are right, Colonel Sir! 'Missing'

and 'Lost'. Two kinds of headings, yet they are supposed to mean the same! Then why have different names?"

The Colonel looked at me. He grinned naughtily and said, "Haldarmashai has raised a serious question, Jayanto! Don't take it lightly. This is really a part of *shabdarthatatwa,* the science of language."

I said, "Oh no! Please don't bombard me with such difficult and serious things on such a lovely morning."

"It is not a very serious matter, Jayanto! Haldarmashai was reading the advertisements of the second page of your *Dainik Satyasebak*. May be you should also read them once!"

It was now my turn to be surprised. Had the Colonel been able to sniff some mystery in the ads of the second page? I did not seem to notice anything like that after scanning the paper myself. Under the heading 'Missing', there were two ads, one after the other. The first said:

"Baba Amu! Please return home immediately. Your mother is on her death-bed. If you need money, let me know on the telephone. – Baba."

The second was:

"Putuda, Whatever you wanted will be done. Come back, wherever you are. – Bhutu."

After this, under the heading 'Lost', there was a photograph of a strongly built boy in shorts and a half-shirt. Under it was printed:

"This is a photograph of Shriman Dipak Kumar Roy. He is almost 14 years old, fair-complexioned, and has a scar on his chin. Any information about his whereabouts will earn the informer a reward of Rs. 10,000.

Pitambar Roy, 8-1-C Ghoshpara Lane, Calcutta 46."

Following this, there were advertisements of astrologers and taantriks. I raised my head from the newspaper and said, "Oh! No! The headings are at the mercy of the people in the advertisement section."

The Colonel brushed some ash from the cheroot off his beard and said, "Haldarmashai is right. 'Lost' and 'Missing' are the same thing. But after reading the advertisements, you should have been able to decipher the different senses in which they have been used."

Whenever Haldarmashai gets a little enthused, the pointed ends of his moustache start quivering a little. I noticed that at this point, he had got somewhat excited. Suddenly, he sat up straight and said, "Yes! I have understood. The heading of ads for people who leave home voluntarily is 'Missing'. And for those who are somehow forced to leave home and then made to disappear by somebody or some people, or possibly even murdered…"

I had to intervene. "Good heavens, Haldarmashai! Please don't say such ominous things."

The Colonel said, "After looking at the photograph of the lost boy, one does feel bad even to hear the word 'murder'. So

Haldarmashai, let us put in end to this topic. That you have understood the colloquial use of the two words in the headings is enough."

The private detective was still looking agitated and absent-minded. A little later, he said softly, "Colonel Sir!" The Colonel smiled, "I can guess what you are about to say. Your curiosity and enthusiasm has been aroused about the lost boy."

Haldarmashai tried to smile and said, "Not for ten thousand rupees. Not even because my detective agency has no case in its hands at the moment. The point is, when do people give such ads? After the police have failed to trace the person?"

"You are right."

"I feel like meeting the gentleman."

"Good idea. The address is here. Copy it and go and meet him."

The detective put his hand inside his sweater and took out a small notebook and a ball point pen. Then he copied Pitambar Roy's address and asked, "Approximately where would Calcutta 46 be?"

The Colonel extended his hand and took out a street directory from the drawer of his desk.

The private detective K.K.Haldar consulted it, stood up and quickly left the room.

I said, "Let it be. Haldarmashai was regretting the dearth of baffling cases in the country these days. There are a lot of thefts, picking of pockets, murders and bloodshed. But all these are quite transparent and simple cases. Even to murder somebody and make him vanish is not so uncanny any more. So let's see if he is able to unearth an enigma by going after this incident... not bad, eh?"

The Colonel had parted his lips to say something when the doorbell rang. As usual, the Colonel called out, "Shashthi!"

A few moments later, two gentlemen came in and greeted the Colonel. One was wearing a shirt, trousers and a jacket. He was quite an imposing, middle-aged person. The other was wearing a dhoti, kurta and shawl. The Colonel said to the former, "What a surprise! Isn't it Mr. Adhikari? Sit down, sit down. Shashthi, we want coffee. And promptly."

Mr. Adhikari said, "I have been meaning to come for quite some time now. Ultimately, I had to. Let me introduce you to my friend, Kumud Ranjan Bhattacharya. He used to teach in our school at Raigarh. He retired last year. Kumud! You must have guessed that this is the famous Niladri Sarkar."

Then the Colonel introduced me to them. The retired schoolmaster's face seemed somewhat abstracted. He had dark circles under his eyes. There were lines on his forehead, and a deep imprint of sadness on his face and eyes.

Mr. Adhikari's full name was Krishnokanto Adhikari. He glanced at me once and said in a gentle voice, "I want to have a few words with you, Colonel Saheb. The matter..."

The Colonel said quickly, "Jayanto is my confidant. In all

matters, he is my assistant. However confidential your subject may be, don't hesitate to say it before him."

Mr. Adhikari said, "I was away on business in October-November. I came back in early December. After hearing about the incident, at first I tried my best through police sources, but ultimately decided to come knocking at your door. Kumud is my childhood friend. He is very close to me. I am prepared to go as far as possible to help him."

"What is the incident?"

"Kumud! It is better that you should relate it. Colonel Saheb should hear about it from the horse's father's mouth."

Kumud coughed a little, cleared his throat and said, "You have been to Raigarh. You have probably seen the playing field towards the extreme south and the dense woods next to it!"

The Colonel said, "Yes. The woods have a peculiar name. The forest of Harmatmatia, which sounds like the rattling of bones. Of course, I have not heard the sound of any bones rattling."

Mr. Adhikari said, "I think I told you that sometime in the past, somebody spread a ghostly story about hearing the sound of the wind on the dried-up trees. A ghost is believed to roam around there. And you can hear the sound of bones rattling. Bogus! Kumud, tell us briefly what happened."

Kumudbabu said, "It was the day after Lakshmi Puja. My only son, whose name is Sudipto, a student of Class 10, good at studies and games, but a bit stubborn and reckless, had gone to play football with the boys of the club. They don't have any fixed time for playing. They are usually still preoccupied in their game at the time of sunset. There is a goal post towards the woods. Dipu has a very strong kick. With one kick from him, the ball flew headlong over the goal post and went into the jungle. So Dipu went into the jungle to retrieve the ball."

At this moment, Shashthicharan brought in the coffee. The Colonel said, "Have some coffee. It strengthens your nerves."

At Krishnokantobabu's behest, Kumudbabu picked up a cup of coffee, albeit unwillingly. After drinking a few sips, he took a deep breath and said, "An eternity passed after Dipu's going into the forest. Today is the 14th of January, and Dipu still hasn't come back."

The Colonel said, "Please explain more fully. I can guess your mental state. Even so, if you don't tell me everything, I can't move a step."

Kumudbabu said, "After a long time, when Dipu still did not come back, his friends started calling out for him. Getting no response, they went inside the woods from where Dipu had gone in. The night had just set in. After much searching and crying out to him, they got scared. Animals could have been at large in the forest, although one hadn't heard of bears or tigers. So they came back to Raigarh and apprised the people of the locality about what had happened. I rushed there when I heard the news. Then we went into the woods with torches, sticks and guns. It was autumn, and the wood had a thick carpet of fallen leaves. We would not have been surprised to come across snakes there."

Kumudbabu seemed to have finished. The Colonel asked, "The forest is quite big. Did you go through all of it?"

"No. There is a big pond in the wood. We saw some fresh blood on its bank. And…"

"Yes?"

"When we were looking at the blood, we heard a weird, inhuman cry from inside the woods. No. It was not even a cry. It seemed like the howl of somebody whose throat had been slit. A sharp, quivering, and ferocious sound. We could hear it without a break for at least a minute. Krishnokanto has a gun. His brother Barada fired twice... but we did not have the courage to proceed any further. Seeing the blood, we concluded that Dipu had not been able to escape the clutches of some wild animal. It's true one hasn't heard of tigers or bears there but, after all, it is a forest. Such animals could have strayed into it. We still haven't figured out which wild animal cries out in that inhuman way."

"What did you do then?"

"We informed the police that very night. But they didn't agree to enter the forest in the dark. In the morning, the *Bara Babu* of the police station went in with a few armed constables, and seeing the blood stains on the bank of the pond, inferred that Dipu had been carried away by a tiger. By that time, the news had spread. The people of the area rummaged through the forest with weapons that could protect them, but no sign of Dipu was found anywhere."

After hearing Kumudbabu out, the Colonel said, "If this is all there is to the story, then you certainly wouldn't have come to me, Mr. Adhikari."

Krishnokanto Adhikari said, "You are right, Colonel Saheb. Kumud, now please tell the rest of the story."

Kumudbabu said, "After ten days or so, a postman came and delivered an envelope. Its cover had my name and address on it. But inside, there was just a coloured photograph of Dipu."

The Colonel gave him a piercing look and said, "The photo of your lost son?"

"Yes. I was taken aback. But I got more surprised when I turned it around. It was written in red ink at the back of the photo: Dipu is alive. He will return home when it is time."

Mr. Adhikari said, "It's a strange case. Kumud knows his son's handwriting. He claims that both the English handwriting on the cover of the envelope as well as the Bangla handwriting at the back of the photograph are not Dipu's."

Kumudbabu said, "Yes. Neither of them is Dipu's writing. Somebody else has written them."

Mr. Adhikari said, "Give the envelope and the photo to Colonel Saheb, Kumud."

Kumudbabu took out an envelope from his pocket and gave it to the Colonel. The Colonel took out the photograph from inside the envelope, and looked at it from both sides. Then he asked, "Okay. What happened next?"

Kumudbabu said, "A few days later, another envelope came by post. There was a letter in the same handwriting. The letter says..."

Mr. Adhikari said, "Why don't you give the letter to the Colonel?"

Kumudbabu took out another envelope from his pocket and gave it to the Colonel. The Colonel took out the letter and started reading it softly:

"Look inside Dipu's study table, and you will find a mathematical puzzle. The puzzle is surrounded by the number 32 on all sides. If it is not in the drawer, please search his books and exercise books inside out. You are sure to get it. After you find it, put the piece of paper with the puzzle on it in an envelope, and go and secretly keep it in the forest of Harmatmatia, on the southern bank of the pond, and cover it with a stone. Beware! Do not breathe a word of this to the police or to anybody else. And don't try to keep watch over the place covertly. Otherwise, you will not get Dipu back."

After reading the letter through, the Colonel said, "Did you find the puzzle?"

"In fact, no. Not knowing what to do, I drafted a letter very carefully and left it where he had asked me to leave the puzzle. I wrote that since I was unable to lay my hands on the puzzle, I may be given a grace period of another two weeks."

"And then?"

"Exactly two weeks later, another letter arrived by post, wanting to know whether I had found it." Saying this, Kumudbabu gave another envelope to the Colonel.

Mr. Adhikari said, "Kumud left another letter there, asking for some more time. Sometime later, I returned from Hong Kong. Kumud related all the events to me. I took him to the police D.I.G. of our range, Sukumar Bhadra. Mr. Bhadra laughed it off. He didn't entertain our misgivings. He said that the son is playing truant with the father, and that if we wait for some more time, Dipu will come back on his own."

Kumudbabu said, "We just couldn't make him understand that Dipu is not that kind of a boy. The D.I.G. Saheb refused to admit the seriousness of the bloodstains seen inside the woods. He said that he has the report of the Raigarh police station on this case. It seems the Adivasi exorcists secretly sacrifice chickens near the pond."

Mr. Adhikari said, "However, that information is correct. To the east of the woods, there is a slum inhabited by Adivasis. In my childhood, I have seen them going into the forest and singing and dancing to the beat of drums as part of their religious rituals. Now they have become Christians. Even so, some people secretly continue to practise their primitive customs. Anyway, our appeal to Colonel Saheb is that he should try to unravel the mystery of Dipu's disappearance."

After talking for some more time, they went away. I then

said, "This is a mysterious incident, Colonel. There must be something precious associated with the riddle of number 32."

The Colonel was scrutinizing Dipu's photo. Suddenly, he pulled the newspaper and started looking at the photo in the column 'Lost'. Then he took out a pair of magnifying glasses from the drawer of the table, compared the two photographs, and sat up straight. He said, "Another angle of the puzzle of 32 is very strange, Jayanto! The printed photo of the lost Dipak Kumar Ray in the newspaper and the photo of Kumudbabu's lost son Sudipto alias Dipu are alike as two peas in a pod!"

Startled, I said, "Let me see, let me see!"

Looking at the two photographs, I was stunned. The two photographs were indeed of the same person!

The Colonel took some more time to examine the photograph and the picture in the advertisement. Then he leafed through some more Bangla and English newspapers of the same day and shook his head. "No! Pitambar Roy advertised only in your paper."

I wondered, "Why only in one newspaper? The person who wants to give a reward of ten thousand rupees to trace the lost Dipu could surely have advertised in other newspapers as well...Shouldn't he have advertised in one English paper at least?"

The Colonel agreed and said laughingly, "Indeed!" "But it could be that Pitambar Roy has assumed that it is sufficient to advertise in a popular and widespread Bangla newspaper."

"I am surprised about one other thing, Colonel!"

"What?"

"The *Dainik Satyasebak* must be reaching the people of Raigarh also."

"It should. But it probably gets to be evening by the time the morning's newspaper gets there."

"No, what I mean to say is that didn't Dipu's father and his friend Krishnokantobabu read the newspaper on the way to Calcutta? Specially a popular paper like the *Dainik Satyasebak.*"

"They didn't. Or the advertisement could have escaped their notice. Otherwise they would have said so."

"I think they will hear about the advertisement when they reach Raigarh today. It is bound to have caught somebody's attention."

"Yes, you are right."

The Colonel cut out the advertisement from the paper and wrote the name of the newspaper and the date on its back in red with a ball point pen. Then he took out a big envelope from the bottom drawer of his desk and put the advertisement, the photograph and the two letters given by Dipu's father inside it.

Just then, a question struck me. I said, "Tell me Colonel, could the advertiser be a relative of Dipu's father? He could have somehow heard the news from Kumudbabu and inserted the advertisement."

The Colonel was putting the envelope in the drawer. He paused and said, "Pitambar Roy has made Dipu into Dipak Kumar Roy in the ad. But Kumudbabu's son's name is Sudipto Bhattacharya or Sudipto Kumar Bhattacharya."

I said, "Let's assume that Pitambar Roy is not Kumudbabu's relative. He could be a well-wisher or a friend. He heard 'Dipak' instead of Sudipto by mistake."

"Careful, Jayanto. You seem to be getting lost in a maze. Why don't you recharge your grey cells with some coffee instead?" Saying this, he called out for coffee.

Shashthicharan brought in some coffee for us a little while later. While drinking the coffee, I remembered the private detective Haldarmashai. I said, "By now, Haldarmashai must have scanned the colony called Ghosh Para Lane. Let's see what news he brings."

The Colonel said," Yes, at last you have been able to get out of the maze."

"Does that mean that Haldarmashai will be able to solve the mystery of Dipu's disappearance on his own? Am I right in assuming that you won't have anything to do with it?"

The Colonel did not respond to what I said. Reclining on his easychair, he shut his eyes and kept smoking his cheroot.

The phone rang. Without opening his eyes, the Colonel said, "Attend to the phone, Jayanto."

As I stretched out my hand to pick up the receiver, I could hear the voice of the private detective come trailing in, "Colonel Sir!"

I said quickly, "Say, Haldarmashai!"

"Is that Jayantobabu? What is the Colonel Sir doing?"

"He is at his meditation. Where are you calling from? And why are you panting so much?"

The Colonel snatched the receiver from my hand and said, "Yes, Haldarmashai!... Yes... Then?... What are you saying?... You come to me instead... You are right. I'll hang up now."

I said, "What's the matter?"

The Colonel said with a smile, "You are in the habit of pulling Haldarmashai's leg. But in this instance, it has not been appropriate to do so, especially when he has just managed to reach a safe place to telephone you after fighting a real wrestling match."

I was startled. "What do you mean by 'a wrestling match'?"

"You'll get to hear about it from the horse's mouth."

A little embarrassed, I said, "But how was I supposed to know that? Besides, I wasn't really teasing him."

"There seemed to be a hint of teasing in your voice."

"Sorry!"

The Colonel laughed loudly. He said, "No, no. You didn't do anything so terrible that you have to apologise for it. But be prepared. Haldarmashai is bringing yet another riddle for you to solve."

The great detective arrived after almost twenty minutes. Tension was writ large all over his eyes and face. His right thumb was bandaged. He slumped into the sofa. "I made a mistake – I forgot to carry any firearms."

"Have some coffee first," the Colonel said. "We can then talk about all those things. Shashthi! Get some coffee for Haldarmashai."

It was then that I noticed that there were blackish blotches all over Haldarmashai's sweater. The bottoms of his trousers were wet. All this was in addition to the bandaged thumb. It meant that the wrestling match must have been a tough one.

A little later, Shashthicharan brought some coffee, and left the room, looking at Haldarmashai from the corner of his eyes. As usual, Haldarmashai fanned his coffee and started drinking it.

Then he suddenly started giggling. "What a drama!" he said. "He just walked into my trap. I pushed him into the gutter and gave him a good drubbing."

"Please finish your coffee first, Haldarmashai," the Colonel reminded him.

The detective now started relishing his coffee. After finishing the coffee, he characteristically took a pinch of snuff, and told us his story, which I recount briefly.

Ghoshpara Lane, he explained, is a crowded alley. There is

an open drain on either side. The street ends in front of the wall of a factory. 8/1 is a two-storeyed house that must have been built two generations back. There are rooms for lodgers on the upper floor. The three people who occupy the three rooms have different occupations. One works in a non-government office, one is a driver, and the third is a newspaper hawker. There are both Bengalis and non-Bengalis living there. Since it was Sunday, all the occupants were out. On the terrace of the first floor, there is a shed with a tin roof, which is used as the kitchen. Haldarmashai got all this information from the manager of the boarding house, Adinath Dhara.

He had gone to meet Pitambar Roy. But it seemed that every Saturday, Pitambar Roy goes back to his home in the village. He returns on Monday morning to go directly to his office. Then he gets back to the boarding house in the evening. On some days, it is nine in the evening when he returns. The other inmate of the room in which Pitambar Roy stays is a man called Ramesh Sharma. Ramesh is the driver of some businessman.

While he was collecting all this information, Haldarmashai asked for Pitambar Roy's home address. Adinathbabu had looked up the register and copied it down for him. Then Haldarmashai noticed that a copy of that day's *Dainik Satyasebak* was lying on his table.

Pretending to read the newspaper, Haldarmashai showed the ad to Adinathbabu and exclaimed, "What! I didn't know

Pitambar's son is not to be found." Adinathbabu was shocked to see the ad, because Pitambarbabu had never told him about such an incident.

While the two were talking, somebody was standing in the verandah, holding on to the railing. Sensing this, Adinathbabu addressed the man and said, "What is it, Gobindo? What are you doing standing there? Come on in."

Adinathbabu let Haldarmashai know by some kind of sign that the young man is a goonda of the locality. Gobindo did not deign to enter the room, and left without saying a word. Adinathbabu told Haldarmashai that Gobindo was a great friend of Pitambar, and that he had warned Pitambar about it many times but he had not paid any heed to it. He also said that although Pitambar may be a friend of Haldarmashai, Adinath did not like his ways, and that he believed that Pitambar was himself responsible for the disappearance of his son or younger brother – whoever it might be.

The discreet Haldarmashai thought it better not to let the conversation proceed any further and went out after noting the phone number of the boarding house. On the way, he came face to face with Gobindo on the deserted street and tried to make friends with him by starting a conversation about Pitambarbabu. This itself brought on the disaster that took him unawares. All of a sudden, Gobindo took out a knife from his trouser pocket and pounced on him. Haldarmashai is a retired police officer, and has been in such situations many times during his career in the police. He kicked Gobindo very hard on his shin, upon which Gobindo fell into the dirty drain on the side. Then Haldarmashai tried to snatch his knife, and cut his thumb accidentally in the scuffle, although he was able to retrieve the knife in the process. By that time, some people had gathered in the street. They were watching the scuffle from a distance, but not one of them had come forward to intervene. Haldarmashai had then stamped on Gobindo's face with his shoes, and let him wallow inside the dirty water and garbage in the drain for two minutes. He then walked away confidently, without looking back even once.

On the main road, he bought a bandage in the pharmacy, and applied some first aid on himself. It is from there that he had called the Colonel on the phone.

Giving us this vivid description of the incident, Haldarmashai produced the spring knife, from which a blade, almost four inches long, came out when pressed. The sight alarmed me.

The Colonel was listening silently. At last he said, "Now give me the address of Pitambar Roy's home in the village. The address is possibly Raigarh in the disrict of Burdwan."

Haldarmashai started as he took out a piece of folded paper from his trouser pocket. His eyes widened, and the extremities of his moustache started quivering in excitement. He could not help asking how the Colonel knew this.

The Colonel took the paper from him and said casually

that it was a pure guess.

The great detective took another pinch of snuff and said, "What a wonder!"

I said, "Behind this wonder there is a greater wonder, Haldarmashai."

Haldarmashai stared at me with his wide eyes and exclaimed, "What are you saying?"

The Colonel said laughingly, "Jayanto is just teasing you. Don't pay any attention to what he says. You proceed in your work just as you had planned."

"That I will," said Haldarmashai seriously. "I have to get to the bottom of why Pitambar has employed such an anti-social person. Why did Gobindo try to stab me just because I was going to meet Pitambarbabu? I'm really quite bewildered as I wonder about it."

"You have a license as a private detective. If necessary, you can even ask for police assistance."

Haldarmashai smiled a little and said, "I won't need police assistance, Sir. Let me tell you what my plan is."

"Yes. Please don't do anything without first informing me."

"Have I ever done so?" said Haldarmashai, taking out a small notebook from inside his sweater. Then he said, "I have taken the phone number of Pitambarbabu's lodging. Tomorrow is Monday. I will call him at night. I will tell him that I know the whereabouts of Dipak Kumar Roy, so he should meet me soon. I will tell him to come to my private detective agency in Ganesh Avenue."

The Colonel relighted his extinguished cheroot and said, "Does that mean that you will reveal to Pitambarbabu that you are a private detective?"

"Yes."

"Wow! Your plan is wonderful. Isn't it natural for private detectives to interfere in such cases?"

"I don't think Pitambarbabu will go to you," I said.

Haldarmashai laughed. "If he doesn't want to come to me, I will threaten him, and frighten him by naming the police."

The Colonel said, "As a private detective, you always take a photograph of your client, don't you? I need a photograph of Pitambar Roy."

The detective said with assurance, "You will get a copy of Pitambar Roy's photograph. I will meet him by hook or by crook. I will also manage to take his photograph."

"Give me the phone number of their lodgings." Haldarmashai gave the number to the Colónel from his notebook. Then he grinned and said, "You named Raigarh in Burdwan district. Give me some hint of what has transpired in the meanwhile which has caused you to refer to it."

The Colonel took a few puffs from his cheroot and stubbed it out on the ash-tray. Then he said, "Right now, it will suffice to say that I have been to Raigarh about twice. The first time was almost five years ago. There are some ruins of an ancient fortress there besides a dense forest. I had gone with my friend Dr. Debabrata Chattaraj. Dr. Chattaraj is an official of the central archaelogical department. His team was trying to explore some ancient history by digging around the ruins. You already know that I also have an interest in such subjects. However, there I was introduced to a big businessman called Krishnokanto Adhikari, whose head office is in Asansol. His ancestral home is in Raigarh. I roamed about a lot in the Raigarh forest with this man. In his younger days, Mr. Adhikari was a skilled hunter. Under his guidance, I was able to take photographs of some rare species of birds. Next year, Mr. Adhikari met me when he came to Calcutta on some work of his own. Now let me tell you the real thing. The forest there is called Harmatmatia (the forest of rattling bones) because it seems that in the deep of night, some strange creature or spirit moves around there and makes such crackling sounds. So I went to Raigarh again with Mr. Adhikari in order to unravel this mystery."

Haldarmashai was listening with his ears pricked. "Did you hear the sound of rattling bones?" he asked.

The Colonel said, "I went in the month of March. At that time, there are strong gusts of wind at night. It's true that I heard many strange sounds. But the affair of the rattling bones has remained a mystery to this day."

"Pitambar Roy's house is in Raigarh, you said. Do you know him?"

"No! But I seem to have heard the name." The Colonel looked at me in a meaningful way. I understood that it was a warning not to reveal everything to Haldarmashai just yet. I pretended to be engrossed in the newspaper.

Haldarmashai took his leave, reiterating that he would somehow meet Pitambar Roy, and take his photograph.

"But this time you must be a little alert!"

"Yes. I'll carry my licensed revolver with me."

The private detective went out speedily. Then I asked, "Why didn't you let Haldarmashai know the background?"

The Colonel said most solemnly, "If I had, he would have immediately rushed to Raigarh. At the moment, *I* want to know Pitambar Roy's background, and it is *I* who has to get to the bottom of why he put in such an ad."

A question occurred to me. I said, "Colonel! You talked about excavating an ancient ruin in Raigarh to discover some ancient history. Could there be a connection between Dipu's disappearance and some precious treasure belonging to that place?"

The Colonel surprised me by saying, "Yes, certainly. And that is possibly the riddle of thirty-two."

Hearing that there was some connection between Dipu's disappearance and the discovery of some archaeological treasure from the ruins of the ancient fortress at Raigarh, I stared at the Colonel in amazement. Having committed himself to such a statement, he had turned rather serious. He kept smoking.

A little later, I said, "You seem to be absolutely certain about the reason for Dipu's disappearance."

The Colonel gulped as if he was agreeing to what I said.

"But what could that ancient treasure be?"

"I have not had the good fortune of seeing it. I had heard about it from Dr. Chattaraj. It looks like a small box, but is not actually a box. Besides, it is made of some unknown metal." The Colonel opened his eyes, sat up straight, and continued, "What a strange coincidence! It was stolen from Dr. Chattaraj's camp."

"You were saying that it is possibly associated with the riddle of thirty-two."

"Why I said 'possibly' is because Dr. Chattaraj said that the rectangular, black box had some minute inscriptions on it, which resembled the Devnagri script. The thief didn't give enough time for it to be cleaned. But Dr. Chattaraj was able to decipher the two figures 3 and 2, written in the Devnagri script, which was more a guess than anything else. But now I think he had figured it out correctly."

"Didn't Dr. Chattaraj let the police know about this theft?"

"I forbade him to do so because it would have started a furore. Dr. Chattaraj would have been answerable to the archaeological department. His reputation would also have suffered."

"But you were there at that time."

After staying silent for a while, the Colonel said, "I was not there that day. I was roaming around in the forest of Harmatmatia with Krishnokanto Adhikari. But it would not have been possible for me to catch the thief even if I were there. There were ten to twelve men in Dr. Chattaraj's team. In addition, they had also employed some local labourers for the digging. It was Mr. Adhikari who had arranged for those labourers, but they were illiterate. Apart from them, even the people of the locality would come and crowd around the place. So you can see that it was like looking for a needle in a haystack for me. More importantly, Dr. Chattaraj did not give much importance to the thing that was stolen."

I laughed and said, "It seems that the thing has acquired a lot of importance now."

The Colonel did not laugh. With the same serious face, he said, "You are right. Dr. Chattaraj retired last year. He lives in Jadavpur. Let's see if we can get hold of him."

The Colonel picked up the telephone receiver and dialed a number. Having got through, he said, "Is Dr. Chattaraj in?... My name is Colonel Niladri Sarkar. I am speaking from Elliot Road... Is he out? Does that mean out of station?... When is he likely to return?... Didn't say anything? May I know who I am talking to? Hallo, hallo!"

The Colonel hung up and said in an irritated voice, "Strange man! He must be a new servant. His old, trusted servant Paresh knows me. This fellow's harsh voice matches the rude manner of his speech."

"Dr. Chattaraj must have a wife and family. You..."

The Colonel interrupted me to say, "His wife is not alive. His son stays in America. His daughter is married and in Delhi. His daughter and son-in-law are both scientists. Dr. Chattaraj stays alone in his Jadavpur house."

Then he leaned back and shut his eyes. From the burning cheroot between his lips blue smoke rings in curious formations rose over his bald pate, which danced momentarily before disappearing into thin air.

At last I understood that the seasoned investigator was trying to discover some link between his memory of Raigarh five years back and what had happened now.

I said, "I'll leave now. It's almost one-thirty."

The Colonel murmured "Hm?"

"You will meditate, and I will sit all alone. What is the point?" I stood up, having made up my mind to leave.

Right then Shashthicharan peered from the curtain on the door leading to the inside and said with a smile, "Dadababu? You are invited for lunch today."

Hearing that, the Colonel broke his meditation. He glared at Shashthi and said, "Okay, we'll eat."

Shashthi said, "Everything is ready, Babamashai!"

The Colonel asked me, "Jayanto, do you want to have a

bath? According to me, if you bathe so late on a winter's day, you might catch a chill, or even come down with fever. Come on, let's go and eat."

After the meal, returning to the drawing room, the Colonel said, "We are going out after a while."

I asked if we were going to Pitambar Roy's lodgings. The Colonel laughed, "No! Let Haldarmashai handle that. After losing the knife, that Gobindo fellow must have procured a sword by now."

"I cannot understand the Gobindo episode. Why did he suddenly attack Haldarmashai?"

"The question occurred to me also. But in that condition, I didn't probe him for any more details. My hunch is that Haldarmashai must have let slip something to the mess manager Adinath Dhara which Gobindo overheard. You know Haldarmashai's indiscreet ways."

A little later, I said, "Colonel, I am troubled by another question."

"Out with it!"

"Didn't Dr. Chattaraj's colleagues know about the black box-like thing which had been dug up from the ruins of Raigarh? If so, they would have mentioned it in the government report. As far as I know, the whole team has to sign on such reports."

"You are right. A list is made of all the things found during the excavations. The members of the archaeological team also have to sign on that. But Dr.Chattaraj had let me know confidentially that he himself had accidentally picked up that thing. He did not think it very important. That is why he had not told any of the team members about it."

"Yet it was stolen from his camp."

"Yes. While refreshing my memory today, I realized what a strange incident this was."

"You said so, but why is it so strange?"

"When Dr. Chattaraj understood that the thing was valuable, why was he so careless about it? I didn't get any satisfactory answer even when I asked him this."

"Is that why you called him today?"

"Yes. As you have realized, after so many years, some great mystery has deepened around that stolen object. That is why it is so important to speak to Dr. Chattaraj right now. Yet I believe he is out of station."

The Colonel was looking agitated. He stubbed out the half-smoked cheroot on the ash-tray and stood up. "One minute. Let me get ready," he announced.

We left at about two-thirty. My car was parked downstairs. The Colonel sat to my left in the front seat and said, "Go towards Hazra Road. Then I will lead the way."

Starting the car, I asked," Who are you going to without an appointment?"

The Colonel laughed. "Your job is only to drive."

After reaching Hazra Road, following the Colonel's directions, we went along a narrow, zigzag path to the right. Finally, at one point, he asked me to stop the car; I saw a wide gate to my left, with a bougainvillea creeper forming an arch over it. The Colonel got down and stood in front of the gate. A man came and opened the gate. The Colonel signalled to me that I could take the car inside.

I turned the car around, and while going up the sloping footpath, I noticed 'Raigarh palace' written on a marble slab. I got excited both by its name and appearance.

The lawn, full of broken stones, plants covered by weeds, a dry fountain-head with a broken statuette and the two-storeyed, ramshackle house, made me feel as though I was entering a chapter in history. The architecture of the house was of the Italian kind. There were huge pillars and windows. After keeping the car under the portico, I got out. The Colonel, in the meanwhile, talking to the same man, had reached the front of a huge door, climbing a few steps. In a trice, the man vanished into the house.

"How wonderful!" I exclaimed.

The Colonel said, "I got a great kick out of giving you a surprise. Come on in."

Then I heard a dog growling upstairs. "Oh no!" I said, "I hope the dog is not unleashed."

The Colonel was about to say something when the fellow came down the stairway in the hall and said, "Please go in, Sir.

The Kumar Bahadur is in the verandah upstairs. He has seen you."

A faded red carpet covered the wooden staircase. I have often had the opportunity of visiting such houses belonging to traditional, aristocratic families with the Colonel.

In the middle of the wide and long verandah, there was a circular portion where an aged gentleman was sitting in his wheelchair. He greeted the Colonel smilingly, and welcoming him, said, "Ever since I woke up today, I don't know why I had an inkling that you'd come to see me." He hollered out to a man called Madhu that Rexy was barking too loudly, that he should be taken downstairs, and that Sabitri should be told that some coffee was needed immediately for the Colonel Saheb.

A black giant of a man with a huge moustache appeared from one of the rooms in the corner and saluted the Colonel. He then untied the dog and took it downstairs.

We sat opposite the Kumar Bahadur. The Colonel introduced me to him. His name was Ajayendu Narayan Ray. His ancestors were once upon a time the Rajahs of Raigarh pargana. He looked quite aristocratic. I got to know during the tete-a-tete that he had fallen down the stairs some ten years ago, and had subsequently lost the use of both his legs. He, therefore, moved around in his wheelchair on the upper floor, but did not come downstairs.

A stout, elderly woman with a similar strong frame as that

of Madhu came in with coffee and some snacks. She bowed her head in reverence to the Colonel. The Colonel said, "How are you, Sabitri? I hope you still visit your village."

Sabitri said softly, "Who would I visit, Colonel Saheb? I have one brother. He has a job in Durgapur and lives there."

After she left, the Kumar Bahadur said, "Raigarh is not the same any more. On rare occasions, somebody from there comes and pays me a visit. Yes, its condition has improved. They have electricity now. There is a college. But political rivalry between different parties and the resultant in-fighting has also increased."

The Colonel said, "Last year, during Lakshmi Puja, while playing football near the forest of Harmatmatia..."

The Kumar Bahadur signalled to the Colonel to stop, and said, "I have heard all that... Keshto Adhikari came to meet me last month. I believe you have also met him. He has made a lot of money. He said he had recently been to Hong Kong."

"Do you know Kumud Bhattacharya, the father of the boy who got lost?"

"Of course I do. Kumud got his teaching job at *my* recommendation some thirty to thirty-five years ago. I was the M.L.A. at Raigarh then. Keshto said that Kumud has retired. And one fine day, his son suddenly disappeared inside the jungle. It was I who suggested to Keshto then that he should take Kumud to see you. Didn't they go to see you?"

"They came this morning."

The Kumar Bahadur smiled and said, "Is that why you have come here, to find some clue?"

The Colonel also smiled and said, "If you believe that, please tell me your opinion of the matter."

"About Kumud's son?"

"Yes."

The Kumar Bahadur kept silent for a few moments and said, "I had given our ancestral house to the government to build a college. Now they have a college there. Our family library was in that house. When Kumud was unemployed, I had entrusted him with the responsibility of making a catalogue of all the books there, some of which were of my grandfather's time. The books were in a disorganized state, and many rare books were getting destroyed. At that time, we could not trace a family history in Sanskrit written by an ancestor of mine. It was a history of many generations of our family and many related facts."

"Was it a printed book?"

"No. There was no printing press in our country at that time. It was a manuscript written on thick, hand-made paper."

I couldn't help asking, "Was there any information about some hidden treasure belonging to your forefathers?"

The Kumar Bahadur laughingly interjected, "No, Jayanto Babu. If there was some treasure, it would have been discovered during my grandfather's lifetime. After the zamindari system was abolished, he could have become a millionaire with the help of such a treasure. I don't have any property except the house that you see here. I have somehow maintained the standard of the place... I don't know how long I will be able to do it, though. May be I'll have to sell it to a promoter and live in some cage of an apartment."

The Colonel asked, "Did you read the Sanskrit manuscript?"

"No! I don't know Sanskrit that well. Neither did my father. However, I always hoped that I would get it translated into Bengali by some Sanskrit scholar and then have it printed. Who knows, perhaps the history of my forefathers could have been of some use in reconstructing the history of the country!"

"Then do you think there could be some connection between Kumudbabu's son getting lost and that ancient manuscript?"

The Kumar Bahadur said with a solemn face, "Keshto Adhikari asked me the same question. He said that since Kumudbabu knows Sanskrit and he used to teach Sanskrit in the school, a connection was likely. He could be right. I asked Kumud to bring Keshto with him. Strange! Today, Keshto and Kumud went to see you. Yet Keshto did not bring Kumud to meet me. Something seems to be wrong somewhere. Since you have taken up this case, I would advise you to go to Raigarh and confront Kumud directly. You will find the missing link about why Kumud's son disappeared from Kumud himself. I firmly believe that."

"I don't know how much Keshto Adhikari has told you.

Did he tell you about the riddle of thirty-two which was mentioned in the anonymous letter?"

"Yes. Keshto Adhikari is a very shrewd fellow. He wanted to see my reaction. I told him that I knew nothing about any riddle. No such rumour was prevalent in my family either."

The Colonel smiled. "I think you do know something."

The Kumar Bahadur said softly, "It's not a hidden treasure or anything of the kind. In the manuscript, I had certainly seen something like a chequer board. In my opinion, it is a secret charm practised by some exotic religious cult, like *tantra*."

"Did you not copy the pattern?"

"No."

"This is a most valuable lead that you have provided. Now we'll take leave." The Colonel stood up.

The Kumar Bahadur smiled and said, "I expect something in return for this, Colonel Saheb."

"Feel free to let me know, please"

"Please retrieve that lost manuscript for me."

"Kumar Bahadur! My first target is the manuscript, because without retrieving that, it will be difficult for me to come to grips with the mystery of Kumudbabu's son, Dipu's, disappearance. Okay, many thanks."

It was six forty-five by the time we reached the Colonel's apartment on Elliot Road. After asking Shashthi to make coffee for us, the Colonel sat on his easychair. Then he took off his cap and kept stroking his bald pate. I asked him when he was going to Raigarh.

The Colonel said softly, "We are going by tonight's train. You go home after finishing your coffee, and come back ready to leave. There is no problem in leaving your car in my empty garage. Let me call Howrah station to find out about the trains."

Just as he extended his hand towards the receiver, the telephone rang. The Colonel picked up the receiver and said, "Who is it? What are you saying? I am afraid my forefathers are not alive…What was that? You will bore a hole through my bald head? Why have you targeted my baldness, brother? …Okay, okay."

The Colonel hung up the receiver, and said with a swollen face, "Somebody threatened me. I think I'm walking on the fangs of a snake. I must be careful"

I am a veteran traveller of trains on cold, wintry nights. But that horrible train journey was a first. The train seemed to be sleeping as it inched forward. And how cold it was! I looked out for intruders wherever the train stopped. The door of the coupe, however, was locked from inside. But the remembrance of the threatening phone call and what the Colonel had said about treading on the fangs of a snake gave rise to a suppressed fear that kept me on my toes, refusing to leave me in peace.

Nobody knocked on the door of the coupe in the night, and I kept track of whether or not anybody had got inside any other coupe by pretending to go to the bathroom every now and then. My licensed revolver, ready for use, was in the inner pocket of my windcheater. Nobody got into the first class coach at any station. Yet my uneasiness remained.

We were supposed to reach Raigarh at about five-thirty in the morning. It was seven-thirty by the time we reached there. It was a quiet station, with no sign of human activity anywhere. Other than us, a few passengers got down and crowded around the tea stall. They were common, rural folk.

The Colonel said laughingly to me, "That train has caused you a lot of distress. Now drink a cup of coffee here."

I said, "Distress? It made me shiver inside my bones."

"A more severe winter is awaiting you, Jayanto. Its name is Harmatmatia."

The tea-stall keeper offered the cup of coffee to me with great hospitality and asked, "Where are the Sirs going to?"

The Colonel said gravely, "Didn't you hear me? I said we're going to Harmatmatia."

But the tea-stall keeper did not as much as smile. He said with a look of fear in his face, "Sir! Are you going to go to the new forest bungalow in Harmatmatia?"

"Indeed."

He suppressed his voice and said, "Be careful, Sir."

"Why do you say that?"

Yesterday, my cousin Jatin went to Calcutta by the nine o'clock train. I heard from him that Harmatmatia has devoured yet another human being just behind the forest bungalow."

"Really?"

"That is what Jatin told me."

"Is your home also in Raigarh?"

"No, Sir. It's in the neighbouring village Hatipota."

"You said the Harmatmatia struck *again*. Has he done this before?"

"Yes, Sir. I have heard that the monster has eaten up the son of a schoolmaster in Raigarh. That boy's body has not been found. Only some bloodstains have been detected. Jatin said that this time, the man's bloody corpse has been found."

"What is your name?"

"Kaanuhari Das."

"This Harmatmatia that you are talking about, is that some kind of a beast?"

Kaanuhari, the tea-stall keeper, said again in muffled tones, "It's not a beast or anything like that, Sir. Some say it is an evil spirit. Others say it is a demi-god. It used to guard the fortress of the Rajas of the Rai dynasty. From there, it has gone and entered the jungle. Whatever you might call it, the monster lives on human blood. Why only blood? I have heard that it eats human flesh too. Didn't it eat up Kumudmaster's son and leave no trace of him? His bones were young and chewable. That is why he ate him up, bones and all. Don't you see?"

"Yes, I see." The Colonel lit a cheroot.

Some passengers came and crowded around the stall. Kaanuhari said to one of them, "Nimaai, I heard that Harmatmatia has eaten up another person from your village?"

Nimaai said with a grimace, "He went there with a wicked intention. So he got his just desert."

"What do you mean by 'wicked intent'?"

"If he didn't have wicked designs, why did Upen go to the jungle and try to dig up hidden treasure? Hearing of the incident from the *chowkidar* of the bungalow, many of us had rushed there. It was a great to-do with a lot of drum beating and carrying of flaming torches. We saw that Upen Dutta was lying next to a ditch. There was a crowbar next to him. The whole thing was very bloody."

"Didn't you hear the Harmatmatia calling?"

"No, we didn't. But the *chowkidar* seems to have heard it." Nimaai sat on the bench, made a face, and said, "Let it be! Don't they say that it is a sin to be greedy, and sinning hastens one's death? I swear by the goddess Kaali, Kaanuda. Do you know that Upen used to come from Calcutta every Saturday and hang around near the forest of Harmatmatia?"

"Really?"

Nimaai sipped his tea and said, "I have seen it with my own

eyes. The boys from the gentlemen's colony would be playing football and cricket. I used to sit and watch their game. And on Saturdays, Upen Dutta would also be there. And at some point, he would enter the forest."

Nimaai and Kaanuhari were still talking when the Colonel suddenly got up. He climbed down the steps to the lower platform and asked, "What did you understand, Jayanto?"

I said, "These are just the superstitions of simple, country folk. Somebody must have called Upen Dutta to the forest bungalow on some pretext, and then killed him when he thought the opportunity was ripe. However, this is also a murder shrouded in mystery. I wouldn't be surprised to see you poke your nose in this one also."

While walking on, the Colonel said, "You are saying it is the superstition of the village people. Educated, urbane people, and even great scholars have superstitions. If you could meet the archaeologist Dr. Chattaraj, he would testify to this."

"But are we going to walk to the forest bungalow?"

"The forest bungalow is just two kilometres by a shortcut. Note that the undulating field of dry mud, laden with stones and dense with bushes, is perfect for our walk. The fog is quite thick even at this hour. It is better to go there under the cover of the fog. If the train had arrived on time, my intention was to reach the forest bungalow without anybody's knowledge. But the train got us here so abominably late."

I imitated his tone and said, "It will be even more abominable if we lose our way in the fog."

The Colonel smiled, "The forest of Harmatmatia is in the direction that we are walking. I hope that evil spirit or god or whatever it is whose bones make such weird crackling sounds will not show its face to us in the daylight. It seems to be a nocturnal creature."

After going some distance, the dry, uninhabited field sloped downward. Then there was a small, narrow river. Walking through bushes and shrubs, the lower part of my body got soaking wet. But thanks to a thick windcheater and a cap on my head, the upper part of my body was protected.

Then a hazy yet huge, black hill seemed to surface from nowhere and stood before us. I asked the Colonel, "Do we now have to go mountaineering?"

The Colonel said, "That is not a mountain. That is the forest of Harmatmatia. It is looking like a hill because the ground gradually rises upwards from here."

We climbed to the top of the hill and found a cobbled path. It took a turn and climbed to a mound. I could see the tiny, yellow coloured bungalow on top of the mound.

In the verandah of the bungalow, the Ranger Saheb was having tea. A jeep was waiting downstairs. He stood up when he saw the Colonel and me. "Welcome! Please come in, Colonel Saheb. When you telephoned last night, I had just got back home from here. I couldn't tell you everything over the phone. But I was very excited to hear that you were coming. Early this morning, I woke up and came here to await your arrival."

The Colonel introduced me to him. The Ranger was called Amal Chaterjee. He immediately asked the chowkidar to make coffee. I noticed that the gentleman had got somewhat excited on seeing the Colonel. Of course, I knew why. We had already heard at the station that the bloody corpse of one Upen Dutta of Raigarh had been found in the forest, towards the back of the bungalow.

Mr. Chaterjee said, "I had told you that we would soon be building a bungalow in the forest, and that you could stay there on subsequent visits. It would be the most suitable place for a nature-lover like you. Now see, the bungalow is ready. But we haven't been able to get an electrical connection as yet. We hope to get it soon."

The chowkidar brought some coffee and snacks in a tray. The Colonel sipped his coffee and said, "We heard at the station why you had to come here last evening."

"Already?" Mr. Chaterjee's eyes shone with excitement. "This is a weird incident, Colonel Saheb. There must be a wild beast in the forest of Harmatmatia. However, it is not just my suspicion, but that of everybody in Raigarh, that Upen Dutta must have gone there in the evening to dig up some hidden treasure."

"The police must have been here already."

"Yes. The police have taken away the dead body. The post-mortem will be done at the Raigarh hospital. But on first impression, their opinion coincides with mine."

"Do you think it was an attack by a wild beast?"

"Exactly. Most people in Raigarh believe that this is the doing of Harmatmatia," the Ranger Saheb laughingly said. "What do the other people believe?" the Colonel asked.

"Upen Dutta was a notorious fellow. He used to buy stolen goods from the thieves and dacoits of the area and run a business in Calcutta. He must have had some differences with one of them over how much money he owed them, and that person must have murdered him so brutally."

"You must have seen the dead body! In what state was it?"

"It was lying on its side next to a hole in the ground. His sweater was torn to shreds. There were scratches made by some sharp nails all over his body. Even his face and head had not been spared."

"I heard that it was the *chowkidar* who first saw the dead body."

Mr. Chatterjee said, "Nakhulal! Why don't you relate the events to the Saheb?"

The *chowkidar* Nakhulal said, "Sir! I heard a strange sound coming from the back of the bungalow. I rushed there with a spear and a torch. I thought it was some petty thief, or perhaps a fox. It's a torch with five battery cells. I went cautiously till the wall at the back. Then I shone my torch on the forest below. Even as I did so, I saw a man crouch in the bushes. I screamed, and then asked who it was. There was no reply. Almost immediately, I could hear the shrill groans of the Harmatmatia."

"Have you ever heard its groans before?"

"Yes, Sir! I have heard the sound three times after this bungalow was built. At first, it is like the sound of the wind blowing. Then it is like the crackling of bones, and then a piercing sound that deafens you. An…n…n…n…n…like that.

"So what did you do after that?"

"I didn't have the courage to stay here any longer. I took the longer, roundabout way to the slum cluster where we stay."

Mr. Chaterjee said, "I believe the Colonel Saheb has seen Nakhulal's dwelling place."

"You mean where the adivasis stay?"

"Yes. They are all Christians. You probably know that also."

"Yes! So Nakhulal! What did you do after that?"

Nakhulal sighed and said, "My neighbours sent me to Raigarh to inform the authorities there. I'll tell you everything openly, Sir! Harmatmatia is our god. Our people call him 'Thakurbaba'. We are his devotees. But I had seen a man in the jungle, who had been devoured by Thakurbaba. At that time, it ocurred to us to inform Raigarh. Why? So that nobody belonging to any other community should incur the wrath of the Thakurbaba."

"Who did you inform?"

"Keshtobabu, Sir. He is the leader of Raigarh now. I heard he has recently come back from Calcutta. But as soon as he heard the news, he took the entire village with him and entered the woods. Then…"

Mr. Chaterjee intervened to say, "Now there is a government rule that you cannot enter this forest without informing the people in the forest department. That is why I was informed. However, I had to come alone with a gun. We have not yet appointed a forest guard."

"After identifying the corpse, was the police informed?"

"Yes."

"Mr. Chaterjee, we want to keep our luggage in the room and go there immediately."

"Certainly. Nakhulal! Open the rooms for the Sahebs."

In a little while, we went out through the rear door of the bungalow. Nakhulal remained in the bungalow. Mr. Chatterjee asked him to make breakfast for us.

It was a sloping ground with pebbles all over. There was a rifle on Amal Chatterjee's shoulder. He was showing us the way.

A little later, we found some flat ground. The forest seemed to have thinned out in this portion. On the dry, barren earth there, we saw that a hole had been dug. We knew the black stains next to the hole to be the blood stains of Upen Dutta.

The Colonel observed everything on all sides minutely with

the help of his binoculars, and kneeled next to the hole. He seemed to go into a deep meditation as he stared into the hole.

Mr. Chaterjee laughed a little and said, - "It's solid and lumpy earth, otherwise there would have been some footprints of the beast."

I said. "Strange!" "Why is this part of the forest so dry? No plants seem to grow here."

"I believe there must be some granite under this. I have seen such dry, lifeless earth in many places around this area. Even grass refuses to grow on these."

"But Mr. Chatterjee, if Upenbabu wanted to hide some stolen goods, why did he choose such a spot?"

"That is what I can't understand. But suppose it is like this, Upenbabu buried some stolen stuff here and came here yesterday in the evening to retrieve it. But where did the stuff go? Yesterday evening, there was so much light and crowds of people here. Somebody would have definitely noticed the thing, don't you think so?"

"It could be that he hurled it quite a distance away from himself while he was being attacked!"

The Ranger Saheb smiled. "I came early in the morning, and looked all over inside the forest. It was foggy. But that was not an impediment. I just couldn't find any such thing."

At this juncture, the Colonel was digging out some things from the earth surrounding the hole. He suddenly stood up and said, "Mr. Chaterjee! Your guess is right. See, there is a lot of black hair around this place."

Mr. Chaterjee examined a few strands of the hair and said, "They belong to the fur of a bear. There is a rumour about bears inhabiting this forest. Now we have got evidence of that. Wild bears are really ferocious. They pounce on human beings when they see any. Yes! That kind of injury mark can only be caused by the nails of a bear."

"You are right. Now let us go back to the bungalow," the Colonel said.

Amal Chaterjee dusted the strands of hair from his hand and said, "Please be a little wary, Colonel Saheb. I am specially saying this to you. I have often seen you are not mindful enough and tend to throw caution to the winds in your fad about rare specimens of birds, butterflies, orchids, or even weeds."

He laughed as he said this, and started striding away. I suddenly remembered the words of Nimaai at the station. That Upen Dutta of Raigarh used to come from Calcutta every Saturday and enter the forest. However, yesterday was a Sunday. Of course, the fact that he would go into the forest every Saturday did not mean that he would not enter it again on Sunday. It looks like he went into the forest on Sunday also, and was taken unawares by the attack of a bear, which killed him.

I sidled up to the Colonel and asked in a hushed voice, "Colonel! Could it be that Upen Dutta is the same as Pitambar Roy?"

The Colonel smiled and murmured, "You understand everything, Jayanto! It just takes you a little longer. Yes. That Upen Dutta is the same as Pitambar Roy. There is no mistake about that. But keep this under your hat right now."

We had just reached below the bungalow when Nakhulal screamed, "Saheb! A bear, a bear!"

The Ranger Saheb got startled, turned around, and fired a shot from his rifle. The birds in the forest started screeching loudly, which gave rise to a pandemonium all around. The Colonel immediately started looking for the bear towards the back of the forest through his binoculars.

The Ranger Saheb kept his rifle ready and asked, "Colonel Saheb! Were you able to see the bear?"

The Colonel lowered his binoculars and said, "I saw it for a few seconds. The beast looks like a bear. But its movements are not like that of a bear."

Mr. Chatterjee said in an excited voice, ""Do you think it could have been a chimpanzee?"

The Colonel smiled. "Chimpanzees don't live in our forests, Mr. Chatterjee! You know that!"

"No, what I mean to say is, in winter there is a fair here. There is a visiting circus troupe. It looks like some circus chimp could have escaped and started living in the jungle."

"That animal was NOT a chimpanzee."

"Then what was it?"

The Colonel said solemnly, "That animal could have been the Harmatmatia. He possibly came to hear our conversation, particularly what we are planning to do."

The Ranger Saheb tried to smile a little and said, "It is impossible to make sense of anything."

After breakfast, the forest ranger Amal Chaterjee left. He said that he had temporarily been given accommodation and also a place that he could use as an office in a portion of the Raigarh Block Development office. His office and living quarters would be built next to the forest bungalow later. However, if we ever needed him, we could always send for him through the *chowkidar.* Besides, if he could find the time, he would give the Colonel company, specially since his curiosity had been aroused by this living creature which was now an inmate of the forest. But in accordance with the laws of wild life conservation, the creature must not be killed.

After breakfast, the Colonel puffed away at his cheroot as he said, "Nakhulal! What is your Christian name?"

The *chowkidar* said modestly, "Joseph Nakhulal, Sir!"

"Is Father Samuel running a school in your slum?"

"No, Sir! The father has entrusted the care of the school to my nephew Philip. His full name is Philip Suren. He has passed out from Dumka Mission School." Then the *chowkidar* lowered his voice, "Suren was a very good friend of the schoolmaster's son Dipu. The day Dipu got lost in the jungle, it was Suren who gathered the sons of all the gentle folk and bravely entered the forest to find Dipu."

"Tell me Nakhulal, did they ever find the football which they lost in the forest?"

Nakhulal crossed his heart, made a fearful face and said, "That day, nobody had their mind on the ball. Suren saw the ball the next morning. Some beast had torn it to shreds. Even its bladder was torn. Please ask Suren about it."

"I will. What is the name of your -er- slum?"

"Ranglidihi. You must have seen that the colour of the earth there is blood red. I have heard from the elders of our clan that Ranglidihi also used to be part of the jungle. And the jungle was right upto the railway line. Now, that side is inhabited."

The Colonel stood up and said, "Nakhulal! Go and do some shopping for our food. The nearest market is in Raigarh. Are you going to go walking?"

"No, Sir.I have a bicycle."

Joseph Nakhulal took some money from the Colonel, hung his shopping bag on the handle bar of the cycle, and disappeared into the trees of the forest.

The winter wind was causing havoc because the bungalow was situated at a height. I entered the room and flopped down on my bed. There was a smell of whitewashing and fresh paint in the newly built room. The window on the western side was open. My eyes followed the landscape, and as far as they could see, it was only intermittently inhabited. On the horizon, one could see the high and low peaks of the bluish mountains. I gathered that the far end was Bihar, and the mountains were part of the Chota Nagpur range.

The Colonel entered the room and said, "If you want to see the ruins of the old fort of the Raigarh Rajas, look at the northwestern side. The river that we crossed just now is filled with water near the fort, because there used to be an abyss under the fort some time ago. Now the abyss has got covered, but the water current is tremendously fast."

I said, "The fog is still there. Let me see through your binoculars."

On adjusting the binoculars, I could see that the ruins were spread over a large area, and one portion extended as far as the forest of Harmatmatia.

Suddenly I saw that two people had come out from behind the ruins and stood in the open space. It was approximately a kilometre away from where we were. But their figures could be clearly discerned through the Colonel's binoculars. One was wearing trousers, a shirt, a windcheater and a cap. He had a kitbag on his shoulder. The other was short and plump. He was wearing trousers, a sweater, and had a muffler covering his head. Their faces were not very clearly visible. They were gesticulating as they seemed to talk to each other.

I reported what I had seen to the Colonel. He almost snatched the binoculars from me to observe the two people.

Then he said, "How strange! What are Dr. Debabrata Chattaraj the archaeologist and Krishnokanto Adhikari doing there?"

I was startled to hear this. I said, "Both of them have entered the forest!"

"Let them be. This is not worth worrying about right now. You might want to lie down a bit to recover from the train journey. After Nakhulal returns, we can bathe and freshen up."

Nakhulal came back after one-and-a-half hours. He said, "I have asked Suren to come here, Colonel Saheb."

The Colonel said, "Okay. Why don't you make me another cup of coffee?"

Nakhulal smiled. "I know, Sir. The Ranger Saheb has told me that you drink coffee all the time."

"I hope there is some provision for hot water for us to bathe."

"Yes, Sir. There is a well at the back of the bungalow. It is covered, but there is a pump attached to the well. I will lift up a bucket of water and heat it for you, Sir.'

Saying this, he retreated to the kitchen at the back of the bungalow. He promptly brought us a pot of coffee within ten minutes. I had to drink coffee at the Colonel's behest against my will. He just keeps repeating that one slogan – that coffee rejuvenates one's worn-out nerves.

I drank the coffee, changed my clothes and reclined on my bed. The Colonel lit a cheroot and went behind the bungalow. I conjectured that he had gone to locate that strange and terrifying creature by the name of Harmatmatia with the help of his binoculars. The *chowkidar* had seen the creature and thought him to be a bear. But although I had not been able to see the creature, I had also not heard any sound of rattling bones. However, the Colonel had said with a serious expression on his face that although the creature looked like a bear, it was not a bear, and it was possibly that Harmatmatia. And it seems he had come to eavesdrop into our conversation. How strange!

A shiver went down my spine as I recalled these words, even though it was in the middle of the day. My drowsiness left me. I also remembered having seen the famous archaeologist Dr. Debabrata Chattaraj and the famous businessman Krishnokanto Adhikari a little while ago on the ruins of the fort. Their behaviour was also somewhat strange.

The Colonel came and sat in the verandah a little later. I got up from my bed. Seeing me in the verandah, the Colonel said, "I thought you were sleeping, all huddled up inside a blanket."

I pulled out a cane chair, sat down and said, "I will sleep after I have had a bath and eaten. But were you waiting behind the bungalow to catch the Harmatmatia?"

"No. I was just chatting with Nakhulal. He is a very simple fellow. Adivasis have this innocence about them. Although they are Christians, all the old people as well as the youth of Ranglidihi believe in the deity of the forest. Didn't you hear Nakhulal talking about the Thakurbaba? This Thakurbaba is a powerful deity. He used to drink the blood of human beings at one time. Now, he seems to be appeased by the blood of chickens. His abode was on the banks of the pool in the jungle which is now completely hidden by the banyan tree. But I got some facts from Nakhulal. On the night that Dipu got lost, seeing the blood on the banks of the pool, the police had said that it was the blood of some chicken that the Adivasis had sacrificed. Nakhulal said that the police were right. On a full moon night in the month of Ashwin, his cousin Manku had made a promise to make a sacrificial offering to God. Manku and Shibu had gone to clean the place in the evening. Although Shibu is a Christian, he has not left his vocation, which is that of an exorcist. He knows various incantations or *mantras.*"

The Colonel lit his extinguished cheroot and exhaled a lot of smoke. I asked, "What happened after that?"

The Colonel said softly, "Manku and Shibu the exorcist saw two people sitting behind some bushes. Hearing them, they hid themselves. Manku and Shibu recognized one of them. It was that same Upen Dutta of Raigarh. They did not know the other one."

"Did they tell the police or Kumud Babu all this?"

"No. They did not unnecessarily want to get involved in any hassle. Moreover, Father Samuel would have got annoyed if he heard anything about making a promise of an offering to the Thakurbaba. They would stop getting any assistance from the Christian mission. So Nakhulal requested me not to tell these things to anyone."

I got excited on hearing these words. I said, "Colonel! That means that Upen Dutta, alias Pitambar Roy, and that hoodlum Gobindo must have kidnapped Dipu when he went into the jungle to find his ball. Then Dipu must have escaped their clutches at the earliest opportunity. This explains the advertisement in the newspaper by Pitambar Roy."

The Colonel laughed. "The puzzle is more complex than that, Jayanto."

"Why?"

"You will know later," he said. "Right now, you have a bath and eat your lunch. It is almost noon."

After the bath and the meal, the Colonel reclined on an easychair in the verandah. I retired for a siesta under my blanket as usual, and soon I fell asleep.

I was awakened by the *chowkidar*'s call. He had brought tea. I rose from the bed and looked at my watch. It was past four. I asked Nakhulal where the Colonel was.

Nakhulal said, "Suren had come here, Sir. The Colonel has gone with him to see our dwellings."

I know how whimsical the Colonel is. There is no use getting angry with him. I stepped down from the verandah to the lawn, and concentrated on drinking my tea, standing in a small patch of the fading sunlight at the end of the day. On either side of the lawn, there was a prettily cultivated garden. There were tamarisks, orchids and some varieties of multi-coloured crotons. I noticed that a gardener was tending to the garden, oblivious of all else. The *chowkidar* went to chat with him.

Nearly a kilometre away, the railway line had curved from the east to the west. A goods train was going along slowly. Beyond the railway line, there was a macadamized road to the east, which touched a side of the Adivasi slum and disappeared to the north. Perhaps that road led to Raigarh. One could see only an occasional truck or a bus there at this time of the day. I even saw a white Ambassador car coming in our direction. The car disappeared to the east of the Adivasi slum.

After finishing his work, the gardener saluted me as he left. He probably thought I was a senior government officer. The *chowkidar* lit a Chinese lantern in the room at the back of the bungalow and came to keep it in our room. Then he kept a kerosene lamp on the table in the verandah. I asked him, "Nakhulal, don't you feel scared to live in that room at the back?"

Nakhulal crossed his heart and said, "No, Sir. I have a spear and a bow and arrow to defend myself with. But, Sir, the Thakurbaba also lives in the jungle, and I wear a cross on my heart. The Lord Jesus is there above all this to protect us. See! By the grace of god, we can see the newly risen moon."

In the middle of these deserted woods, I was in no frame of mind to savour the moonlight. In fact, I had got to a state where I was in constant dread of the weird beast. The slightest rustling of the breeze caused me to look around. By then, I had my torch in my hand, and kept the licensed revolver next to my pillow on my bed.

Every now and then, quite meaninglessly, I shone my torch over the garden defacing the moonlight. In a little while, I heard the Colonel open the wooden gate and enter the premises. He said to somebody, "Now you go back. You really needn't have bothered to come all the way with me."

That somebody said, "How can that be, Sir? I would not have had any peace of mind till I knew that you had reached the bungalow safely."

It was the voice of a young man. His accent was moderate. The *chowkidar* asked, "Did Suren come with you, Sir?"

"Yes", said the Colonel. "Your nephew is a very good boy. He is decent, and has a lot of guts."

Nakhulal said, "The Father has promised to get him admitted in college."

"Very good. But right now, I need coffee."

"Yes Sir. I have put on some water to heat."

The Colonel climbed on to the verandah, pulled out an easychair and sat down. Then he said, "Jayanto? Why aren't you talking? It means you are annoyed with this old man. But there was no point in disturbing your siesta. Now your body is rejuvenated."

I said, "I was not annoyed or angry. I was just standing in the lawn basking in the glory of the moonlight."

The Colonel said laughingly, "Basking in its glory? You were, in fact, slaughtering the moonlight. Seeing your torch flashing from a distance so many times, I got worried. You must have seen the Harmatmatia lying in wait for us."

"Let that be," I said."Tell me how far you went."

Nakhulal left a pot of coffee, milk, sugar and a plate of snacks for us. As he stirred his coffee, the Colonel said, "Suren had come while you were sleeping. The boy is just about sixteen or seventeen. He is very courageous. He took me to the place in the forest where he had found the ball on the day after the mishap. I gathered that the ball could not have reached that far from the playing field. That means somebody deliberately took the ball there, so that Dipu could not find the ball. Anyway, Suren asked me to wait while he went home to get the tattered ball. He brought it in a polythene bag."

"Haven't you brought the ball back here?"

The Colonel opened the kitbag which was lying next to his feet. He said, "At first sight, it will appear as if some ferocious beast has torn it. But after looking at it through a magnifying glass, you will see that somebody has done it with the help of a very fine and pointed instrument. So it seems that the person who did it wanted it to appear as if Dipu had got into the clutches of a wild beast. You can see from this that those who kidnapped Dipu wanted some time to get him safely away to Calcutta."

"Colonel! Then I have reason to believe that the kidnappers

transported him to Calcutta by car, not by train."

Sipping his coffee, the Colonel said, "You are right. That is my theory also."

"But if we could meet Kumudbabu about the Sanskrit manuscript that was stolen from Kumar Bahadur Ajayendu Roy's family library..."

The Colonel interrupted me and said, "But we must know before that why Upen Dutta was digging in such a stony area in the forest. Jayanto! We will go there tonight. I have told Suren that he must come here after dinner by nine."

"I hope Nakhulal will not spread word of all this in the slum."

"Suren will explain everything to his uncle."

About half an hour later, Nakhulal came to take away the trays, wearing a monkey cap and an overcoat. He smiled a little and said. "Colonel Saheb! How did you like Suren?"

The Colonel said, "Very much. A brave boy. Listen! Suren will come here once more at around nine."

Nakhulal's face showed signs of anxiety. He said, "Will he come here alone through the forest so late in the night? Sir, if you permit me, I will go and fetch him."

The Colonel smiled. "You have no reason to worry, Nakhulal," I said. "The cross which Father Samuel has presented to Suren has the words of Jesus Christ inscribed on it. No harm can come to somebody wearing that cross on a chain around his neck."

The Adivasi-Christian Joseph did not seem to be very reassured by my words , but went away with a solemn face instead.

It was getting colder outside. We went and sat inside in the room. The Colonel took out the tattered ball and bladder from his kitbag and showed it to me. I said, "But one thing just doesn't seem to fall in place."

The Colonel said, "What?"

"Looking at the tattered football, I am wondering if Upen Dutta, alias Pitambar Roy, was murdered with the same weapon. It seems his body also had scratches like those made by the nails of a wild beast." The Colonel wrapped the ball and bladder in plastic, and put them back in his bag. Then he said, "Generally, wild bears rent a thing from one end to the other with their nails. The roar which Nakhulal and some other people heard was also similar to the way that wild bears call out. It is not impossible that this forest is inhabited by wild bears. Dipu's kidnapper, therefore, tried to put the onus on bears. But his dead body has not been found to date. Then there is his photograph and the whole affair of the puzzle of thirty-two. But such things are not for public consumption. After this, Upen Dutta's body has been found. People have believed his killer to be a bear or a wild animal of that kind. And those who believe the hearsay about the Harmatmatia think it to be the doing of that strange creature. On the other hand, Upen Dutta used to deal in stolen goods. There are many rumours afloat about that also. From this, we can only reach one conclusion. Which is, that someone, or some people want to create an atmosphere of panic all around."

"Why?"

"We can answer this question if we can by chance find what Upen Dutta was looking for."

"But why in the night? Can't we find that thing in the daytime?"

"There is a problem during the day, because we have discovered Dr. Debabrata Chattaraj and Krishnokanto Adhikari together."

Suren came at nine o'clock as promised. There was an elegance as well as smartness about this boy who had just about acquired the beginnings of a moustache. He greeted me with folded hands and said to the Colonel, "Colonel Saheb! Please allow me to go and talk to my uncle."

We had our dinner at nine-thirty. At ten, we opened the gate to the north of the bungalow and went out. Nakhulal kept standing at the gate with his spear, and his powerful torch containing five batteries.

I was on edge every minute that night on our journey in the moonlight to this place, although going there had not frightened me at all in the morning. In one hand, I carried a torch. In the other, I held my revolver. The Colonel only had his bag slung over his shoulder. Suren had a torch and a crowbar with him.

The trees were swaying in the winter breeze. I sensed a curious mystery all around in the moonlit night. It seemed as if some people were waiting in the shadows, yet they did not seem to be human at all. In a little while, we could hear the sounds of the breaking of dry twigs. Somewhat stunned, we stopped. The Colonel asked us not to use the torch.

The sound stopped after about two minutes. "I have heard this sound very often," said Suren, "But I have never understood what it is."

The Colonel said softly, "Come on! We have reached our destination."

In that empty patch of land, the Colonel reached the hole in the ground and looked all around him. Then he said in a muffled voice, "It is about three feet from the hole that Upen Dutta dug. Here it is. There is no need for a torch. I saw a faint cross sign here in the morning."

He took out a small black thing from his kitbag. A tiny red light shone in it. I recognized it as the Colonel's metal detector. It made a very feeble sound, which stopped when the Colonel shut the switch. The light also went off. He asked Suren to dig carefully.

The Colonel and I stood at a little distance keeping a watchful eye all around us. Seeing that Suren's crowbar was very easily going under the ground, I understood that some sand had been packed in where the earth was. A little later, Suren put the crowbar aside, removed the sand with both his hands and took out what looked liked a small packet. The Colonel took it from him and asked him to fill the hole with sand again, and said he would scatter the area with small pebbles in the morning.

We were on our return journey within minutes. Just as we had got near the bungalow, we heard an inhuman wail behind us. AAAAAAAAAAA.......nnnnnnnn

The Colonel indicated to us to quickly run for cover to the bungalow.

It was a somewhat steep climb to the back gate of the bungalow. We saw Nakhulal emerging from his room with a spear in one hand and a torch in the other. Suren shut the gate and apprised his uncle of the situation in their own language. Nakhulal also said something in reply. But even in the dim light of the lantern, I could discern signs of fear on his face.

Later, sitting in our room, we saw a suppressed smile on Suren's face by the light of the Chinese lantern. I said, "Your uncle seems to have retreated to a corner after hearing that weird roar. But it doesn't look as if you are frightened."

Suren said, "I asked my uncle what he had been doing inside since he was supposed to have been standing at the gate. He said that we had gone on a course which would inevitably incur the wrath of the Harmatmatia. He had been afraid that if he stood alone at the gate, the Harmatmatia would tear him to shreds like Upen Dutta. Actually, my uncle was scared out of his wits hearing that awful roar."

"Didn't you feel scared?"

"No, Sir. I have heard that roar many times. But I have taken courage in my hands and stood for a while to realize that the roar eventually stops. Harmatmatia has never shown its face to me, let alone try to kill me." Then he laughed and added, "I was going to suggest to the Colonel that we should stand defiantly, and nobody would attack us. Besides, you had a revolver."

The Colonel did not laugh. Solemnly, he said, "Suren! We have snatched away whatever the Harmatmatia had been guarding for so long. That is why he was so angry, and was raring to attack us. He would not have got frightened even if Jayanto had fired a shot at him."

Suren got a little surprised and said, "What is in the packet I dug out of the earth, Sir?"

"I will explain everything to you later. It is enough for you to know at the moment that this thing is responsible for the disappearance of your friend Dipu. Anyway, don't try to go back home tonight. Stay on with your uncle."

Nakhulal said something to Suren in their Adivasi language from the verandah. Suren went out again. Then the two of them went off towards the back through the verandah.

He opened the wrapping. I saw a strange-looking object that was jet black in colour, rectangular, six inches long, four inches wide and four inches high. It was beautifully engraved on all sides. On one side, there were tiny, round buttons fitted in a row. The Colonel said, "It is quite heavy. You can pick it up in your hands and see for yourself."

I took it in my hand and guessed that it might weigh half a kiogramme or so. I looked at it carefully from all sides and said, "Although it looks like stone, it is not made of stone, Colonel."

The Colonel took it back from my hands and said, "No. It is made of some lesser known metal. Jayanto! We are really fortunate. I am certain that this was the thing that got stolen from the camp of the archaeologist Dr. Chattaraj. It was Pitambar Roy alias Upen Dutta who buried it in the forest. For some reason, he came back here last night to dig it out again. At that time, the unknown assailant suddenly pounced on him. Without Upen's knowing it, the assailant must have followed him into the forest."

"But if the assailant was a man, why did he brutally tear him to shreds like that?"

The Colonel grinned and said, "It's time you started putting two and two together, Jayanto. There is a rumour that Dipu was killed by an animal. Besides, the Adivasis also believe that there is a ferocious monster or witch by the name of Harmatmatia in the forest. That is why the murderer and his accomplices wanted to establish that Upen Dutta was killed in an attack by a strange beast."

"But is that inhuman roar really that of an animal?"

"I don't know."

"Colonel! Didn't you urge us to run for our lives to take cover in the bungalow?"

"I did. One can't defend oneself with only a revolver in the jungle in the middle of the night. Anyway, let us call it a day now and go to sleep. We must go to Kumudbabu's house first thing in the morning tomorrow."

As soon as I awoke next morning, I saw Nakhulal standing with our bedtea. There was bright sunshine outside. It was not foggy like the previous day. I asked, "Where is the Colonel Saheb, Nakhulal?"

"He went out early in the morning with Suren," Nakhulal said.

"Did you see which side he went?"

Nakhulal pointed to the north west and said, "I saw him going towards the ruins of the fort, Sir."

I am used to having my first tea of the day in bed. But seeing the bright sunlight, I went and sat outside on the verandah. The fog seemed to have retreated a little on that day. Towards the south-eastern side, an occasional vehicle plied on the macadamized road.

Nakhulal came and announced that he had left some hot water in the bathroom, and that the water would go cold if we did not wash up soon. So I entered the bathroom, and came out wearing my shirt, trousers and windcheater, and then proceeded to the western side of the bungalow. A thick mist enveloped the ruins of the ancient fortress. Sometime later, looking at the parched fields and river, I noticed somebody walking in my direction. The figure was a bit hazy, but had a bag slung on his shoulder. I could recognize him only after he crossed the river and came towards the bungalow.

The man was the private investigator K.K.Haldar – our favourite Haldarmashai. But how did he know that we were staying in this forest bungalow?

As he came closer, he waved to me, and increased his pace. I went and stood near the front gate of the bungalow. The great detective took some time to reach it. I welcomed him and asked him how he knew we were here.

He laughed a little stiffly and said, "I followed that fellow Gobindo. I also telephoned the manager of the boarding house last evening. He said that Gobindo had told him that Pitambarbabu is dead. The news had been given to him by Pitambarbabu's nephew. The manager knows that nephew. He used to go and stay with his uncle sometimes. The two of them had taken Pitambarbabu's belongings and gone to Howrah station."

"You must have rushed to Howrah station immediately."

"Let us go inside. I will tell you all. Where is Colonel Saheb?"

"He has gone for a morning walk."

After sitting down in the verandah, Haldarmashai undid the muffler around his head. Nakhulal had come and stood there in the meanwhile. I said to him, "Nakhulal, this is Colonel Saheb's friend. Make some tea for him immediately."

The long and short of what Haldarmashai told me after Nakhulal had left was: He had looked high and low at the Howrah Station for Gobindo, but had not found him. He was thinking of coming back helplessly when he noticed Gobindo and another boy of his age getting down from a taxi with a lot of luggage. He then hid himself and observed them. But the train to Raigarh was at midnight. Haldarmashai enquired about the details, bought a ticket for himself and waited without their knowledge. When the train came to the platform, he boarded the coach behind Gobindo's. When the train reached Raigarh in the morning, Gobindo and his friend got into a truck and went away. Haldarmashai was wondering how he would get out of the station when a group of Adivasis entered the quadrangle of the station. He learnt from them that Raigarh was not very far by foot from there. If he cut straight through their habitations, it would be one-and-a-half kilometres. There were some educated people among the Adivasis, who told him that there is no hotel in Raigarh. Shashthicharan had told him that we were in Raigarh, so he started enquiring about a bearded gentleman. He is, after all, a clever private detective. Moreover, he is a retired police officer. He was able to gather the information that the Colonel had taken up temporary residence in the forest bungalow.

In the meanwhile, the *chowkidar* had brought the tea. Drinking his tea, Haldarmashai concluded his conversation. "I asked the Adivasi gentleman about Pitambar Roy. When I heard that there was nobody here by that name, I said that a man from Raigarh who used to live in Calcutta, had died suddenly. The gentleman said that there was a man who got killed by a dangerous animal in the forest, but his name was Upen Dutta. Then I told him about Gobindo, upon which he said that Gobindo is a *goonda*. Upen Dutta was also a bad sort, and Gobindo was his sidekick"

Now it was my turn to tell Haldarnmashai about Upen Dutta's gory death. I also said that Upen Dutta and Pitambar Roy were the same person. But I did not tell him about the previous night's incident. The Colonel would tell him if he thought it necessary.

The Colonel came back alone at almost nine. As soon as he saw Haldarmashai, he said, "Good morning Haldarmashai! I was taken by surprise when I detected you through my binoculars a little while ago. Your talent as a detective is unparalleled."

"Why do you embarrass me, Colonel Sir?" Haldarmashai demurred, blushing. "I have reached here by trying to follow Gobindo and a companion of his."

The Colonel called Nakhulal and asked him to make arrangements for our guest. He need not worry, since the

Colonel would inform the Ranger Saheb himself. He requested Nakhulal to open the room next to ours, and to make breakfast for the three of us.

Nakhulal opened the adjacent room. Then he went to organize breakfast. Haldarmashai peeped into the room, came back and said, "It's a new room. It smells of paint. Is there no electricity here?"

The Colonel said, "No! But it's not inconvenient during winter. Yes, there are mosquitoes, but mosquito nets are available."

In a little while, Nakhulal brought us *luchis* fried in ghee, a gravy made of potatoes and some *sandesh* on a tray. Bread of a good quality was not available there. But their ghee was unadulterated. The *sandesh* was also the finest of its kind. The coffee after breakfast was a fitting finale to our rich repast. The Colonel gave some money to Nakhulal for shopping, and he pedaled away on his bicycle.

In between the sips of coffee, I said to the Colonel, "I saw you roaming around the ruins of the fort with Suren. Did you discover anything there?"

The Colonel said, "There may yet be things to discover there. But that is the task of the department of archaeology. I went to find out why Dr. Chattaraj and Krishnokanto Adhikari were there yesterday. We suddenly saw a cave-like place amidst the ruins. It was veiled by a creeper plant covering the small cave. Suren said that once Dipu had brought him there to see the cave. Seeing some black hair in the cave, they had guessed a bear might be living there. So they had run away immediately, in case the bear chanced to be lurking around. I also saw the hair of a furry animal scattered there."

"Hadn't you picked up hair from the place where Upen Dutta's body lay?" I asked.

"Yes. Nakhulal also saw a bear yesterday and screamed with fright. But I still believe that the beast is not a bear."

Haldarmashai was all attention. He said, "If a bear comes to attack me, I will shoot."

The Colonel laughed and said, "No Haldarmashai. The beast is most probably not a bear. But if you chance to see it, please do not fire a shot. You may point your revolver at him, and then watch him getting terrified."

"You must be kidding, Colonel Sir. A bear getting frightened of a revolver shot?"

"Yes," said the Colonel. "You rest for a while. We will lock up our room and go out for some time. In the meantime, you can sleep peacefully. We will come back around twelve."

The Colonel got onto the road just below the bungalow, and said, "We have sent Suren to inform Kumudbabu that we will be coming. We will take a shortcut through the Adivasi habitation."

The Adivasi habitation was quite neat and clean. The Colonel had his bag on his shoulder, and his camera and binoculars hung from his neck. Mistaking him for a foreign tourist, they were eager to show him their church, school, and the seat of their ancestor, the Thakurbaba, in the forest. But after hearing him speak in Bangla, their enthusiasm waned.

After crossing the habitation, we reached the playing fields to the left. On its eastern side, we could see the proper road. We saw Suren after going a little way along the playing fields. Suren said, "Mastermashai is at home. He is very happy to hear that you will visit him."

"Is his house visible from here?", the Colonel asked.

Suren pointed and said, "See there! You can see an old, one-storeyed house through the banyan tree, almost at the end."

The Colonel scanned all of Raigarh, situated towards the north, through his binoculars, and then said, "Let's go."

Kumud Bhattacharya was standing on the high verandah of his house. He greeted us and led us to his living room. He said, "It was kind of you to grace my house. I am now really hopeful that you will be able to trace Dipu. But a strange thing has happened elsewhere. On the day I went with Keshtobabu to meet you in Calcutta, somebody advertised in the 'personal' column of the newspaper, with Dipu's photograph and all..."

The Colonel cut him short and said, "Yes. I saw the ad after you people had left."

Kumudbabu said, "I was shocked to see the ad when I came back home. I went over to Keshtobabu's place. He said, 'This couldn't have escaped the Colonel's eyes. He will certainly find out more from the address of Pitambar Roy given here.' "

"Yes, I have. He belongs to Raigarh. You will be further shocked to know that his real name is Upen Dutta, who got killed in the forest of Harmatmatia."

Kumudbabu stared incredulously.

The Colonel looked around the room and said, "I have reason to believe that this is where Dipu studied."

"Yes. One minute. I'll just be back."

Saying this, Kumudbabu went inside. There was a divan with a bedcover on one side. Next to it, near the wall was a desk and a chair. Books and exercise books were kept neatly on the desk. There was a wooden rack on the wall. Four of its shelves were stacked with books. The Colonel started looking at old and new books on the rack. He said, "Dipu seems to have been interested in reading books on all subjects. There are books on science, history and sports."

The Colonel pulled out a book on sports, and started leafing through it. After looking at it, he took out another book on sports. Then I noticed that he took out a piece of paper from it and promptly pocketed it.

Kumudbabu came back just then. He said, "Dipu was as interested in sports as he was in reading."

"Yes," said the Colonel. "That is what I observed also."

A young girl in a frock brought in the tea on a tray. Kumudbabu said, "I am only a poor man. I don't have the means to entertain you. I can only serve you some tea and biscuits."

The Colonel said, "We have had a full breakfast. We could have done without all these. But I wouldn't mind a cup of tea. It's nice to have some tea after drinking coffee."

Kumudbabu served Suren a cup of tea with his own hands and said, "Suren is a close friend of Dipu's. After Dipu's disappearance, Suren was the only one among his friends who went around looking for him frantically."

Sipping his tea, the Colonel said, "If I am not mistaken, you were a Sanskrit teacher in the school."

"Yes."

"Before this, I believe you used to look after the library of the royal family of Raigarh."

Kumudbabu addressd himself to the Colonel and said in a hushed tone, "I didn't get an opportunity to tell you one thing before Keshto Adhikari. I can say it before Suren. In the royal family's library, there was an ancient manuscript written in Sanskrit. The Kumar Bahadur Ajayendu Roy had requested me to translate it. I had sent the manuscript, but when I went there after a few days, I heard that it had got lost."

Kumud became silent, and was looking a bit distracted when the Colonel asked, "What happened then?"

Kumudbabu dropped his voice even more and said, "I suspected a member of the staff of the royal household called

Maakhon Dutta, who used to regularly steal things from there and sell them with the help of his brother Upen Dutta. I still firmly believe that Maakhon stole the manuscript. The Kumar Bahadur used to trust Maakhon, and had told him in my presence that there was a secret story about his ancestors in it. Maan Singh, who was the commander-in-chief of Akbar's army, had given a wondrous thing to his ancestors, which contained an invaluable gem inside. But Maan Singh had not told him the code of how to open the box to get the gem. He had asked him to use his intelligence and do some arithmetical calculations in order to get the gem."

"What happened after that?"

"Nobody in the royal dynasty knew how that gift from Maan Singh had got lost. But it was possibly explained in the manuscript. I have not had the leisure to read it in detail. It was hand-written, in the Nagari script. But I had glanced over a couplet which mentioned a complex and strange kind of sum."

"Do you remember the sum?"

"Yes. The numbers from one to fifteen have to be arranged in four rows in a way that on all four sides the sum of those figures will be 32."

The Colonel laughed."Yes, the riddle of 32. But did you tell Dipu about it?"

"Yes, Dipu's strong point is Maths."

"When did you tell him?"

"When I read the couplet, Dipu had not even been born. But I remembered the puzzle. Upen Dutta had come to my house during the last Pujas. He was looking for Dipu,and took him away for some time. When Dipu disappeared, my suspicion fell on Upen Dutta. But Dipu is a strange boy, he never told me what Upen told him in their private encounter. Upen had also bought a lot of books from Calcutta and presented them to him. So I had thought that Dipu must have talked to him about those books; after all, I can't buy him the books he wants to read. Dipu used to call him Upenkaaku. But after this meeting, Dipu would always avoid Upen and said to me that the man was a bad lot."

"How did Upen get along with Mr. Adhikari?"

Kumudbabu kept quiet for a while and then said, "I have heard that Upen used to run a business in Calcutta. But he was known here as someone who deals in stolen goods. He had some business interaction with Keshtobabu. "

The Colonel lit a cheroot and said, "So although you were surprised to see Dipu's photo in the newspaper ad, you had not realized that Upen Dutta was the same as Pitambar Roy."

"No, Sir. Nor did Keshto Adhikari. But we had both suspected that he had kidnapped Dipu, and Dipu had somehow escaped from his clutches. But why did Dipu not come back home?"

The Colonel smiled and said, "Let me tell you my

arithmetical puzzle. Dipu is probably in the custody of the very person who helped him to escape from the kidnappers. It is clear from the anonymous letter that you received that Dipu solved the puzzle of thirty-two. But he had not disclosed the whereabouts of the solution because he did not want to give it to Upen Dutta. He must have said it is somewhere among his books and exercise books."

"But I couldn't find it even after rummaging through his books."

Around this time, somebody called out from outside, "Kumud! Kumud! Oh Mr. Bhattacharya."

Kumudbabu peeped out and said softly, "Its Keshto Adhikari."

Krishnokanto Adhikari entered the room, saw the Colonel, and said, "I heard just a little while ago that the Colonel Saheb has graced our town with his presence, and is living in the forest bungalow. So I thought I would go and visit him there with Kumud."

"But we were planning to go to your place from here," said the Colonel.

Krishnokanto Adhikari's Ambassador car was standing in a lane behind Kumudbabu's house. We took leave of Kumudbabu and got into the car. Poor Suren stood on one side, looking a little left out. The Colonel said to him, "You'd better go to the bungalow and help your uncle with the cooking."

In a while, we left the older settlements and reached the new township. In the course of the conversation, Mr. Adhikari said, "I went to somebody's house in Kumud Bhattacharya's locality. You must have heard that a certain Upen Dutta died of being mauled by a bear. We had some business dealings with Upen. It's true that he was a rascal, but he had a very sharp mind as a business agent. His brother Maakhon Dutta used to be a member of the staff of the zamindar's house. He had sent for me. Since Maakhon is not mobile any longer, I had gone to meet him. I was told there by Maakhon's nephew Bijay that a bearded saheb has come to visit Kumud master. I immediately realized it must be you. In the morning, I had met the Ranger of the Forest Department, Amal Chatterjee, in the market. He mentioned you while talking to me. Amal is the son of a friend of mine. He used to live in Durgapur, but has been transferred here recently."

"Did Maakhonbabu call you to discuss the gory incident of his brother's death?" the Colonel asked.

Mr. Adhikari slowed down his car and said, "Yes. Maakhon suspects that somebody must have murdered his brother and then left his body in the jungle. He wanted me to tell this to the police. But Upen is a notorious smuggler in the records of the police. I can't do anything about it."

"Do you know anybody by the name of Gobindo?"

Mr. Adhikari smiled. "Did Kumud tell you about Gobindo?"

"No. I have heard from a person in the Adivasi settlement that Gobindo was an accomplice of Upen. Apparently, he has come back to Raigarh from Calcutta."

Mr. Adhikari said a little later, "Gobindo is a daring and stubborn fellow. Businessmen here had got the police to keep track of him because he was upto a lot of mischief. Gobindo had then gone to Calcutta and taken shelter in Upen's den. I know from Maakhonbabu that Gobindo has come back here. I am, in fact, a little apprehensive that Gobindo might become the leader of all the miscreants in Raigarh."

I understood by looking carefully at Mr. Adhikari's huge, two-storeyed house that he belonged to an aristocratic family. The ancient house, which was surrounded by a high wall, had been renovated to look more modern. There was a garden with colourful flowers and well-trimmed plants, arranged in their separate beds. The car proceeded along a pathway paved with pebbles, and stood under a portico.

Mr. Adhikari took us to the drawing-room. It had smart modern furniture. The sculptures, flower vases and other objects d'art from different parts of the world spoke of a certain aesthetics that the gentleman possessed, despite being a businessman. It seemed incongruous for such a person to have any relationship with Upen Dutta.

He ordered coffee for us, and then came and sat facing us. The sprawling floor of the room was covered all over with carpets with different patterns on them. The Colonel remarked that the room seemed to have been done up recently.

"That's nice," said the Colonel approvingly.

The two of them started talking. I was wondering why the Colonel was not looking for an opportunity to introduce the topic of the archaeologist Dr. Chattaraj. The Colonel had seen the two together on the ruins yesterday.

The servant brought in the coffee and snacks, and then said to his master, "Please come upstairs for a minute. Bacchubabu has called from Asansol. Memsaheb asked me to tell you."

Mr. Adhikari looked anxious and went inside on hearing the news. During that time, the Colonel asked the man his name. He said he was called Bhujanga. The Colonel asked him if the gentleman who had come from Calcutta had left. "But nobody has come here from Calcutta," he tried to say smilingly. "But Sir, yesterday, a gentleman came to meet the *kartababu.* Then the *kartababu* left with him. From their conversation, I understood that he is staying at the government bungalow next to the river. He is from Calcutta."

The Colonel took out a ten-rupee note from his pocket, and stuffing it into his hand, said, "Don't tell your *kartababu* what has transpired between us. Mum's the word, okay?"

Bhujanga was a little taken aback at first, but soon composed himself, and said in a low voice, "Yes, Sir. What can I say to you, Sir? My *kartababu* is stingy to his bones. All that I get for a month's work is twenty-five rupees, and food."

"Are you a resident of Raigarh?"

"No, Sir. My house is in Madanpur. It's been six months I have been employed here. I want to leave this job as soon as possible. Sir! Can you get me a job in Calcutta?"

"I'll see. You meet me secretly in the forest bungalow."

The man looked grateful, saluted the Colonel and left. I asked, "How did you know that you could extract information about Dr. Chattaraj by bribing Bhujanga? If he lets Mr. Adhikari know, even by a slip of his tongue..."

The Colonel intervened, smiled and said, "It's my observation, Jayanto that when the servant of such an aristocratic family brings in a tray for visitors, one can see from his gestures and his facial expression whether he is used to such work or not. Servants of such families are much smarter. I understood by one look at Bhujanga that he is rustic to the core, and has not been able to adjust himself to his surroundings so far."

The Colonel paused to sip his coffee. I did not want to drink coffee, but had to take the cup in my hand anyhow. Mr. Adhikari returned after a while and said, "I am sorry, Colonel Saheb. There was an urgent call from the Asansol head office. I have to leave by car right now. Most probably, I will return tomorrow morning. No, no. You finish your coffee. Let me go and get ready. I will drop you somewhere near the forest bungalow."

"Don't worry about us," the Colonel said. "I have come to Raigarh after three years. I want to roam around a little."

We quickly drained the rest of the coffee. Bhujanga entered smilingly and took away the cups. Then Mr. Adhikari came out, dressed in a suit and wearing a tie, with a briefcase in his hand. We both took leave of him and went out of the gate. Then the Colonel started walking in the opposite direction. We turned back once to see Mr. Adhikari's Ambassador car speeding away.

The new township was clean, and every house had flowers and fruit trees in the front or at the back. At the conjunction of four streets, where Netaji's statue stood on a platform, the Colonel said, "If only we could get a cycle rickshaw!"

"Where do you intend to go?" I asked.

"To the dak bungalow."

"Goodness! Don't tell me you are going to meet Dr. Chattaraj."

"What is so frightening about that?" the Colonel asked. "If he can come to Raigarh for a change of air, so can we. He knows that Raigarh is my favourite historical spot."

After we had walked a little along the street to the left of the cross-road, we found a cycle rickshaw, and the Colonel asked the driver to take us to the dak bungalow.

Just as we crossed the new township, the road wound to the right. Towards the left, we observed the narrow river acquire a different kind of beauty. The trees on its bank seemed to stand like sentinels to prevent the edges from disintegrating. The river flowed parallel to the row of trees. Then I noticed the government dak bungalow. The one-storeyed, old-fashioned bungalow had been renovated. It had a roof of red tiles, and a verandah ran all around it. There were seasonal plants and beds of Indian as well as exotic flowers on both sides of the lawn.

The Colonel said to the rickshaw driver, "You wait a little. We will come back soon."

To the left side of the lawn a man, who looked like an important government officer, was sitting in a cane chair, basking in the sunshine. He looked at us just once. A man in uniform was sitting on the steps leading to the verandah. He promptly got up and saluted us.

The Colonel said, "We want to meet Dr. Debabrata Chattaraj. Please inform him."

"There is nobody here by that name, Sir," he said.

"Then I must have heard his name wrong. There is a gentleman who has come from Calcutta. He is fair, tall, has a grey beard, and wears spectacles…"

"I know who you mean, Sir. Is it Keshto Adhikari's friend you are enquiring about?"

"Yes. You are right."

"Sir! He left a little while ago. I called a rickshaw for him."

The Colonel looked at his watch, seemed visibly disappointed, and said, "How strange! He was supposed to meet me. Why did he go away so suddenly?"

The man said, "Mr. Adhikari phoned him a little while back. That is why he left in a hurry."

"Has he said he will not come back?"

"Yes, Sir!"

"I can't recollect his name. I met him on the train when we were coming here. Was it Dr. Debabrata Chattaraj..."

"No, not Chattaraj. Chaterjee Saheb. D. Chaterjee. A high-up government officer"

"You are right."

We left. And only after we had got into the cycle rickshaw again did I offer an opinion, "It's too complicated an affair for me, Colonel."

The Colonel said with a solemn face, "I see that Mr. Adhikari is a deep sea fish. I had become suspicious about him ever since I heard about him from the Kumar Bahadur. But I think that he did not know the basic reason behind Dipu's disappearance when he came to meet me with Kumudbabu. Possibly, Pitambar Roy, or Upen Dutta, came here and contacted him. Thereafter, Upen must have, according to Mr. Adhikari's instructions, gone to dig up the ancient treasure chest from the forest..."

"You are right," I intervened. "It's possible that Mr. Adhikari got Upen murdered in order to get the treasure chest for himself at no cost."

The Colonel pointed to the rickshaw driver and said, "Shh! Don't say anything now."

The rickshaw driver asked after a little while, "Are you going to get down near the crossroad?"

"No," said the Colonel. "Continue along the highway. We will get down at the turn to Ranglidihi."

I had forgotten that Nakhulal's settlement was called Ranglidihi. The highway took a bow-like turn towards one end of the settlement, and continued further to the south. After getting down there, it took us about fifteen minutes to negotiate our way through the rough terrain of reddish earth and reach the forest bungalow. The road became steep as we entered the jungle. Haldarmashai was standing at the gate of the bungalow. On seeing us, he said excitedly, "There is an animal in the forest. I didn't get an opportunity to fire. But what I have heard from Nakhulal is not false."

The Colonel said, "Why haven't you bathed yet? It's a quarter past one."

Haldarmashai said, "I forgot my bath in the excitement of all that happened. Come in. Let me tell you."

The Colonel unlocked our room. I opened the windows to the south and the west. Nakhulal came in and reported that Suren had just gone home after waiting for us. He would come back after lunch, and had wanted to know when they intended to go.

The Colonel said, "At one-thirty. It's one-fifteen now."

I will give a gist of what Haldarnmashai said after Nakhulal left:

After resting for a while, he had gone to the back of the bungalow, chatting with Nakhulal. He heard from him about the strange creature called Harmatmatia. Then he found his way to where Upen Dutta's mutilated body lay. Suddenly, he heard a sound like that of dry twigs breaking to the left. He took out his revolver and cautiously advanced in that direction. After seeing a black bear-like animal very indistinctly, he fired from his revolver, but the beast disappeared within a moment. He bravely went towards the bushes, where he saw a lot of black fur. He gathered it was not a bear, because wild bears go straight for human beings when they see any. But the strange matter was how the bear disappeared. The forest at the back is dense. A cat can't slip in and out of it let alone a bear.

The Colonel said, "Don't worry about these things. And please do not go into the forest alone. Let us eat now. Then we can sit and discuss everything."

After the meal, out of sheer habit, I wrapped a blanket around myself and tried to get a nap. The Colonel and Haldarmashai sat in two chairs on the grass and were talking in whispers. I realized that the Colonel now wanted to give Haldarmashai an update, with all the background information that he did not already know.

I was woken from my siesta at the Colonel's call. By that time, the winter sunshine had acquired a pallid golden hue. It was already four o'clock. When I sat up, the Colonel said, "Get ready fast. And carry your firearms with you."

"One could have done with a cup of tea or coffee to tone up one's spirits right now." I complained.

The Colonel smiled. "See, your cup of tea has been kept covered on the table. Haldarmashai and I have had coffee just now."

I sipped my tea and said, "I suppose Haldarmashai is going with us."

"He left a little while ago."

"Where have you sent him?"

"I sent him to Mr. Adhikari's head office in Asansol. He has a house there too. Suren has gone to see Haldarmashai off and put him into a bus at the turn of Ranglidihi. It will take him about three hours."

"Why have you sent him to Asansol?"

The Colonel was ready with his kitbag, his binoculars and camera hanging from his neck. He gave me a dirty look and snapped, "No 'whys' please. Drink your tea and get ready. Why do you have so many *why*s all the time?"

I literally gulped my tea and got ready. Then the Colonel looked at me approvingly and said, "There! That's more like what I'd expect of you."

The Colonel shut the windows, locked the door, and informed Nakhulal that we were going out. Like the previous day, Nakhulal was busy chatting with the gardener. He saluted and asked the Colonel when we would return.

"If it gets a bit late, don't worry."

The Colonel stepped down from the bungalow and went forward on the rough forest path made of red earth. "Colonel! You were speaking just like a minister of ours when you said, 'Why do you have so many *whys*?'" I said, imitating him. "But that gentleman would go further and make a face at the gathering of journalists and say, 'What a dust-bin of *whys*!'"

"Your nerves seem fine now," said the Colonel. "Now listen. Suren will be waiting for us at the turn to Ranglidihi after seeing Haldarmashai off. With him, we will go to Maakhon Dutta's house."

"Isn't Maakhon Dutta the elder brother of Upen Dutta?"

"You can't seem to remember anything certainly. However, you are going there as a journalist, which is your real identity. You have come from Calcutta to collect some information about Upen Dutta's death. Is that clear? Now listen carefully to what I have to say further. You have also been to Kumudbabu's house in the morning to get the facts of Dipu's disappearance from him. Okay?"

"Right, Colonel."

"You will also talk to Upen Dutta's wife. Try and console her. Also, offer to write in *The Dainik Satyasebak*, asking for government assistance. Remember to bring up the topic of the Raigarh palace and the royal library as you talk to

Maakhonbabu. Then mention the Sanskrit manuscript at an opportune moment..."

The Colonel could not finish what he was saying. All of a sudden, somebody pounced on him from the hedge on the left of the narrow and rough pathway. I was taken aback and stood still. Then I saw that the Colonel kicked the assailant on his lower abdomen with amazing dexterity, and with his boots on, which caused him to scream and collapse on the ground immediately. The Colonel pinned the man down and sat mercilessly on his back, and as he took out his revolver, he said, "I hope you are aware of what will happen if I pull the trigger."

Then I saw that the knife in the assailant's hand had fallen to the ground. Its blade was almost six inches long. I picked it up, holding my revolver in my hand.

The person on whose back the heavy Colonel had ensconsed himself was bleeding from the nose and mouth. The Colonel pulled his hands behind his back and said to me, "There's a rope in my bag. Take it out quickly."

I took out a nylon string from the knapsack on the Colonel's back. I know that this bag of his contains everything, starting from the simplest screwdriver. The Colonel tied the assailant's hands tightly behind his back, and got off his back. Then he caught him by the hair and made him stand. He was panting and his face was bleeding all over. The Colonel boxed him on his ribs and said, "You must be Gobindo, aren't you?"

The assailant was a young man. He was looking quite gory with such a bloodied face. He did not reply. The Colonel smiled at me and said, "Come, let us tie this villain to a tree in the forest. Harmatmatia will pick at his raw flesh and eat it with relish."

Just as the Colonel made a gesture as if to pull him into the forest, he cried out in his cracked voice, "I will never do it again, Sir! Greed made me.... Oh God!"

The Colonel said, "First tell me if your name is Gobindo. If you tell a lie, I will go and tie you to a tree."

"Yes, Sir. I am Gobindo," he groaned.

"Tell me who asked you to murder me for money." The Colonel shook him in a way that his hair stood on end.

Gobindo panted and said, "Keshtobabu, Sir! Before going to Asansol today, he told me that he would give me five thousand rupees if I could murder the bearded Colonel Saheb."

The Colonel pulled him by the hair again and said, "Where is Kumudbabu's son Dipu?"

"I swear by the goddess Kali, Sir, I have no idea. Upenda had kept him in somebody's house in Calcutta. But Dipu ran away from there."

A group of Adivasi labourers were returning from the Raigarh railway station at this time. They looked visibly excited, and started making a lot of noise in their own language. One of them said in Bengali to the Colonel, "Saheb! This is Gobindo, the goonda. He was hounded out of Calcutta by the police.

This villain of a fellow used to regularly go to our slum and extract money from people after beating them up. When this goonda entered Ranglidihi, our wives and daughters would get so frightened that they would retreat inside their homes. You should hand him over to the police."

He said something else in his native tongue. Two of them ran away from the scene. At the instruction of the Colonel, I folded Gobindo's knife, and put it in his trouser pocket. The Colonel related what had happened to us to the Adivasis. An elderly one among them suddenly hit Gobindo on the back and said something in their native tongue. I could make out that Gobindo must have harmed him greatly on some past occasion.

A little later, I saw some people, playing on their bell-metal plates and drums, arrive from Ranglidihi. The Colonel said, "Jayanto! They will probably beat him to death. Before that, we must fire our blank cartridges to try and scare them away."

With this noisy mob having suddenly descended on us, and two of the Adivasis fleeing from the scene, it was natural for the Colonel and myself to be a little unmindful of Gobindo, specially since he had both his hands tied behind him. Taking advantage of this opportunity, Gobindo ran off into the forest just as he was.

I was not prepared for this event, and just about managed to scream, "Catch him! Catch him! He is running away."

The Colonel put a foot forward to run after Gobindo, and then stood still. The Adivasi mob had also noted the event, and a group of them noisily entered the forest with their rods, spears and choppers.

At last, some words emerged from the Colonel's mouth, "Goodness! Gobindo will probably not be able to run in that condition. These men will murder him."

The beating of drums and the playing of bell-metal plates had stopped by then. The mob had got startled, and were saying something among themselves with their faces turned towards the forest. The Colonel said to them, "Some of you had better quickly go to the police station and report what has happened. I will explain to them in detail later."

One of them said, "Sir! The police will not arrest Gobindo. Even today, I saw Gobindo going towards the market in Keshtobabu's car. The police try to stay on the right side of Keshtobabu."

Around this time, Suren came running to us, and said pantingly, "I have heard everything on the way, Sir! Gobindo apparently tried to kill you!"

The Colonel said, "Suren! Take this card of mine and go to the police station immediately. Before coming here, I had spoken to the D.I.G. of police, Aurobindo Mukherjee, about the reason for my intended visit. He must have let the Raigarh police station know about me."

He gave his card to Suren, and Suren had just about taken a

few steps forward when the armed mob came out of the forest. One of them yelled something in their language, which made the restless crowd transform itself into what seemed like a painted picture of lifelessness.

"What happened, Suren?" I asked.

Suren said in a terrified voice, "Baba Harmatmatia has killed Gobindo."

The Colonel was startled. "What! Call one of them, Suren. Let me hear what happened."

At Suren's call, a strong looking young man with a cane in his hand and a fearful countenance came forward, saluted us and said , "Sir! Gobindo could not go very far. In exactly the same way as Baba Harmatmatia had done to Upen Dutta, he also ripped open his follower Gobindo's body from his skull to his ribcage. The goonda is lying flat on his back."

A companion of his said, "We heard that Gobindo tried to murder you. We think that the Thakurbaba had followed him while he came in through the jungle to murder you. The Thakurbaba always punishes the sinful and the wicked..."

The Colonel interrupted him and said, "Suren! You take one of them and go to the police station. The police will come back to see Gobindo's state. Hurry up!"

Suren called the strong young man and rushed away with him. The people in the mob looked at one another in a daze and left. I realized that they were scared of the police. They also fled the scene as the police might think them to be

Gobindo's murderers.

The people who had entered the forest to catch Gobindo were also going away one by one. The Colonel said, "I request you not to go away. You have no reason to be afraid. Why don't you give your weapons to the others and come with us? I want to see Gobindo's corpse."

Three young men agreed to go with us. The others took all their rods and lances and walked away towards the settlement. The winter sun had just about descended and hidden itself behind the hills in the distance. The Colonel and I had torches with us. We switched on our torches and followed them. It was dark inside the forest. The swaying breeze made a strange sound in the trees and the bushes. Avoiding thickets and brambles, we took a path under the tall trees and were quietly proceeding towards the north by the light of our torches.

The youth turned towards the west a little later. Then we came across a grassy spot, and when we reached the end of it, we heard the creaking of branches. They stood startled, bowed in reverence, and made the sign of the cross on their chests. I realized that these Christians had also not given up their belief in the religion of their forefathers. But what was the creaking sound? It was coming from inside the jungle.

They put out their hands and looked inside the bushes. The Colonel and I went forward and stood dazed. It was a grotesque sight.

Gobindo had collapsed with his hands still tied behind his back. Blobs of fresh blood still oozed from his head. His sweater was torn to shreds. The Colonel looked for a while and turned his head. He said solemnly, "It's all my fault, Jayanto. I have never beaten up anybody like this. But the instinct of cruelty to one's fellow being or some residual habit of my martial life made me box the poor chap. I deeply regret it now. This unfortunate young man had wanted to murder me, no doubt, but I could have just defended myself and then restricted his movements."

An Adivasi youngster understood what was troubling the Colonel's conscience and said, "Sir! The criminal has got his just retribution. This is no fault of yours. The Lord Jesus has said that the punishment for sin is nothing short of death."

Another one of them was going to say something, when we suddenly heard that mysterious roar – Aaaaaaaan......... aaaaaaan!

The Adivasi boys immediately ran helter skelter without any direction. The Colonel took out his revolver and said urgently, "Jayanto! Be ready. Keep your eyes open all around you. But be careful and don't shine your torch."

I held a revolver in one hand, and a torch in the other. I alertly observed all around me. This time the roaring continued. One could not make out from which direction it was coming. I muttered, "Colonel! Let's fire one round."

"No," said the Colonel, and crept a few steps on all fours and shone his torch suddenly. For a fleeting instant, I saw a bear-like creature diappear into the bushes. I report it to be about as big as a bear, but in that instant I also knew it was not a bear. It was more like a chimpanzee or a gorilla. Yet it was imposible for chimpanzees or gorillas to be in this forest!

The roar had stopped immediately after the Colonel's torch had shone. At least there was no doubt that the strange creature had been making the noise.

Right then, the Colonel amazed me by his famous loud laugh. "What is the matter? What is there to laugh at?" I asked. He sat comfortably on the grass, lit his cheroot, and said "Sit down. We can't do anything but wait till the police arrives."

I was compelled to sit down, but was still restless. Asking the Colonel many times did not yield an answer about his inappropriate laughter. A little while later, we saw the moon above the trees. The moonlight created an eerie sensation inside the forest. The winter breeze made the light and shade all around quiver. I felt all the time that the weird creature was probably roaming all around us, and would pounce on us unawares any time, not giving us time to open fire.

Sometime later, we saw a bright light in the direction from which we had come. Then we could hear Suren, "Colonel Saheb! Colonel Saheb!"

The Colonel stood up and said, "It's possible that Suren's companion can't find this place." He lit his torch and started guiding them to that spot. Their bright searchlight gradually located where we were sitting, and they arrived there. A police officer saluted the Colonel and said, "We got your message. We also knew that you are staying in the forest bungalow. Anyway, where is the corpse of that rogue Gobindo?"

"Are you the officer-in-charge Mr. Tapesh Sanyal?" asked the Colonel.

"Yes, Sir."

The Colonel took him to see the mutilated corpse. A constable had brought a lantern, which he busied himself in lighting. It was a regular armed police brigade which had landed up there. Everybody went forward towards Gobindo's dead body. The constable kept the lantern near the body after lighting it. There were two other police officers. They scanned the nearby bushes with the help of the searchlight. Suren and his companion were standing on one side. I went to them. Suren whispered to me, "His name is Chhakua. Peter Chhakul Murmu. Please ask him what he saw."

Chhakua said softly, "Sir, I caught a glimpse of Thakurbaba."

"What does he look like?" I asked.

Chhakua said, "He is black. His hands are so long as to touch the ground. He has big nails, Sir. He must have killed Gobindo to drink his blood, but vanished when he saw us."

I understood that the young man was educated. I asked him, "Have you seen the Thakurbaba on any other occasion?"

Chhakua said, "No, Sir. But my father had once come into the jungle to cut some branches from the trees. Sitting on the branches, he had seen that the Thakurbaba was hiding inside the bushes. It is very strange, because there is no reason for my father to lie."

"What is strange?"

Chhakua whispered, "My father saw Keshtobabu standing, with a gun, right next to the Thakurbaba."

I was surprised and said, "But didn't your Thakurbaba kill Keshtobabu?"

"That is what my father could not fathom. Keshtobabu went away after a little while. Then my father got down from the tree and fled. He told me not to say this to anybody. But I told it to Suren today, and he said I must report it to you."

Suren said, "I think it is some ferocious animal that is now a pet of Keshtobabu."

I said, "You may be right."

I saw some people coming with a bright searchlight beaming at us. Suren said, "They are coming from the hospital with a stretcher on which they will take away the dead body. They have some armed police with them. See!"

After the hospital staff had gone away with Gobindo's body on a stretcher, and the armed police had left, the officer-in-charge, Tapesh Sanyal, said, "We have nothing left to do here. Let us go, Colonel Saheb. I will drop you at the forest bungalow and then get back to the police station. We have a jeep and a car waiting near Ranglidihi."

The Colonel at last introduced Mr. Sanyal to me. Tapesh Sanyal folded his hands in greeting, and said laughingly, "You are a journalist. As an eyewitness, you will publish a report in your paper. But the occurrence of two incidents like this in quick succession only establishes that there is some fierce, bloodthirsty animal in this forest. We will inform the forest department and the wild life conservatory. It is essential to lay a trap and catch the beast."

As we talked, we walked in the same direction that we had come from. After turning towards the south and walking for about ten minutes, we reached the rough path. Suren came with us but Chhakua slipped away.

The Colonel said, "We can go back to the bungalow now, Mr. Sanyal. You don't have to bother to come with us. But I hope things will be done according to what I told you."

Mr. Sanyal said, "Certainly, Sir. The D.I.G. has strictly ordered us to cooperate with you. Besides, I am personally very curious to see the outcome of this case. You have further awakened my curiosity."

I reached the forest bungalow and saw that Nakhulal was standing with a torch and a spear, anxiety writ large all over his face. The Colonel said, "Nakhulal! Quickly make us some coffee. It is very cold tonight. Suren! Narrate the story to your uncle. Do you see anything in your uncle's face?"

Suren tried to laugh and said something to his uncle in his mother tongue. Then both of them went towards the back of the bungalow. A lantern was burning in the verandah. But it was bitterly cold outside. The Colonel opened the door to our room and lit the Chinese lantern. Then he kept his kitbag on the table. He examined his camera and binoculars and said, "I thought I had damaged these two instruments in the guerilla war that I had to fight in self-defence against that wretched Gobindo. But it looks as if they are both unscathed."

Then I told the Colonel about the incident I had heard from Chhakua about his father getting to see Baba Harmatmatia and Keshto Adhikari together. But there was no sign of surprise on the Colonel's face. He spread out his legs, leaned back, took off his cap and simply said, "It's all a magic show."

"What do you mean?" I asked.

The Colonel did not pay any heed to what I said. Absent-mindedly, he said, "I am now beginning to get worried about Haldarmashai, Jayanto. I had never imagined that Keshto Adhikari was such a dangerous man. Of course, Haldarmashai will sport a disguise to get inside Keshto Adhikari's fort. But even then..."

He suddenly stopped and started stroking his beard. A little while later, Suren brought in some coffee and two plate of snacks. I requested Suren to repeat the experience of Chhakua's father. But the Colonel said, "No, Suren. Go and chat with your uncle and replenish your energy with a cup of tea or coffee. Tell him you will eat and stay in the bungalow tonight."

Suren left silently. I understood that he had wanted to tell Chhakua's father's story. But the Colonel himself looked like the embodiment of some great mystery. Seeing his attitude, I sensed that something untoward might happen again.

But nothing out of the ordinary happened that night. Around ten, after we had finished our dinner, the Colonel lowered the flame of the Chinese lantern and smoked his cheroot while ordering me to go to bed. The tiredness that gets you after a bout of great excitement numbed me as I got bed. I covered myself with the blanket all over except my face. The window to the west was shut, but the window to the south had been left open. I kept waking up, thinking that the grotesque creature we had seen might extend its long arm and tear me to bits with its sharp nails. Then I turned my face once to see that the Colonel still sitting at the table, his head lowered, with the lamp turned towards him. Since his back was towards me, I could not see what he was doing.

I was awakened by Nakhulal's call. He had come to serve us bed-tea. A foggy, dull sunrise greeted us from outside. I took my cup in my hand and saw that the Colonel's bed was empty. His kitbag, binoculars and camera were not there. Nakhulal said, "Colonel Saheb took Suren with him and went somewhere early in the morning."

After a little while, when the fog had cleared, I went and

stood in the sun in the lawn outside. As usual, the gardener was watering the flowers. Just then I saw Suren rushing towards the bungalow from the road.

He opened the gate, entered the lawn, and said, "The Colonel has sent for you. He has asked you to get ready quickly and report to him."

I was somewhat surprised and asked where he was.

Suren paused to take a breath and said, "In the early morning, he took me with him to see the fort of the Rai dynasty. From there, he went to the police station. Then he went to Maakhonbabu's house. He is still there."

His last words made me recall that on the previous evening, the Colonel had asked me to see Maakhon Dutta as a representative of the *Dainik Satyasebak*. That was when Gobindo had taken him unawares and pounced on him with a knife. I got out as fast as possible. I took my reporter's notebook in the pocket of my windcheater. I also had to take my revolver in my rucksack, as the Colonel had sent me a coded message to 'get ready' and report to him. It was a signal to be prepared to face any eventuality.

Suren said, "Let me go and tell my uncle that you will not have breakfast. Colonel Saheb has instructed me to do so."

Nakhulal was approaching from the rear end of the bungalow with a solemn face. They talked among themselves in their native tongue. Then Suren came and said, "Let us go, Sir!"

Walking along the rough path, Suren laughed and said, "My

uncle is very worried about me. He thinks that Baba Harmatmatia will now kill me and drink my blood."

"You don't believe in any Thakurbaba Harmatmatia, do you?" I asked.

"It's all bogus, Sir!" Suren responded, and continued, There is an exorcist by the name of Shibu in Ranglidihi. He has instilled this fear in everybody. Like Chhakua's father, Shibu also claims to have seen Harmatmatia. He says he follows the practice of sacrificing chickens in the name of the Baba. The Baba's abode is supposed to be at the edge of the pool, which Shibu seems to have seen. Baba was eating the blood of chickens there, but had raised his arm in blessing when he saw Shibu."

As Suren laughed out loud, I realized that he was a rational young man. He took me to the highway from the southern edge of Ranglidihi where there is a bus stop, and a few shops selling tea and cigarettes. Some cycle rickshaws stood there. Suren waved to a rickshaw driver he knew and said, "Jhabbuda, take us to Maakhon Dutta's house."

Jhabbu sized me up and said it would take three rupees to transport us there. Before Suren could say anything, I said, "It's okay. Hurry up."

The highway took a turn and was adjacent to Raigarh throughout. There was a chilly wind all around, and Jhabbu should, in fact, have demanded ten rupees. It took us about half an hour to cover a distance of one kilometre. When we turned into Raigarh, we had to go through a narrow alley before

Jhabbu brought the rickshaw to a halt in front of Maakhon Dutta's ramshackle house. He saluted me when I handed him a five-rupee note. How simple these Adivasis are even now!

A high verandah had rough patches of cement on it. Suren got up, peeped in and said, "Sir, the Chota Saheb is here." I entered and saw the Colonel sitting on a rickety chair. There was a mat on a divan laid out before him. An old man was sitting on it. He stood up and greeted me. "Namaskar! I am a fan of the *Dainik Satyasebak*. I, therefore, know both of you. But I never expected that I would see you with my own eyes. Jayantobabu! You sit next to me. Suren, you sit here, okay, son?"

The Colonel smiled mischievously and said, "Jayanto, I hope you are following what Maakhonbabu is saying."

Maakhonbabu lowered his voice and said, "Upen was indeed my younger brother, but I had nothing but contempt for him. I knew what he was upto with the assistance of that devil of a Gobindo. The royal palace now houses a college. Before that, Upen had stolen a lot of priceless things from there and sold them in Calcutta. Although I knew all this, I didn't have the guts to open my mouth. He would not have spared me although I was his elder brother."

The Colonel said, "Your assistance will be very valuable to us, Maakhonbabu. That Sanskrit manuscript belonging to the royal palace..."

Maakhonbabu intervened, "That is Kumud's idiocy. Or it could even be his greed. He should have confessed it by now. But he has not told you yet. Do you mean to tell me that Kumud didn't know why Upen kidnapped Dipu? Dipu is an innocent boy. His father had showed him that manuscript. Dipu had mentioned it to his friends. It didn't take long to reach Upen's ears. Now let Kumud confess the truth before me. He is a Brahman. I challenge him to swear by his holy thread that he did not sell the manuscript to Upen for a mere fifty rupees."

In amazement, I looked at the Colonel. The Colonel said, "Let it be. Let bygones be bygones. But please retrieve it for us somehow from Upen's wife now."

Maakhonbabu said, "I will send some tea for Jayantobabu. Then I'll go and see if Upen's wife Rama is there."

Maakhonbabu went inside. A girl came in to serve me tea. The Colonel was looking rather serious. He whispered to me, "The O.C. Mr. Sanyal searched Upen's room in the morning but he couldn't find it. Maakhonbabu said that Keshto Adhikari had come here yesterday morning. He had met us at Kumudbabu's house. But he had come to speak to Upen Dutta's wife. I believed that Keshtobabu has laid his hands on the manuscript. But Maakhonbabu said that Upen's wife Rama had left a suitcase with him last night, which she requested him to keep in his custody. But the keys are with Rama, and that is why he has gone to locate her."

After an agonizing wait, Maakhonbabu came back and said with an annoyed look, "What a villainous woman! What else could one expect from Upen's wife? While Colonel Saheb was talking to me, she took the suitcase from its hidden place and left. My elder daughter Sutapa said that her aunt left for her parents' place about five minutes ago. Suren! Please take these gentlemen to the bus stop just now. You are sure to find her."

Suren was about to go out. The Colonel said, "Sit down, Suren! It is no use running about like this."

Maakhonbabu said with surprise, "What are you saying, Colonel Saheb? If Rama disappears with the suitcase, we will never retrieve the Sankrit manuscript."

The Colonel smiled and said, "Don't worry, Maakhonbabu. I told the police to keep a watch on your house. No. They are not uniformed police. They are disguised in white gear, and are taking turns to await anything untoward that might happen here. By now, your sister-in-law must be in police custody."

Maakhonbabu looked relieved and said, "This is a wonderful move you have played."

The Colonel was silent for a while, but finally said, "I have just one request, Maakhonbabu."

"What is it?"

"Your brother Upen's room is locked."

"Yes. But if you so desire, I can try and open it. There is a man called Nanku in the market. He makes keys for locks.

Nanku is very much in demand when anybody loses his keys by chance. Suren knows him."

The Colonel said, "Suren, please hurry up and call Nanku here."

Suren went out. Maakhonbabu's daughter Tapati peeped into the room and said, "Baba! Aruda is asking about my aunt. What shall I say?"

Maakhonbabu said, "Ask him to sit down. I am coming."

"Who is Aru?" asked the Colonel.

"Sir, he is my nephew." Saying this, Maakhonbabu lowered his voice. "I feel ashamed to acknowledge Aru as a nephew. Upen ruined him. He's another one like Gobindo."

I remembered that Haldarmashai had followed Gobindo and Upen Dutta's nephew all the way from Calcutta. I said, "Colonel! This is the same Aru who brought Upenbabu's belongings from Calcutta with Gobindo."

Maakhonbabu said, "Let us call Aru here, Colonel Saheb."

The Colonel said, "Let it be. You go and see what he has to say. Then bring him here if you think it is necessary."

"He entered from the back door. It means he is avoiding the police."

Maakhonbabu entered the house. The Colonel's cheroot had got stubbed out. He lit it with the help of his lighter, blew out a few rings of smoke, and said, "I am anxious about Haldarmashai. He is supposed to call the police station and let me know his whereabouts. But I had assured the Kumar Bahadur that I would retrieve the Sanskrit manuscript of his forefathers."

I said, "The police must have caught Rama Dutta with the manuscript by now."

Right then, we heard Maakhonbabu's raised voice, "Have you come to fight with me on behalf of your younger aunt? Don't you feel ashamed, you scoundrel? What can I do if your aunt was nabbed by the police? What are you doing? Why are you opening Upen's room? Where did you get the keys? Aru! I forbid you to open the room."

The Colonel went inside. I followed him. There was a well in the middle of the courtyard. There was a new house at the other end of it. It was all ready for the construction of the first floor, with steel frames rising out of the construction. The staircase in the centre was not plastered as yet. A strong young man was opening the lock of one of the rooms. His skin was copper-coloured. His hair style was like that of film heroes. He had on a blue tee-shirt and jeans. As he opened the last lock, the Colonel put a hand on his shoulder.

He got startled and turned back. Then he saw the Colonel and said, "Leave my shoulder, please." The Colonel pressed his shoulder further, smiled and said, "Where did you get the keys to your uncle's room?"

Arun tried to extricate himself with a jerk, but could not. He asked his other uncle if he knew who the old gentleman was. But the entire household had been stunned into silence. Maakhonbabu's wife, daughter and two sons were staring at the scene without batting an eyelid. Maakhonbabu suddenly roared, "He means death for you, you ungrateful monkey! How do you have the audacity to want to enter Upen's room? First tell me who gave you the keys."

Arun snapped back at him, "You think that just because your brother is dead, you will grab this house by surrendering your sister-in-law to the police?"

"Why are you entering the room, Arun?"

Arun said, "Chotomaami has asked me to stay in her room and guard the house. You don't know, Sir, that Boromaama will grab Chotomaama's house and throw Chotomaami out of it."

The Colonel removed his hand from his shoulder and said, "Okay. If your Chotomaami has given you the keys, you are the owner of the house. Maakhonbabu! Please don't obstruct Arun."

The Colonel stepped aside. Aru opened the last lock and went inside. I had, meanwhile, got up on the verandah, and was standing next to the Colonel. The room was dimly lit inside. I noticed that Aru took out a sheaf of papers from under the mattress. The Colonel lit his cheroot and said, "Let's go, Jayanto. We'd better not pry into their family affairs."

By that time, Aru had come out with the papers and was locking the door. The Colonel suddenly pulled out the papers from under his arm. Immediately, I saw a knife glistening in Aru's hands. Maakhonbabu, almost dumbstruck, could only utter, "Hey! Hey!"

The Colonel was ready. Using the method of toppling his enemy to the ground, he kicked him in the stomach, and Aru fell on the verandah groaning. The Colonel pointed his revolver at him. This time, I did not become stupefied into inaction. Since Aru's knife had fallen aside, I quickly picked it up. Aru was doubled up with pain. Obviously, the Colonel's kick had been a hard one. He gave me the packet of papers, pulled up Aru by the hair, and made him stand. Then he pushed him inside the room. The keys were lying near the door. The Colonel closed the door, put three locks on it, and came down. He said, "Maakhonbabu! Don't worry about your nephew! I will inform the police. I hope you and your family will report to the police whatever you saw."

Maakhonbabu stood dumbfounded. We went out and were on the road when we saw Suren rushing towards us. He gasped for breath and said, "It will take a while for Nanku to reach here."

The Colonel said, "We won't need Nanku any more, Suren. We are going to the police station. You go to the forest bungalow. Your uncle is really scared. He will be reassured to see you."

On the main road, the Colonel hailed a cycle rickshaw. He said, "We will go to the police station."

As the rickshaw started moving, the Colonel took the tapes off the outer wrapping of the papers that he had taken from Aru. Then he opened up a few more paper wrappings and saw one side. I saw a satisfied smile on his face. Even I could see what it was. It was that Sanskrit manuscript. It was a family history written on copper-coloured, thick paper. Before we could read anything else, he wrapped it up, opened the chain of his satchel and put it inside.

I said, "So the police will not get anything in Aru's aunt's suitcase."

"They could lay their hands on something else. I realize that Rama did not know what was wrapped in the packet. Aru had not told her. But I am surprised why the police could not find this when they searched Rama's house. One possibility is that it was with Aru. After the police left, he quietly entered that house and kept it under the mattress. By that time, Maakhonbabu and his family were asleep. He had taken it upon himself to come and retrieve it now. Keshto Adhikari had possibly told one of his men to get in touch with Aru."

I assented and said, "I can't find any logical explanation except this."

The O.C. Tapesh Sanyal was waiting for the Colonel. He welcomed us and asked us to sit down. Then he asked a constable in a white uniform to bring us coffee. He said, "Upen Dutta's wife has been arrested while she was going to the bus stop. In her suitcase, two packets of heroin have been found under her clothes. Its estimated value is two and a half lakh rupees. There was also an idol made of the eight basic metals, but it could not be ascertained what exactly the idol is. Two years ago, such an idol was stolen from the house of the zamindar of Sonadihi. It seems to match the photograph that they had given. We have informed Sonadihi."

The Colonel said, "You were looking for Aru, Upen Dutta's nephew. Well, I have just pushed him into a room and locked him in it. Please give this key to some officer and send him just now. This boy wanted to stab me suddenly with a knife, just like Gobindo. Upenbabu's brother Maakhonbabu and his family witnessed the entire incident.

Tapeshbabu immediately called a sub-inspector, gave him the keys, and acquainted him briefly with the situation. He went off at once.

The Colonel said, "I had told you about Mr. Haldar. His..."

"Yes. Mr. Haldar called from Asansol about half an hour ago. He asked me to tell you that he has to go back to Calcutta. Keshto Adhikari's friend is returning to Calcutta by the same train. Mr. Haldar will call the police station late at night, or early tomorrow morning. "

A boy brought some coffee and biscuits. I realized that there was a shop selling tea and coffee right next to the police station. I did not want to drink coffee, but had to take a sip at Tapeshbabu's insistence. The Colonel, of course, is happy to drink coffee anywhere, and at any time. While drinking his coffee, he said, "Are you free at two in the afternoon?"

Tapeshbabu smiled, "I am never free. But I can make myself free for you."

"Please bring an S.I. and an armed constable with you. We also need a spotlight."

"Won't you give us a hint about where we will go?"

The Colonel smiled. "It's more or less an adventure. So please choose your companions with care. They shoud be competent and courageous. Yes. Maakhonbabu was saying that there was a deadly dacoit in Raigarh by the name of Banka. It was rumoured that he died in a skirmish with the police. But the then O.C. of this police station, Mr. Bhaduri, had spotted him on a hilltop in Lohapur. However, he was not able to find him in that rough hilly tract."

Tapeshbabu sat straight and said, "Yes, Banka. I have seen his case file. The Bihar police are also keen to find him. I have read Mr. Proshanto Bhaduri's report. The dacoit Banka has a gunshot injury on his leg. Proshantò saw him limping."

The Colonel looked at his watch and said, "Whatever it is, I also want to lodge an FIR, against Aru."

"Certainly. Why don't you write it yourself?" said Tapeshbabu, and gave the Colonel a sheet of paper.

The Colonel quickly took out a pen from his pocket, wrote his complaints about Aru, and gave it to Tapeshbabu. Then he got up and said, "Remember, two o'clock. I will be waiting in the forest bungalow."

After coming out of the police station, it took us only about half-an-hour by cycle rickshaw to reach the bend at Ranglidihi by the highway. This was because we were going towards the south, in the direction of the roaring winter wind. After paying the rickshaw driver, the Colonel looked through his binoculars to scrutinise the pathway through the southern side of the uneven woods. He stepped forward only after looking around in all three directions.

Suren was standing in front of the bungalow. He smiled on seeing us. He said, "My uncle has got very anxious."

The Colonel said, "Has he seen a bear again, or has he heard the creaking of bones?"

Nakhulal was approaching from behind the bungalow. He had heard all the words. With a salute and some sorrow on his face, he smiled a little and said, "Nothing goes in through Suren's ears. His hearing has changed after learning to read and write. Sir! I have twice heard the steps of the Thakurbaba towards the north of the bungalow."

Saying this, he crossed his chest and forehead from habit. The Colonel said seriously, "Don't feel afraid, Nakhulal. Raise your spear and shout to the Thakurbaba that his creaking sound must stop soon. Shibu the exorcist has gone to call his teacher."

Suren started guffawing with laughter. Nakhulal said, "Lunch is ready, Sir. If you want to have a bath, please go ahead. The hot water is ready."

The Colonel said, "Jayanto will have a bath. The day for my bath is tomorrow."

I entered the room and said softly, "You have snatched a packet from Aru. Aru or Maakhonbabu could report that to the police."

The Colonel looked at me with deceitful eyes and said, "Go and have a bath. It is half past twelve. We'll have lunch at one. Tapeshbabu will come here at two."

After my bath, I was habitually sprawled out on my bed. The Colonel was smoking a cheroot in the verandah. I saw Suren after a little while. He sat down on the grass in the sunny patch of the lawn. A little later, I heard the Colonel saying to him, "You saw the hole. But did you tell anybody?"

Suren said, "I had told Dipu. Dipu had warned me not to tell anybody else."

"Did you or Dipu ever try to get inside it?"

"Once we were about to. We heard a muffled roar from inside, and came running out in fear. The fortress of the Rajas of the Rai dynasty was covered by the woods. Some people came from Calcutta to clear it once. But that side had not been cleared. Neither had it been dug up. Dipu had said it was because the government was not prepared to pay any more for the operation. The excavating work has stopped since then."

"Okay. The O.C. Tapeshbabu will come around two. When we go there, you will come with us."

My eyes were closing in their habitual need for a siesta. The winter was really at its worst in this bungalow. One had to use two blankets even during the day. But just as it had got warm inside the blanket and I had fallen asleep, the Colonel lifted up the blankets and said, "Jayanto! That's enough. Get up."

Although irritated, I had to get up. The O.C. Tapesh Sanyal, another officer and two strong-looking armed constables were standing on the lawn. I saw that the Colonel had got ready for the expedition. I went to the bathroom immediately, and splashed cold water on my face. Then I changed my clothes, put my small weapon in my pocket, and came out.

I saw the police jeep waiting next to the lawn of the bungalow. I could not figure out how so many people would fit in the jeep. But we had to go walking with the Colonel to the northern side of our bungalow, near the small gate. Nakhulal opened the lock of the gate. The Colonel said to him, "Let the gate remain open. We'll be back in no time."

After we stepped down into the woods from the bungalow, the Colonel turned towards the west after walking for a while. After going through some impenetrable thickets, he again turned to the north on the right hand side. Then he signalled to Suren. Suren was carrying a chopper with which he could cut away the thickets in the forest. He said softly, "The stone slabs are a little lower down, Sir."

The dense, impenetrable forest had sloped downwards towards the west. Suren cut away the copse in front of him with one stroke of his chopper. Then I saw to my amazement the remains of a room made of stone. At one end of it, there seemed to be a hole like a well on which creepers hung like a screen. The hole was actually a perfect square. Over it, a short, leafy tree grew which did not let the rain get into the hole.

The Colonel whispered, "Mr. Rakshit! You and another armed constable should keep a vigil on this hole. But please do not fire a shot. Take your positions inside the copse in a way that anybody coming out of this hole can't see you. The rest depends on your intelligence and adroitness. We'll go now. We'll see you at the appointed time. Be sure to come."

The O.C. Tapeshbabu, an armed constable, the Colonel, Suren and I went back again to the bungalow. Then we got out through the front gate of the bungalow, and walked diagonally towards the Northwest. Black pebbles of various sizes and shapes were strewn all over the hard and dry surface of the road. There were thick copses, though very few and far between. The Colonel observed the ruins of the fortress with his binoculars from time to time. After walking for one kilometre, we saw the river. We carefully stepped on the stones in the water to cross over to the other side.

When we reached the ruins of the fortress, we started walking towards the right, following Suren's instructions. The winter sun had dulled because it was early evening by now. In the distance, one could see a screen of hanging mist. The wind was not roaring as it had been in the morning. I saw a little while later that towards the east of the fortress, there were many mounds with overgrowths on them. We had to tread very carefully. There were stone slabs everywhere, and plants peeped out of each. At one place, Suren showed us a mound, which was the remnant of a room. A part of its roof was still intact. Thick creepers hung down from the ceiling. The Colonel signaled to Tapeshbabu and showed him something. I peeped in and saw that over the growths of reeds and under the creepers, there were a few clumps of black fur. I had seen this kind of fur in a cave with the Colonel.

Tapeshbabu looked at the reedy overgrowth and said, "The middle of this place seems to have got pressed by the weight of the animal."

The Colonel said rightly, "Jayanto, you understand everything, but somewhat late." The aim of the thrilling adventure on that day became clear to me. But an unknown terror seized me, and made my heart freeze.

The Colonel whispered, "Not a word more. You are all armed. But let me tell you one thing: whatever happens, don't fire. Give me the spotlight. I will get down first. Tapeshbabu will be by my side. Behind us will be constable Narasimha and Jayanto. Suren will come down last. Jayanto! Take out our pistol, but don't shoot under any provocation."

The Colonel removed the curtain of creepers. I saw a rectangular doorway made of stone which was almost six feet high and four feet wide. But the panel of the door was missing.

The Colonel paused and said in a very low voice, "I don't know how far we have to get down. This tunnel goes under the river."

Tapeshbabu said softly, "My estimate is that we may have to go down thirty feet. The stairs may be very steep."

The Colonel peeped and said, "Yes. The stairs are at an angle of forty-five degrees. Careful! Nobody should slip and fall. There is no need to hurry. We will go slowly and try not to make any sound. We will put on the light only intermittently. Take the support of the wall with one hand as you go. Two people should walk astride."

I could not figure out why the Colonel was forbidding us to shoot time and again. We had already got proof of the fact that the nails of the wild chimpanzee or whatever were very sharp. Would we have to suffer passively even if he attacked us?

As the Colonel and Tapeshbabu got down, they turned back to ensure that Suren was there. Suren went forward with his long, pointed chopper quite impassively. The Colonel once shone his spotlight on the stairs at the bottom and said, "Wow!"

I shivered as I got one glimpse of the smooth, one-foot wide, black, stone stairway. Human beings probably feel such an uneasy sensation as they descend down a well. After that, there seemed no end to our descent. Every moment, I shuddered to think what would happen if the tunnel gave way.

We counted forty steps as we descended, and then the Colonel paused for a few seconds to put on the spotlight. After this, there was a flat, smooth, stony path. The Colonel turned on the spotlight once again. We observed some wooden crates arranged on the side, adjacent to the wall. Tapeshbabu whispered, "Whose godown is this?"

Immediately, that horrible roar deafened us. An........ an........an !

That inhuman and horrible cry, resounding inside the deep tunnel, created a nightmare. We had all become immobilized with terror. But the bellowing stopped soon after. The light from the spotlight was directed towards the front. Whether the beast was a chimpanzee or the Adivasi's 'Thakurbaba' Harmatmatia, it had probably moved away from the area described by the bright light.

After the Colonel turned off the spotlight, the O.C. Tapeshbabu switched on a torch. He examined the shelves of crates to his left on the wall, and said in hushed tones, "No doubt these are stolen goods. But if we leave them behind and walk ahead, the smugglers might use the opportunity to remove everything."

The Colonel passed his roving eyes over the plywood crates and said, "Tapeshbabu! You were right. The name of a Swedish company appears on these."

"What are you saying?" said Tapeshbabu, and tried to get one of the crates down from the top, but he couldn't.

The Colonel shone his spotlight in the front again and said,

"Baba Harmatmatia will not come here any more. One thing is clear. That creature is very scared of fire arms. Let us quickly do one thing. With the help of Suren's chopper, let us open a crate and see what is inside. Jayanto! Hold the spotlight. Light it now and then to see what is before and behind you."

Tapeshbabu said, "You are right. It could be that some of the smugglers have seen us going down this tunnel."

The Colonel had, by then, got down one of the crates from the top. After hearing Tapeshbabu's words, my terror had multiplied manifold. There was no chance of our survival if Keshto Adhikari's team attacked us unawares with guns and pistols inside this tunnel. The smugglers were even more treacherous than the prehistoric beast.

As Suren ripped open one side of the crate with his chopper, the Colonel said, "Full of weapon parts."

Tapeshbabu asked, "Weapon parts? What weapons?"

The Colonel said, "My hunch is that these are pieces that make fire arms. If you put them together, you will know them to be automatic rifles or some even more formidable weapon."

"Good heavens!" said Tapeshbabu, startled. "Colonel! Then we must immediately seize these crates and send them to the police station. We will deal with the beast later."

The Colonel said, "Tapeshbabu! I have reason to believe that the beast guards these crates. There is a rumour about the beast in the locality. In fact, people have assumed that Dipu was devoured by the beast. Then Upen Dutta was also killed in an attack by it. So whether it was the ring of smugglers or Keshto Adhikari's team, they were certain that nobody would have the courage to enter this secret tunnel!"

Inside this tunnel, even these hushed whispers raised ghostly echoes. Suddenly, Suren said, "Sir! Why don't the constable dada and I sit at the entrance to the tunnel? If anyone dares to come this way, we will try to get at his leg with this chopper."

In this grim situation, the Colonel suddenly laughed. "You are intelligent, Suren. If you wait outside the entrance to a tunnel, one person can keep a hundred of the foe's army at bay. Tapeshbabu! Instruct the constable that as a police officer, in order to defend himself, he can first fire in the air to ward off the enemy, or later shoot him in the leg if he fails to do so."

At Tapeshbabu's directions, Narasimha and Suren went ahead. Lighting their torch now and then, they disappeared through the same stairs by which we had descended. The Colonel said, "Come on! Let us go ahead now."

The Colonel was in front, Tapeshbabu on his left, and I was on their right, a little behind them. We all had loaded revolvers. The Colonel was keeping track of the path by lighting the area by means of his spotlight now and then. There were stony bricks below us, and also on our side on the wall, but the ceiling contained huge, black, and smooth stone slabs.

I had often been on blood-curdling expeditions with the Colonel, but this one was unique. In some ancient age, some Raja of Raigarh, fearing attack and defeat by the enemy built this secret tunnel, which passes under the river-bed, so that he could escape with his family. The forest must have been more remote and widespread then. And now, many ages later, we were going to confront a living nightmare in this very passage. I got quite carried away imagining this terror, and conceptualizing its wondrous aspect.

We kept on going. The dense blackness all around us was interrupted only by the intermittent flashes of the spotlight in the Colonel's hand. I did not remember to look at my watch. I shuddered to think that the ferocious creature might appear at any time, because it would naturally get more and more desperate. The other entrance to the tunnel was guarded by the armed police. It might get even more fierce on seeing them.

The Colonel had said that the beast is afraid of fire arms. I do not know why he had come to this conclusion. Sometime later, the Colonel spread the light of the spotlight and said, "We are now going under the river. See Tapeshbabu! There is a leakage through the roof of the tunnel."

Tapeshbabu pointed at the roof and said, "I hope it won't cave in."

"There is no reason for it to cave in. The masons and artisans of those days were so skilled – you get examples of that everywhere in the world. The drops of water are falling through the stone bricks and blending into the sand below. But yes, some of the way is slippery. Tread carefully."

Walking through a tunnel under the river-bed was a novel and unique experience. Who could say with any confidence that its roof would not come crashing down any minute? We were going ahead with our lives in great danger. At one point, the Colonel said, "We have crossed the river. But be even more careful now. The path is on the rise."

Before he could finish his words, we heard that deafening roar again. An..an..an..an..an..an! My blood froze when I heard this roar inside the tunnel. When it stopped, the Colonel stopped. Startled, he said, "I have heard that chimpanzees and gorillas make this kind of a sound. But..."

He suddenly paused. Then Tapeshbabu said, "But what?"

Actually, the Colonel was listening carefully for something. He said, "After the roar stops, every time I have heard the sounds of dry twigs breaking. Listen! The sound is very strange."

Tapeshbabu and I both clearly heard the 'mat' 'mat' sounds. We had heard this in the forest of the Harmatmatia also. But inside the tunnel, the sound was the cry of some unknown nightmare. It was as if some prehistoric beast was advancing towards us. This sound was the sound of his steps.

After the sound stopped, the Colonel went ahead again. Now the pathway was ascending. Our shoes were slipping on the stones. So I was leaning against the wall and walking. The Colonel spread the light from the spotlight and said, "Careful!

It seems like a snake."

Tapeshbabu said, "Where? Where do you see a snake?"

"Right in front of you. It is raising its hood."

"Then it is a poisonous cobra. They raise their hoods when they see light."

Tapeshbabu tried to go ahead, past the Colonel saying angrily, "I can see the snake. I will shoot it and break its hood into pieces."

The Colonel would not let him go ahead. He said, "Is the snake Baba Harmatmatia's pet? If it had bitten him, we would have known. One minute! Let me play with the snake for a while."

Before Tapeshbabu could say anything, I said, "Colonel! Colonel! I know you have often encountered venomous snakes during your military career, but all you have in your hands now are a spotlight and a revolver. You have told me that you have often caught such snakes with the help of a stick. But you don't even have a stick now."

Tapeshbabu said anxiously, "It doesn't make sense wasting time in play, Colonel Saheb. We haven't come here to play with snakes."

But the Colonel did not pay any heed to his words. He said, "You have a baton hanging on your waist. That is enough to catch a snake. Pass it to me."

The O.C. Tapesh Sanyal said irritably to me, "Here. But it

is smaller than a lathi."

The Colonel said, "The Vaids of Kerala use lathis of this size to catch poisonous snakes. See! You just bring your spotlight and stand next to me, so that I can see the snake."

At last I saw the snake with its intricate patterns and its raised hood. The hood was swaying a little. It sent shivers down my spine.

The Colonel crouched on his knees, about two feet away from the snake, with his baton in one hand and his revolver in the other. Then he surprised us all by laughing out loud. He said, "When I saw this snake, it seemed as if it was advancing towards us. And why not? It is because the snake was coming down from a higher to a lower level."

He caught hold of the snake by its head. "What is all this?" exclaimed Tapeshbabu.

The Colonel laughingly said, "It is not a real snake. It's a rubber snake, meant for amusement. Somebody has hurled this snake at us from the dark to frighten us. That person has deliberately done it so that our progress is slowed down. He thinks we are going to shoot the snake. What he does not know is that the other entrance to the tunnel from the side of the forest is also blocked by our men, ready to pounce on them."

The Colonel gave the baton back to the O.C. Tapeshbabu and started walking rapidly with his spotlight. Tapeshbabu said, "I can't understand one thing. The beast can go to the other entrance and see if anybody is waiting there."

The Colonel said, "It is still daylight there. The beast does not want to be seen during the day. Of course, if his keeper Krishnokanto Adhikari is there, it's another thing."

Tapeshbabu asked, "Is it Keshtobabu's pet?"

"Yes. But be careful now. I think there are stairs leading to the top ahead of us."

The Colonel went a few steps ahead, put on his spotlight, and raised the light to an area above us in the front. Like the other side, I could see stairs on this side also.

Tapeshbabu looked up and said, "Colonel! I can see the chimpanzee or gorilla or what-have-you. But why is the rascal not roaring any more?"

The Colonel said as he climbed up carefully, "He is not roaring any more because his voice needs a break. See, it is going up."

Just as we had climbed up ten or twelve stairs, we suddenly heard gunshots and a loud uproar. The Colonel said, "Hell! Did the sub-inspector or constable kill it by mistake?"

Tapeshbabu said, "I have forbidden them to shoot. Probably, Mr. Rakshit fired a blank shot to scare the beast. It sounded like a shot from a revolver."

The Colonel said, "Poor Harmatmatia has landed himself in a soup. See! He is standing at the end of the stairs and begging, with folded hands, for his life, from us.

I saw to my utter amazement that the gorilla-like creature was standing with both his hands folded. In the glow of the spotlight, its nails were shining. Two teeth were protruding on either side of his mouth. The teeth were pointed and crooked, like a sharp knife. Tapeshbabu said, "Colonel Saheb! Tamed animals can display a lot of skills at the behest of their master. Even the way he folds his hands is learnt. But we have made a mistake. We could have arranged for a lasso or rope or cage if we had informed the conservation department of the forest earlier. I don't know how you will catch it in this state."

The Colonel smiled and said, "He knows that there is no way for him except to give himself up. He is now begging for his life. Come! Keep the revolver ready and come right behind me. Doesn't Baba Harmatmatia know that if he decides to attack us, we can send him to hell with three shots?"

He raised his face and smiled at the beast. "Thakurbaba! O Baba Harmatmatia. Please go up. Nobody will shoot you. Why don't you go up and pay your obeisance to Mr. Rakshit? Come on, up!"

It seemed to be Krishnokanto Adhikari's pet, because it understood the language of humans. It went up. I could hear Mr. Rakshit shout, "If you come one more step forward, I'll fire at you. But this beast is doing a *namaskar* to me. How strange! What is this? Don't come forward, I say. What a wonder! Is it an orang-utang?"

The Colonel went up to the entrance of the tunnel and

said, "Mr. Rakshit! It is a wonder indeed. Don't worry; it won't try to escape. It knows that if it tries to do any such stunt, we will break its leg."

Tapeshbabu and I followed the Colonel. The forest still had fading sunlight, and was swept by a cold breeze. I breathed freely after having returned from the world of perpetual darkness to my known world. Then I looked at the beast.

It was colossal. Its two hands were abnormally long. It had black fur all over its body. But how strange! Its eyes seemed very similar to the eyes of humans.

The Colonel lit a cheroot, looked at the beast and said, "Why are you going on with it, Baba Harmatmatia? Now come out of your mask. Or do you want me to help?"

Immediately, the beast cried out like a human being, "Sir! It is not my fault at all. I am reduced to this in the clutches of Keshto Adhikari."

The Colonel smiled. "I know. So you are Banka the famous bandit, aren't you?"

Tapeshbabu was standing there, dumbfounded. "Banka?" he asked. "There are innumerable cases of dacoities and murders against him in Bihar and West Bengal."

The Colonel said, "Banka will not be able to get out of his chimpanzee or gorilla disguise. Keshto Adhikari is extraordinarily cunning. He has fitted a miniscule battery-operated microphone and tape recorder on his neck. You have to press a button to hear a roar, and press another to hear the sound of bones creaking, or twigs breaking. Keshtobabu has really made Banka disabled."

Saying this, he freed Banka from his outer covering of an animal. His body was enormous. His hair was a mixture of black and white. He was wearing shorts and a sweater. He knelt down, covered his face with both his hands and started crying.

The Colonel pressed a button on the mini tape-recorder and said, "The battery is finished. He had to play the tape many times during our journey through the passage today. In the last two or three days also, there have been several occasions on which he has had to play it. It is no fault of the battery."

Tapeshbabu was examining the nails and teeth of the animal skin. "This seems to be made of steel," he exclaimed. "It is like a sharp, pointed knife."

The Colonel said, "Tapeshbabu! Suren and Narasimha are waiting at the other end of the passage. Please explain the matter to Mr. Rakshit. Ask him to go and wait there. You take Banka, along with his animal skin, escorted by the constable. After that, we need at least one armed constable to go and retrieve the stolen boxes of arms from the tunnel and bring them back in the police van."

Tapeshbabu took out a cell phone from his pocket and said, "There is no problem. I will let the police station know. The SDPO will inform the SP. We knew that soldiers sometimes surreptitiously supplied weapons here and there. But I had never imagined that we would discover such weapons. Actually, I have also heard many rumours about this tunnel. But we had never tried to connect the two or seize the weapons. How did you know about them?"

The Colonel said, "Suren knows this area like the back of his hand. He did not discover the tunnel alone. He did it with the help of his friend Dipu. Both of them used to be seen a lot with Dr. Debabrata Chattaraj when the archaeological excavation office was set up near the fort. Dr. Chattaraj was the chief executive of that office. He has retired now.

After Tapesh had informed the police station on his mobile, he said, "The police force will arrive soon. I request Colonel Saheb to give me company till it arrives."

By that time, Mr. Rakshit had handcuffed Banka, and the constable had tied a rope around his waist.

After almost half an hour, a police officer came forward with his spotlight and said, "The police van has arrived, Sir."

Tapeshbabu bid farewell to the Colonel and said, "It is late in the evening. I don't want to trouble you any more in this inclement weather. See you."

The Colonel said, "For the time being, one of my tasks is accomplished. The other can wait. I am getting restless for coffee right now. Goodbye."

We went, as the crow flies, to the bungalow through the path in the forest. I did not feel any terror any more.

Nakhulal was waiting for us, anxious. On seeing us, he said excitedly, "I have heard gunshots in the forest, Sir! I hope Suren hasn't landed in any danger."

The Colonel reassured him and said, "No, Nakhulal. In fact, we have good news. The person whom you believed to be Baba Harmatmatia is actually a man. He used to wear a black animal skin and frighten people, so that people would not enter the jungle. You had said that it was a bear-like beast. He is actually a notorious dacoit. His name is Banka. He has murdered Gobindo also."

Nakhulal said with surprise, "I have heard of Banka the dacoit, Sir! So he used to roam around the jungle dressed as a beast! Have you been able to catch him?"

"Yes. Now please quickly arrange for some coffee. Don't worry about Suren. He will come after a little while."

Saying this, the Colonel went round the bungalow to the verandah in the south. Then he unlocked the room and said, "Jayanto! Please light the Chinese lantern."

It was dark outside. The moon had not risen yet. I lit the lantern and said, "There is one thing I still can't understand. You said that Banka can't undress himself. How did he manage to eat and drink?"

Seated on the easychair, the Colonel took off his cap, smoothed his hands over his bald pate and said, "You would have realized it if you noticed carefully. Banka could take off certain portions of his face and head, and he could also take off the portion that covered his hands like a glove. But he could not take off any of the remaining portions of his body without somebody's help."

After some time, Nakhulal brought some coffee. One could make out from his attitude that he was keen to hear about the incident. The Colonel said, "You will be able to hear all the details from Suren, Nakhulal. You stay silent, because even after we leave, Keshto Adhikari's people will remain in Raigarh. If you stay silent like Suren after knowing everything, you will not get into trouble in their hands. Understand?"

Nakhulal went away quietly. I asked, "Did Suren know about the tunnel?"

The Colonel said, "Yes. Even his friend Dipu knew. But Suren did not know what was in the stolen casket. That was known only to Dipu. Dipu had solved the tangle of the riddle of thirty-two. That is why Upen Dutta had kidnapped him."

"But we have not yet traced Dipu."

The Colonel said slowly, "Possibly, Haldarmashai has followed a lead about Dipu and followed Dr.Chattaraj to Calcutta. Let us see what he can do."

I said a little later, "Colonel! Firstly, the casket that was stolen from Dr. Chattaraj's tent is with you. My hunch is that you have managed to retrieve the solution to the puzzle of thirty-two from one of Dipu's books. Now why don't you open the tiny metal box to see what is inside?"

The Colonel said, "Shut up, for heaven's sake! Even walls

have ears. And listen! We can hear police vans and jeeps going past the bungalow. My erstwhile friend is now in the process of becoming pure and simple Keshto Adhikari – no strings attached. Jayanto! This is the strangest incident related to this case, isn't it?"

That night, when the police brigade seized the crates of secret weapons from the tunnel, and was taking them away, they dropped Suren at the bungalow. The O.C. Tapesh Sanyal stood with the Colonel in the lawns of the bungalow, discussed some matters and went away. By then, we saw a moonlit sky all around us. That moonlight was both misty and mysterious. Suren had deposited his long, sharp chopper in his uncle's room and come to our room. Nakhulal had just brought in a second round of coffee for the Colonel. Suren also drank some coffee with us. According to the Colonel, after such a spine-chilling experience, even Suren needed some coffee to revive his nerves.

Suren said, "I had kept watch and seen about three people coming towards the fort. The darkness had just set in. When I told Narasimhada, he stood ready with his rifle and asked me to light the torch. When they saw the policeman bearing a rifle in the light of the torch, they ran away. Narasimhada also shouted, 'Who is it?' "

Suren guffawed with laughter as he said this. The Colonel asked him, "I hope they didn't get to see you."

"No, Sir. But I think they have gone to Asansol to inform Keshtobabu."

"I suppose they would. The police will inform the Asansol police station tonight. They will search Keshto Adhikari's office, shop and house as soon as possible. It is also essential to arrest Keshtobabu. Otherwise, Dipu's life may be in danger."

Suren said, "Why? Dipu has not done anything against Keshtobabu."

"Suren! Even if Dipu has not done anything, everything that has happened so far has been centered around him. One has discovered the proverbial snake in trying to dig up worms. So Dipu is likely to bear the brunt of Keshtobabu's anger."

"Sir! Do you think Dipu is in Keshtobabu's clutches?"

"I don't know. But I can't say – he may be. Let us see."

At around ten, we had had dinner and dropped off to sleep. In the morning, I was awakened by Nakhulal's call. He brought in the bed tea. The winter morning was looking gloomy in the mist. The cold seemed to have suddenly increased that day. Nakhulal had draped a blanket over his sweater. He said, "Today, the cold really seems to have settled in here."

I said, "Yes, I can feel it. But the Colonel Saheb seems to have gone for his morning walk even in this bitter cold. Hasn't he told you anything?"

Nakhulal said, "No, Sir. I have seen him going towards the fort with Suren."

I could not, for the life of me, imagine why the Colonel had again braved the jungle surrounding the fort. Keshtobabu's cronies could suddenly attack him there."

The bitter cold made me go out after a while, and stand in the lawn wearing my trousers, shirt, sweater and thick windcheater. The sunshine was feeble. It was almost eight o'clock. Yet one could not see anything even a little distance away in the dense fog. After almost half an hour, the fog cleared up a little. At that time, I saw a man coming up the path to the guest-house, wearing a monkey cap, high-collared coat and trousers, with a bag slung on his shoulders. As soon as he stood near the gate of the bungalow, I recognized him. It was the private detective Haldarmashai.

I addressed him – "Good morning, Haldarmashai. You were supposed to call us. How is it that you have come in person?"

The master detective said a little wearily, "Don't ask me, Jayantobabu. I just went to Calcutta and came back. I didn't even get a seat. I came standing all the way."

I called Haldarmashai to our room and ordered coffee. I saw that he was wearing gloves. He took off the gloves and the monkey cap and sat on a chair. I said, "I will listen to the news later. Let the coffee come first."

The private detective asked, "Where has Colonel Sir gone?"

I said, "For a morning walk. Nakhulal saw him going towards the fort with Suren."

Haldarmashai undid a button of his high-collared coat and took out a piece of folded paper. He unfolded it, showed the paper to me and said in a soft voice, "I have brought a map of the fort. You can see 'tunnel' written beside this black spot.

I said with surprise, "Where did you get this map?"

The great detective giggled a little stiffly, "I followed Dr. Chattaraj. How would he know me? We had seats next to each other in the air-conditioned chair car."

"What are you saying? You must have had to pay a lot for the ticket."

"No, it was not all that much. What could I do? The train was jam-packed. Yet I had to follow Chattaraj."

"I see. But this map…"

Nakhulal entered with coffee and snacks. He saluted Haldarmashai and went out. Haldarmashai sipped his coffee and said, "Dr. Chattaraj took out a diary from his briefcase. A piece of paper fell out of it near his feet. He did not realize it. When he went to the bathroom, I quietly pocketed this piece of paper. Now do you understand?"

Haldarmashai laughed and concentrated on his coffee once again. I saw the map and realized that it was a map of the ancient fort at Raigarh with the letterhead of the government archaeological department. This was not an original map. It was a copy of the ancient map preserved in the government records. There was a line showing the fort and the tunnel. Besides a sign showing a rectangular room, it was written 'treasury'. On the eastern side of the tunnel, I could see a sign showing the jungle.

While drinking my coffee, I was looking at the map in detail, when I heard the Colonel. He came to the verandah and addressed Haldarmashai, "Good morning. I am not surprised to see you come back so soon from Calcutta."

Haldarmashai was excited to see the Colonel. He said in a low voice, "I have traced Dipu. He was in Dr. Chattaraj's house. Dr. Chattaraj had gone to get him. After that, he came back to Asansol by the night train. He has possibly taken Dipu to Mr. Adhikari's house in Asansol. I did not get down at Asansol because I thought it is essential to let you know."

Suren had gone to tell his uncle to make some coffee. At this time, he returned. Seeing Haldarmashai there, he stood back in surprise. The Colonel said, "Suren! You call Shibu the exorcist's son from Ranglidihi. There's no hurry. It will be okay to get out at ten."

Suren left. I asked the Colonel, "What's the matter?"

The Colonel kept his cap, binoculars, camera, etc., on the table and said, "There is a ruin, on top of it there is a gigantic tree on which I saw an exotic variety of weed. Shibu the exorcist's son is a master at climbing trees. However, I have been able to fit a telephoto lens and take some pictures."

Nakhulal brought in some more coffee. The Colonel was visibly relishing his coffee. I asked him why he was not at all surprised to see Haldarmashai come back. He did not pay any heed to what I was saying. Instead, he said, "Now let us hear Haldarmashai's exciting story."

The sum and substance of what Haldarmashai said was this: In accordance with the Colonel's instructions, it was not difficult for him to find Krishnokanto Adhikari's head office. Keshtobabu is a well-known businessman there. When he asked a worker about Keshtobabu's house, the gentleman said, "Adhikari Saheb lives on the second floor of this office. His home is in Raigarh. But you will not be able to meet him now. He is very busy."

Haldarmashai took up his abode in a hotel nearby. His room was on the second floor of the hotel. So it was easy for him to keep watch over Keshto Adhikari's room over his office. He phoned the Raigarh police station at night to say that there was no news so far. He would phone again in the morning. The next morning, Haldarmashai saw two people drinking tea or coffee on the terrace next to Keshtobabu's room on the second floor. From the description of Dr. Debabrata Chattaraj's appearance that the Colonel had given him, he was able to recognize him at once.

After lunch, Haldarmashai saw Keshtobabu and Dr. Chattaraj getting into a car. He quickly got down, hired an autorickshaw, and followed the white car. The car made its way to the railway station. He then saw Dr. Chattaraj getting into the chair car of the train. He too got into the chair car, and arranged for a ticket for himself by requesting the ticket checker. The chair car was almost empty. He sat next to Dr. Chattaraj, and was luckily able to lay his hands on the map of the ancient fortress of Raigarh. He had told me earlier how he got it. Now he told the Colonel in detail and told us the rest of the story of his adventures.

After the train crossed Burdwan, he started a conversation with Dr. Chattaraj. Haldarmashai could gauge that he was causing him irritation by thrusting himself upon him. But Haldarmashai cleverly started discussing the difficulty of finding a taxi at Howrah station. Dr. Chattaraj then said that his car would be waiting at the station. Haldarmashai humbly requested him to drop him near the latter's house, as he had a heart ailment. Moreover, he said he lives in the vicinity of Jadavpur.

The detective was thus able to procure a seat for himself in Dr. Chattaraj's car when they reached Howrah stataion at half past four in the afternoon. A tough-looking fellow had come with the driver. Dr. Chattaraj asked him how master Dipu was. Haldarmashai was all ears when he heard this. But his eyes were shut. After all, he was a heart patient.

The man said that Dipu was acting in a very spoilt manner.

Dr. Chattaraj said, "I will take him by the twelve-five train tonight. I will go myself. It will be a little strenuous for me, but there is nothing else to do."

Dr. Chattaraj dropped Haldarmashai near his home. After this, Haldarmashai returned to his own house on Lake View

Road. Then he wore his monkey cap, changed his attire, put on his glasses and reached Howrah station in time to catch the train. While waiting at the platform, he had been able to make out from Dipu's gestures that he had run away from Upen Dutta's den and had taken refuge in Dr. Chattaraj's house on Saral Biswas Road. Dr. Chattaraj had detained him on the pretence of getting some assistance from him regarding the stolen treasure. Dipu had, of course, shown some enthusiasm about this. Haldarmashai had heard Dr. Chattaraj say, "Mr. Adhikari will drop Dipu home. We will go to Raigarh in Mr. Adhikari's car. Don't worry. But we should first find the lost treasure."

The Colonel was smoking his cheroot with his eyes shut so far. As soon as Mr. Haldar finished, he opened his eyes and said, "The police is supposed to have been on watch in Keshtobabu's office and godown in Asansol yesterday. If the police had found Keshtobabu, Dr. Chattaraj, and Dipu there, some news of it would have come to the Raigarh police station and it would have reached us by now. So we can deduce that the shrewd Keshtobabu has taken cover somewhere on the pretext of dropping him home. Dr. Chattaraj had probably guessed that and gone away from the station. Haldarmashai could have got down at Asansol and telephoned us."

I said, "He did not know what happened yesterday. How would he even know that the police would raid Keshtobabu's office in Asansol?"

Haldarmashai was sitting dazed, listening to the Colonel's words. Now he only said, "Huh?"

The Colonel said, "Yes. You are right, Jayanto. But Haldarmashai has brought very valuable news."

Haldarmashai said softly, "Why has Dipu got into Keshtobabu's clutches? Will Keshtobabu keep him in his hold like Dr.Chattaraj did? Jayantobabu said a lot of things happened yesterday. What happened?"

The Colonel said solemnly, "Keshtobabu is now desperate. You will know why while you have your breakfast. We also went on an exciting adventure yesterday. Besides, some other momentous things have happened. Please have some patience. Go to your room, wash yourself in warm water, and change your clothes."

A little later, the Colonel narrated all the events of the previous day to Haldarmashai in our room. The great detective intermittently kept saying in an agitated voice, "Oh! Look what I missed."

Hearing that the beast was the formidable dacoit Banka, the private detective rolled with laughter. He said, "I had a glimpse of him. Thank goodness I didn't shoot."

I said, "I have understood now why the Colonel used to say that the beast was afraid of firearms."

Haldarmashai said, "Yes. Why should a beast be afraid of fire arms? Do beasts understand fire arms?"

Around a quarter past ten, Suren brought a thin-looking boy of his own age. The Colonel said smilingly, "So this is Don!"

Suren said, "Yes, sir. Our father has given him the nickname of Don. His Christian name is Daniel Kaliprasad Besra. He has left the Mission School, and roams around in the forest in fear of the father."

The Colonel said, "Haldarmashai! You have been awake all night. Please rest for a while. Jayanto, do you want to accompany me?"

I said, "Am I mad? I am always ready to go with you on other expeditions. But when you want to explore the woods and copses for birds, butterflies and orchids, I'd rather not be with you. I have learnt this after a lot of misadventures I've had."

The Colonel went away laughingly with Suren and Don. Haldarmashai and I sat down on two chairs in the lawn. Haldarmashai said, "I don't understand one thing. Why will Keshtobabu keep the boy as a hostage?"

I agreed and said, "You are right. What does Keshto Adhikari gain by holding Dipu captive? The one thing that was necessary for solving the riddle of thirty-two has come into the Colonel's hands after Banka the dacoit murdered Upen Dutta in the guise of a chimpanzee..."

Haldarmashai said, "What did you say? Say it again!"

Just as I was about to answer his question, I saw Kumudbabu

open the gate and enter the lawn of the bungalow in a flurry. He was almost in tears, and said breathlessly, "Where is the Colonel Saheb? Something dreadful has happened here."

I said, "What has happened, Kumudbabu?"

Kumudbabu took out an envelope from his kurta pocket and said with a pathetic face, "This letter was pushed inside through the outer door. I had not noticed it. Sometime back, Dipu's mother noticed it when she was cleaning the floor. This is a letter written by Dipu. Please read it."

I opened the letter and saw what was written in it:

> Baba
> The thing that was stolen from Chattaraj Saheb's camp is with some Colonel Saheb. Please show him this letter, and ask him to leave the article next to the pond in the Harmatmatia forest, at ten in the night. They will kill me if you let the police know. If they get the thing, they will set me free. If they don't get it, they have resolved to kill me at one in the morning.
> Dipu.

Haldarmashai's face was very close to mine as he read the letter. I could clearly hear the sound of his gasps as he read. Restless, he said excitedly, "We must inform the Colonel Sir immediately."

Kumudbabu said in a broken voice, "Where has the Colonel gone?"

I said, "He is out on one of his fads! He has gone to the forest near the fortress to get some parasitic plants. You wait for a while."

We went and sat in the verandah. Haldarmashai said a little later, "Where is that forest? If I had known, I could have informed him. Doesn't Jayantobabu know it? Kumudbabu, you must know where it is."

Kumudbabu said, "I am in quite a sorry state. It cost me a lot of pain to reach here. It is about one kilometre to the north-west, across the river. Of course, the river does not have that much water."

"Please show me where it is." Saying this, the ace detective stood up.

To tell the truth, I had become somewhat nervous after reading the letter. Kumudbabu got down from the verandah and pointed out the forest adjacent to the ruins of the fortress. Haldarmashai took the letter from him and went out.

I called Nakhulal and asked for tea for Kumudbabu. Nakhulal said *namaskar* to Kumudbabu and went off.

When the Colonel came back with Suren and Don, it was almost twelve. I saw that he had with him a thick branch on which there was a red flower and a green filigree leaf. Some herbs were hanging on both sides. The Colonel saw Kumudbabu and said, "Please give me a minute. Let me tell Nakhulal to plant it in the ground."

I asked, “Where is Haldarmashai? He had gone to call you.”

The Colonel arched his eyebrows and said, “Haldarmashai? I have not met him.”

The Colonel went towards the rear of the bungalow. Kumudbabu said, “It is impossible not to have met them because the place is like a circular maze. It is possible that he is still looking for the Colonel Saheb.”

A little later, the Colonel returned and gave some money to Don, who went away happily. Suren went to his uncle. The Colonel came back, lighted his cheroot and said, “I can see that something has happened. Tell me, Kumudbabu.”

Kumudbabu reported the incident of the letter and wiped his eyes with his handkerchief. The Colonel said, “Why did Haldarmashai take the letter away? I needed to see the letter.”

Kumudbabu said, “It is written in Dipu’s hand.”

The Colonel said, “Okay. Don’t worry. Please go home and wash and eat your meal. For heaven’s sake, don’t mention the letter to anyone.”

Kumudbabu stood up and said, “Krishnokantobabu is not at home. He…”

Upon his words, the Colonel said, “Kumudbabu! Please understand that it is Krishnokanto Adhikari himself who has held your son back. But be careful! Nobody except you should know about this.”

Kumudbabu was startled. After standing with his face

lowered for a while, he went out dejected.

The Colonel had gone to the western side of the bungalow, and was watching the forest next to the fortress. I was observing him from the verandah. He came back after almost fifteen minutes. He looked serious. He looked at his watch and said, "It is time for lunch. We will go out after lunch. It is no use waiting for Haldarmashai. He can have his lunch whenever he wants to."

"I hope he hasn't run into any danger," I said.

"I can't say. The problem with Haldarmashai is that he is arrogant and obstinate enough to think of himself as he was when he used to be a police officer."

The Colonel went to change in the bathroom. We waited for half an hour, and ate at a quarter past one. At two o'clock, the Colonel took the last puff of his cheroot and said, "Jayanto, Haldarmashai has possibly walked into Krishnokanto Adhikari's snare without realizing it himself. Come! Let us go in search of him. I will call Suren. He knows the forest like the back of his hand."

The Colonel, Suren and I walked for almost one kilometre, with the Harmatmatia forest on the right, and the river running parallel to it on the left, and finally reached the ruins of the fortress. We crossed the river, and entered the western ruins. The Colonel was intermittently looking all around through his binoculars. After entering the maze of the fortress, he said, "Suren! Can you see what that is?"

Suren stepped forward and picked up a dirty handkerchief. I was startled and said, "This is the handkerchief with which Haldarmashai wiped the snuff off his nose."

We walked around on the right and left for some more time, and stopped at one place, where the Colonel said, "How strange!"

Suren cried out, "Sir! See how some people have put an enormous rock at the opening of the tunnel."

The Colonel went forward, pushed the bushes aside, and said, "Jayanto! Suren! Come, let us try to remove the rock. Let us see why Keshtobabu's people have blocked the small opening of the tunnel with this rock."

Removing that heavy rock from the opening of the tunnel on that freezing winter evening caused us to sweat. After a lot of effort, we could barely move aside. But at last, a gap was made through which one person could enter the tunnel. The Colonel climbed on a mound to observe all four sides. Then he got down and said, "There is only one problem now. If we go inside, some member of Keshtobabu's team who may be hiding in the tunnel may open fire, and we won't get any chance for self-defence."

I said, "You are right. Keshto Adhikari is a smuggler of fire arms. So his lackeys may very well be in the tunnel, guarding Haldarmashai with some fire arm in their hands."

Suren said, "Sir! That Mr. Adhikari's people have caught

him and forced him into the tunnel there is no doubt about. But I hope they have not killed him inside the tunnel."

The Colonel said, "Keshtobabu does not gain anything by killing Haldarmashai. It is more likely that he will hold him captive, and demand from me the box with the riddle of thirty-two as ransom. Dipu and Haldarmashai must both be in the clutches of Keshtobabu. This has given him an opportunity to pressurise me further."

Suren said, "Sir! In the jungle of Harmatmatia…"

The Colonel said, "The age of Harmatmatia is over, Suren. Can't you understand that Keshtobabu had employed the services of Banka the dacoit for many days, even years, to carry on his shady business safely? He had put a mini Japanese tape recorder around his neck with 'mat-mat' sounds recorded in it, so that a situation was created in which people were afraid to enter the jungle not only in the evening, but also in the day."

I said, "But it is getting closer to sunset. Let us do what we should do right now. "

Suren said, "I am just thinking of one thing, Sir! Have Keshtobabu's people covered the other opening to the tunnel in the middle of the jungle like this?"

The Colonel said, "Suren! Can you please do one thing? If you leave this place, after you cross the river, there is an empty field on the north eastern side. Can you run across the fields and go to the Raigarh police station?"

"Of course I can, Sir."

"Then please go and deliver this letter to the O.C. Tapeshbabbu or the duty officer. Don't come back alone. Come back with the police."

Saying this, the Colonel took out a notebook from inside his jacket and wrote a note on one of its pages. Then he gave his visiting card to Suren and with it, the page on which he had written, which he tore out. Just as Suren had stepped forward, the Colonel said, "One minute! You might run into some trouble while getting out of the jungle. Come, I will see you off till the bank of the river. Jayanto! Take out your revolver and keep it ready in your hand. Please also hide behind the bushes near that mound. Nobody should be able to see you. Be careful."

The Colonel went to leave Suren till the bank of the river. According to his instructions, I sat with my revolver behind the bushes. I must admit that the sense of an unknown terror had numbed me. Every moment, I feared that Keshtobabu's followers would pounce on me and take me captive like Haldarmashai. Even he had a revolver with him when they captured him.

But nothing like that happenend to me. Seeing the Colonel return, I came out of hiding. The Colonel grinned and said, "I hope the ghosts didn't throw stones at you."

"No," I said. "Did they throw any at you?"

"They did, just as I was returning."

"Heavens! That means Keshtobabu's cronies are somewhere in the vicinity even now."

"Yes. They were stupid enough to let us know that."

"It's a mercy they didn't fire a shot."

The Colonel lit a cheroot and said, "If I am killed by firing from behind covers, Keshtobabu knows very well that he will not be able to lay his hands on that Mughlai treasure chest. Anyway, let us sit on top of this mound till the police arrive. Be careful as you climb. You might break a limb if you slip and fall."

We climbed up a denuded heap of the ruins and sat there. These remains of the fortress were so filled with stones that no weed had ever grown on it. The daylight was fading. At this time, one could hear the birds chirping to proclaim the end of the day.

The Colonel was looking on all four sides with his binoculars. I noticed that it was four o'clock. Why did the day end so early in this place, I wondered. I understood a little later that everything was looking hazy because of the fog. After a while, the Colonel looked towards the east and said, "Great! Tapeshbabu and company are here. Come, let us get down.

Just as we had got down from our seat at the top, we saw a red, dusty face peering from the opening of the tunnel. The Colonel ran up and said, "Haldarmashai! So Keshtobabu's fellows let you go at last."

Haldarmashai's mouth was sealed with tape. As soon as the Colonel pulled off the tapes, he cried out in agony, and said, "My hands are tied at the back. You will have to lift me.

The Colonel and I pulled him up from both sides and got him out. The Colonel then took out a knife from his kitbag and cut the strings that tied his hands. Haldarmashai's entire body was covered with dust and a reddish mud. After getting used to his new freedom, he said, "Why did those creeps have to tie me at all places? They suddenly pounced on me, and...oh!"

The Colonel asked, "They tied you and pushed you inside the tunnel. Did you see Dipu there?"

"Yes, I have seen him. They didn't tie him. I could recognise him by the light of the torch that Keshtobabu had put on. A little while ago, somebody came with a flaming torch from the other side and said, 'Sir! Things don't look too good. I have seen Suren running. He has possibly gone to inform the police station. Even the fixing of the rock on the western opening of the tunnel has not been perfect.' Then Keshtobabu said, 'Let this detective remain tied here. Come, let us go into the jungle with Dipu.' They went away. Both my feet were tied. At one place on the wall, one of the stone tiles was protruding a little. I rubbed the strings against that in the darkness till they frayed, and then stood up."

At this juncture, Tapeshbabu reached there with his team. He said to Haldarmashai, "What a state Mr. Haldar is in! I have, of course, heard from Suren about finding his handkerchief."

"I hope your people are there near the eastern opening of the tunnel, in the forest," enquired the Colonel.

The O.C. Tapesh Sanyal said, "After getting your letter, the first thing I did was to send two officers and two armed constables inside the jungle. They have gone in a jeep. After crossing the playing field, it is not difficult to drive a jeep through the jungle. I had, in fact, noticed that last night. The bushes and overgrowths are no impediment. Now tell me what I should do. If we clear the blockade to the tunnel by removing the stone, one of us might have to lose his life in case they open fire."

Before the Colonel could say anything, Haldarmashai said, "Keshtobabu and two of his fellows have gone to the opposite side with Dipu in their custody."

"How long ago was that?" asked Tapeshbabu.

"I don't know. Perhaps more than half an hour. I can't remember the exact time."

"That means they have escaped before the police force could reach."

The Colonel lowered his voice, "Let us do one thing. Let us cover the opening of the tunnel with the stone, and keep the police force under cover in the bushes nearby. Keshtobabu's people were here in the jungle even a little while ago. They might run away on seeing you. Or they might wait till the police leave. You instruct an officer accordingly. If they find Keshtobabu's people confronting them, they should be adequately prepared."

"What next?"

"What next? Let me see... Come, let us go to the eastern opening of the tunnel near the jungle. It is necessary to know what has happened."

Tapeshbabu called an officer and gave him instructions accordingly. Then he said, "Colonel Saheb! One of our officers there has a mobile phone. I have not received any messages yet. It means that Keshtobabu and company must have left earlier, or hidden themselves in the tunnel after hearing the sound of the police jeep. Let me try to ring them up instead."

Tapeshbabu also had a mobile with him. He dialed and asked for a code number. Then he listened into the phone for sometime and said, "Okay. We are coming."

He hung up and said, "The S.I. Mr. Mitra said that there is a thick foliage of bushes over the opening of the tunnel. He caught a glimpse of a face in between. But the face vanished immediately after he saw it."

The Colonel said, "It means they have not yet been able to get out. Let us hurry, Tapeshbabu. Inside the tunnel, the only danger is that of a possible exchange of gunshots. We'll attend to the situation after we gauge it over there."

We worked our way out of the jungle of the fortress and

reached near the police van after crossing the river. Tapeshbabu instructed the driver and two armed guards to wait there. Then he headed forward. The forest of Harmatmatia sloped downwards on this side. The Colonel said softly, "We have to go a little further to the right and enter the forest silently."

At this point, there was a beeping sound on Tapeshbabu's wireless. He responded, and said in a low voice to the Colonel, "Keshtobabu is a formidable man. He must have held a revolver to Dipu's ear and got out of the tunnel. His two associates are with him. Keshtobabu is saying that unless they are allowed to go, he will shoot Dipu in the head. After that, even if the police shoots them, they don't care."

The Colonel saw the forest all around in the murky light of dusk, and said, "I know the place now. We have to crawl through these bushes as silently as possible. It is winter, so the fallen leaves are likely to make it noisy. But inside the bushes, there is no risk from fallen leaves."

Suren was behind the Colonel, I was behind Tapeshbabu, and Haldarmashai was on our right. We crawled up the slope like wild creatures. The Colonel, Tapeshbabu, Haldarmashai and I had revolvers filled with cartridges in our hands. At this time, there was a nip in the air, which was to our advantage. The Colonel stopped at one place. Then we saw a really frightening sight.

Outside the opening of the tunnel, Keshto Adhikari was holding the nozzle of a revolver to the ear of a boy of about

Suren's age, and going forward step by step. Two strong looking men next to them had rifles of a foreign make with them.

They had their rifles pointed at the police as they moved forward. Two police officers and constables had raised their rifles and had positioned themselves a little apart. The situation was so tense that any moment, a battle of fire arms would begin. Then Keshtobabu roared in a muffled kind of voice, "We will die. But before that, Kumud master's son is going to die. I am asking the police babus to reconsider. Let us get away without any obstruction. See? My two friends have automatic Kalashnikov rifles. Every two seconds, two shots can be fired. You will be blown to smithereens."

Suddenly, something else happened. We had not noticed but Haldarmashai had crept up to them. He pounced on Keshto Adhikari unawares, and knocked him to the ground. From this side, the Colonel and Tapeshbabu leapt on Keshtobabu's two associates. Two police officers quickly went and pushed their Kalashnikov rifles under the soles of their feet. They were also similarly grounded. Like Keshtobabu, the two of them were also pinned dwn by two heavy and armed people sitting on their backs – the Colonel and the O.C. Tapesh Sanyal. Keshtobabu's revolver had been flung to one side. Haldarmashai showed his revolver and said to Dipu, "What is this boy doing? Why are you standing? Pick up Keshtobabu's gun."

Dipu was still staring blankly. In one leap, Suren picked up

Keshtobabu's rifle. Then he giggled and said to Dipu, "Hey! You had gone wearing a tee-shirt and shorts, but have come back wearing trousers and a sweater. Who bought these for you?"

Dipu smiled somewhat stiffly and said, "Chattaraj Saheb!"

By that time, the police had handcuffed the grounded Keshto Adhikari and his two companions, and dragged them up to stand on their own feet. Tapeshbabu said, "Mitrababu! Please take the culprits away carefully. Let me call the police force back from the fortress in the jungle. I will go down, and then return in the jeep. Colonel Saheb…"

The Colonel rapidly said, "I will return and have some coffee at the bungalow. I am taking Dipu with me. Suren, please inform his father. Let's go!"

Tapeshbabu smiled and said, "We will require both you and Dipu."

"I know. You will get all of us tonight to file a case against Keshto Adhikari and company. I will make the retired Dr. Chattaraj a royal witness in the case as soon as I get back to Calcutta. I take your leave."

After returning to the bungalow, the chowkidar Nakhulal saw Dipu and almost screamed, "Dipubabu! Where were you all these days? Suren has been crying with worry about you. Where is he?"

The Colonel said, "Suren has gone to inform Dipu's father.

Nakhulal! I want a cup of coffee quickly. And we also need a bucketful of warm water for Haldarmashai to bathe in. He is covered with a light-coloured dust all over; he has become a pure *saheb*."

Haldarmashai smiled, "It was a hard scuffle. I was alone against the four of them."

A little while later the Colonel said, as he drank his coffee, "Why aren't you drinking coffee, Dipu? Your body and mind will get reactivated if you drink the coffee. Drink some coffee. Have you had anything to eat today?"

Dipu said, "Keshtobabu had brought some food inside the tunnel in the afternoon. I have never had to do with inadequate or bad food. It was only Upenda who had kept me captive in a room in a slum with Gobindo. He used to threaten me with a dagger. He would keep the place locked."

"How did you run away from there?"

"On one night, Gobindo had come to the room in an inebriated state. He used to lock the place from inside at night but he was in such a state that he forgot to lock it. I took the opportunity to run away. I knew the address on Dr. Chattaraj's name card by heart. After a long search, I reached his house. I gave him the sum with the riddle of thirty-two in it. But he forebade me to go out. He used to say that Upen Dutta's people were looking for me. Later, I understood that he had also kept me captive."

"Hm. I know the rest. See, I found your riddle of thirty

two from a book of yours."

The Colonel showed an old, folded piece of paper which was in his knapsack. Dipu said, "But you haven't found the treasure chest."

The Colonel said, "Let the treasure chest be. Drink your coffee quietly. After your father arrives, we will go to the police station together. Then we will return to Calcutta by the train that leaves at 1 a.m. You will not be allowed to get into any more scrapes."

Kumudbabu arrived with Suren a little later. He held Dipu to his chest and cried his heart out.

The police jeep dropped us to the Raigarh station that night. After returning to Calcutta, the Colonel took Haldarmashai and me to Kumar Bahadur Ajayendu Ray's house in Hazra Road.

Ajayendubabu greeted the Colonel and addressed him; "Colonel Saheb, I hope your expedition was successful."

The Colonel laughed a little and said, "Yes. But there is one thing. Did you know that Krishnokanto Adhikari used to supply arms to warring people in various areas?"

Ajayendababu was shocked and said, "How awful! I had no idea!"

"Whatever the case, and it's a long one, Keshtobabu has been caught with his entire team. I will tell you the details later. Right now, I want to strike a secret deal with you. Please bolt the door from inside. There should be nobody eavesdropping outside."

The Kumar Bahadur made the necessary arrangements by getting me to bolt the door from inside. He was looking restless. He said in a low voice, "Have you been able to recover the Sanskrit manuscript?"

The Colonel first delved into his kitbag and gave him the Sanskrit manuscript folded in a newspaper. Then he said, "You will not recognize what I'm going to show you now. Your ancestor had received it as a gift from the Mughal general Maan Singh."

Saying this, he took out something in a packet from his kitbag. I recognized it the moment I saw it – Suren had dug this out of the bare earth near Upen Dutta's dead body in the forest of Harmatmatia. The Colonel had detected it through his metal detector. But he had not told me about it, and had evaded my query about it.

The Colonel took out the small cube and said, "This is a treasure box. Now see, I will open it according to the cue I have got from the riddle of thirty two. However, the credit for solving the puzzle is not due to me, but to Dipu, the son of Kumudbandhu Bhattacharya. The Sanskrit manuscript had a passing referrence to this magic square. Please see for yourself."

The Colonel took out from his pocket the paper he had found inside Dipu's book and laid it out flat. He said, "One has to arrange the figures one to fifteen in a quadrangular pattern so that the sum of each side is 32 (Because there are sixteen squares, one of the numbers will appear twice). See how Dipu has solved the puzzle.

Ajayendubabu saw the treasure box and said, "I see that the 300-400 year old thing is still quite spotless."

The Colonel said, "It was not clean. I have cleaned it with a brush. Now, I will see it with a flint glass and press the numbers written in Nagari script according to Dipu's design. If you press the figures on all sides four times, the box will open."

With the help of his index finger, the Colonel pressed the figures from one to fifteen, in the order in which they were written consecutively. The box opened in two equal halves. A priceless, multi-coloured necklace sparkled inside. The Colonel picked it up and said, "It's a historic necklace embedded with diamonds, rubies and emeralds. Its price would be lakhs of rupees now. This necklace was gifted by the Moghul general Maan Singh to your ancestor. Legally, therefore, you are its heir."

He put the necklace around the Kumar Bahadur's neck. Haldarmashai said laughingly, "What a furore! Why should there not be a fight over such a historic piece of jewellery?"

Ajayendubau took off the necklace and said, "Please put it back in the box. I will keep it safely in my iron chest. Then I will call you and sell it. With the money I'll open an orphanage."

The Colonel put the necklace back in the box, and shut both its lids. The treasure chest was closed again. The Colonel tugged at the box and said, "This will not open unless I do it by the earlier method. So please keep this paper with Dipu's solved puzzle in it. There is another thing – Kumudbabu is a poor man. If you could contribute a small part of the sum for Dipu's studies…"

At his words, Ajayendubabu said, "I am responsible for Dipu's education. I will write to Kumud today. Let me go and keep this in the iron chest then tell me the whole story while we have coffee."

After he opened the door and left the room, Haldarmashai spoke. "I haven't said something so far. Let me say it now. When I had got on Keshtobabu's back, I felt a tumour there – or perhaps it was a hump. I exerted a lot of pressure on it!"

The Colonel roared with laughter on hearing this.